CW01501755

INDICTMENT

(Capital Murder)

The Grand Jury of Quartz County charge that before the finding of this indictment Destiny Grace Harper, whose name to the Grand Jury is otherwise unknown, did intentionally cause the death of Brooklyn Harper and Lydia Harper, children less than fourteen years of age, in violation of §13A-5-40(15) of the Code of Alabama. AGAINST THE PEACE AND DIGNITY OF THE STATE OF ALABAMA.

Bail fixed at $ No Bond
/s/ Kelsey M. Kerr
District Attorney.

THE OUT-OF-TOWN LAWYER

THE
OUT-OF-TOWN
LAWYER

ROBERT ROTSTEIN

BLACK STONE
PUBLISHING

For Daco

CHAPTER ONE

Twenty miles east of Laredo, Texas. Heading nowhere, waiting for my next assignment to somewhere. My phone rings.

Hazel Ruth Curnow's antique voice crackles like tires rolling on gravel. That voice is so familiar, yet even after five years working for her, I've never met her in person. A former legal icon, Ms. Curnow became a hermit nineteen years ago, after her son died of an accidental overdose of fentanyl and Xanax (though the gossipy legal community questions how accidental it was). Her son died long before Ms. Curnow plucked me out of the back alleys of the law and offered me a job as, shall we say, her surrogate on the ground. Why was my legal career in extremis? I don't share my secrets, just as I don't ask Ms. Curnow hers. She wouldn't share them with me anyway. We don't really know each other. When she calls, I answer; when she assigns me a case, I take it. That suits me fine. Never get too close to your boss.

"Our new client has been charged with capital murder in Quartz County, Alabama," says Ms. Curnow. "Trial starts in four-and-a-half weeks."

My Ford Transit van swerves into the opposing lane. "As in

Cole's Crossing? My hometown? I don't want to go back there. Four weeks and change to prepare? No damn way."

"Margaret Booth will meet you tomorrow afternoon, 4:15 p.m. sharp, at the Quartz County jail, where you'll interview the accused. When I hang up, contact Margaret for a briefing. Go save a girl's life, Elvis." The phone line dies.

I utter a few more expletives and accelerate the van, passing a billboard touting a personal injury lawyer with offices in eight states and a couple of billion dollars in jury verdicts. He surely doesn't drive from state to state trying cases like I do. I pass another billboard reading, *Who in their right mind would hire a billboard lawyer?* Amen.

In my years on the road, I've become an aficionado of billboards. Billboards can feed you, fill your tank, get you drunk, even save your soul. The next billboard captures my attention— *Lola's Gentlemen's Cabaret and Adult Superstore, Fully Nude, 6 Miles, Exit 72 at Hansen.*

I get off the highway at exit 72. I've always wanted to see Hansen.

CHAPTER TWO

The Quartz County detention center is all concrete, metal, and glass—hard construction materials for hardened human beings. Alleged baby killer Destiny Grace Harper sits slouching at a table in the attorney-client conference room, the Holy Bible open in front of her. That book got her into this scorching mess, but she still clings to it. Is her Bible a true believer's Bloody Mary, the zealot's version of *hair of the dog*? Harper wears the jail's standard-issue lime-green jumpsuit. Her auburn hair is stringy and unkempt—rubber bands and scrunchies can turn into implements of violence in a jail. A tattoo inside her right upper arm reads, in brownish ink, *grace upon grace JOHN 1:16*. Interesting—her church likely frowns on body alterations. An homage to Jesus or not, I bet she'll regret the tattoo someday. I regret my Kurt Cobain tattoo, though at the time, it seemed like a good way for a boy named Elvis to say *Fuck you*.

I sit across from Harper. Our firm's paralegal, Margaret Booth, sits at the far end of the table. Although we came into the room a couple of minutes ago, Ms. Harper hasn't acknowledged us. She's praying, I suppose. She finally looks up from her Good Book and sends a shy smile my way. I send a winning smile back. "I'm Elvis Henderson. Call me E."

"Thank y'all for coming, Mr. Henderson." A soft, fluty voice, laden with Alabama country. "You okay, sir? You look a little raggedy." She crinkles her nose and swipes at the air.

"I look and smell this way because I drove eleven hundred miles in fourteen hours to get here, with only a brief stop to spend some time with a few fully nude women," I say. "I haven't showered in three days. All for the privilege of helping you out."

She recoils ever so slightly but doesn't stop smiling.

I introduce Ms. Margaret Booth. Destiny Grace's smile vanishes, and she lowers her eyes.

Margaret purses her collagen-enhanced lips and primps her long brown hair, tangled in July's humidity.

"Something bothering you, Ms. Harper?" I ask.

Destiny Grace sits straighter in her chair. "I don't want Ms. Booth working on my case. No offense, but she won't help with the judge or jury."

You'd think the younger ones would be more enlightened, even in this part of America. Or at least you'd think the desperate would show more gratitude. Margaret's first name at birth was different, matching the *M* on her birth certificate, a fact still evident in her physiognomy and unlikely to win her many friends in this part of the Yellowhammer State.

"Well, this won't be the first time a client has fired us," I say. "I'm sure Aruna Higgins will do a fine job for you after all." Higgins is—or was—Harper's inexperienced court-appointed attorney, who last week had the bad sense to recommend that Destiny Grace plead guilty to second-degree murder and serve forty-four years in the Julia Tutwiler Prison for Women in Wetumpka. Julia Tutwiler might've been known as the angel of the prisons, but the penitentiary named for her is hell. Higgins told us how Destiny Grace fired her on the spot and reached out to Hazel Ruth Curnow. Only Ms. Curnow would agree to jump into a capital murder case on four weeks' notice, pro bono, no less. Easy for her to volunteer when I'm the one on the front lines.

Margaret and I get out of our chairs, and I bid Destiny Grace Harper adieu. I left this town twenty-eight years ago, just after I turned eighteen, never intending to return. I have no desire to stay.

"Wait, sir," says Destiny Grace. "I want *you* to represent me, just not . . . No offense intended, Ms. Booth. Like I told you, I worry the judge and jury won't agree with . . . you know."

Margaret starts to say something, but I hold up a hand. "Are you a fan of billboards, Destiny?" I ask.

"It's Destiny *Grace*."

"Are you a fan of billboards, Destiny Grace?"

"They're eyesores, sir."

"Yes, but eyesores can be informative, and that can be beautiful. For example: speeding through Texarkana to get here as quick as I could, I saw a billboard reading, 'Two are better than one, because they have a good reward for their labor.' From the Bible. Ecclesiastes, as I recall. The sign was advertising a soft-serve ice cream shop in Homan, Arkansas, but my point is, you work with both of us, or you work with neither of us. And I *will* fire you—the only lawyers who don't fire problem clients are desperate lawyers. I am not a desperate lawyer. Are you a problem, Destiny Grace?" I keep my index finger poised near the buzzer, giving her a moment to ponder her future.

She tugs at a strand of hair and picks off one split end after another. Finally: "Yes, sir, I understand. I can't afford to be fired." A conciliatory nod toward Margaret. "Thanks for coming to help me, Ms. Booth. No offense intended."

"We're all good," says Margaret, and I know she means it. She's genuinely a forgiving person—far more than I am. Destiny Grace Harper is hardly the first client to shun Margaret at first sight. We've represented White supremacists in the past, and Margaret won them over—well, a couple of them maybe.

When Margaret and I sit back down at the conference table, Destiny Grace closes her Bible, raises her arms above her head, and stretches. "Y'all know I didn't murder my babies, right? It ain't like I had an abortion or took drugs while pregnant or nothing. All I did was entrust my babies to the Lord, and He decided to embrace them in His loving arms."

Destiny Grace's unborn fetuses suffered from TTTS, which stands for twin-to-twin transfusion syndrome, a rare condition afflicting only identical twins. Almost always fatal to one or both of the babies if left untreated, the condition is highly treatable via specialized laser surgery on the fetuses. Destiny Grace refused the laser procedure on religious grounds—her church scorns modern medicine.

I fight to keep myself from sighing. I wish I could change her views on a pregnant woman's rights and the lifesaving capabilities of medical care, but I doubt I will. No matter. I have one job and one job only—to convince a local jury not to murder *her*. The State of Alabama seeks to transport her to the William C. Holman Correctional Facility death chamber, strap her to a gurney, and inject into her petite body a lethal combination of 100 mL of midazolam hydrochloride, 40 mL of saline, 60 mL of rocuronium bromide, and 120 mL of potassium chloride. Legalized murder. I've witnessed two executions, but I don't talk about that.

"Let's start from the beginning," I say. "Who the hell are you, Destiny Grace Harper?"

CHAPTER THREE

"Oh. Okay. So, like, I feel like I made some poor choices in my life. In middle school I started hanging out with the wrong people. My mother was a single parent working all the time to make ends meet, so she left me on my own. Don't get me wrong, I ain't blaming her. She worked hard all her life. Worked as a secretary, and as a landscaper, and then doing taxes and bookkeeping for our church and other people. But I started drinking alcohol when I was twelve; weed at fourteen, harder drugs when I was fifteen. I got caught shoplifting at the Dillard's down in Huntsville. Spent two nights in the juvenile detention center. At sixteen, I got caught possessing meth. Lucky I was still a minor. So, anyway, the judge showed leniency when the pastor of my church, Reverend Jeremiah Tipple, stood up for me. After spending ninety days in juvie, I attended the drug and alcohol rehab program through the Church of Our Lord's Rapture. Reverend Tipple saved my life. Real understanding man back then. I finished high school, and I was on the right track. Teaching the preschoolers at the church. Thinking about going back to Calhoun Community

College to get my associate degree until . . ." She lets out a deep sigh. "My mama caught the ovarian cancer, and she couldn't work for almost a year. That was about a year and a half ago."

"Sorry to hear it," I say. "I hope your mother didn't rely on the power of prayer to treat her illness."

"I apologize for E's snarky comment," says Margaret. "We don't judge our clients' beliefs."

"Margaret doesn't, Ms. Hazel Curnow doesn't, but I do," I say. "I'm going to make full disclosure, Ms. Harper. That's lawyer-speak for making a confession. I disagree with your church's views on medicine. To say that I'm not a fan of the choice you made regarding your babies is an understatement. But rest assured my personal views won't affect our defense of you in the slightest. Just the opposite. If that doesn't work for you, we can fire each other again."

"I ain't sure I get what you're saying, but Mama did decide to go to a doctor, and that's when all the problems started," says Destiny Grace. She explained how her mother, LeAnn Harper, suffered from agonizing gut pain, which worsened despite the holy oil and the healing prayers. Desperate, LeAnn consulted a medical doctor down in Birmingham, who diagnosed stage 3A ovarian cancer. She underwent surgery and chemotherapy—less forgivable in the eyes of her church than breaking the Ten Commandments. The church excommunicated her. "The last scan was clean, but you know how scans and doctors go. Can't trust them. Anyway, Mama didn't have insurance, and she couldn't work. She went into a lot of debt. Mama declared bankruptcy. I kept teaching the little ones at the church school, but I also got a job as a maid, cleaning hotel rooms at the Quartz Inn. Two jobs and a sick mama took up all the hours in the day. Then I ended up pregnant, and here we are." She sighs. "That's who I am, Mr. Henderson. Not a very interesting person."

"Oh, you're quite interesting," I say. "You just left out the interesting part. You know, the part about your babies having a serious medical problem and you running off so they wouldn't get medical care. And then they died. Do I have that right?"

When the Quartz County DA's office sought a court order forcing Destiny Grace to have the laser surgery to cure the TTTS, she fled the jurisdiction and went into hiding. Last November, she gave birth. One baby was stillborn, the other alive for some minutes. The State of Alabama arrested her for capital murder and seeks the death penalty.

Destiny Grace clenches and unclenches her jaw. "Those are mean words, sir."

"Maybe so. Just like doctors have to perform painful surgeries to save a patient, sometimes a lawyer has to ask hurtful questions to defend the client."

"You know how I feel about doctors and surgeries."

"Did you understand what TTTS is?" I ask.

A sigh, at once impatient and patronizing. "It means one of my babies was like a vampire, draining the blood from the other." A vivid but accurate description. "But like I said, I didn't do anything to harm my babies. I just prayed. This is the South, where most people believe in God and accept Jesus. No one will convict me for praying that the Lord heal my babies. We believe in freedom of religion down here, and the right to keep the government out of your private business. And my body is my private business."

"Unfortunately, it doesn't work that way," says Margaret. "Ever since the US Supreme Court legalized abortion in *Roe v. Wade*, there's been a long tradition among conservative people, especially in the South, to value the life of the unborn over a woman's right to control her own body—and not just in abortion cases but also in cases a lot like yours, and it's only gotten worse since the *Dobbs* case overturned *Roe*. Way back in 1982, a couple from Frankfort, Kentucky, was charged with homicide when their baby was stillborn. Like you, they were members of a church that believed in the power of prayer to heal, and just like you, they refused medical treatment that could've saved the baby's life." Margaret pauses to let this information sink in. "In another case, the Supreme Court of Georgia gave a government welfare agency temporary custody of a fetus after its mother on religious grounds refused a cesarean section that was necessary to save her baby's life. And many courts, North and South, have ordered pregnant mothers to undergo blood transfusions despite the women's staunch religious beliefs."

There were other cases that Margaret could've mentioned. A court in Washington, DC, ordered a pregnant, terminally ill cancer patient to undergo a C-section over her objection; the mother and baby both died excruciating deaths. After a pregnant woman failed to have a court-ordered C-section, a Utah prosecutor charged her with first-degree homicide. A woman down in Birmingham was charged with killing her own baby after provoking a fight and getting gut shot. (The shooter wasn't charged; she was only standing her ground, the grand jury found.) And after the US Supreme Court overruled *Roe v. Wade* and held in the *Dobbs* case that the states could illegalize abortion, prosecutions against pregnant women for the accidental deaths of their babies have skyrocketed, especially in the Deep South. Appeals to freedom of religion and the right against government intrusion couldn't stop these prosecutions and wouldn't guarantee acquittal for Destiny Grace Harper.

"What Margaret means is that many Southern jurors won't care about your religious belief or the government's intrusion if they think your beliefs killed your babies," I say. "And that goes for some jurors who might be pro-choice. Surely your former lawyer told you that."

"Aruna didn't put it so blunt," she says. "But I just can't believe the law would do that in a free country. Good lord, people around here who aren't even in my church fought against those vaccination shots the government forced on us when the Covid came."

"Vaccinations don't involve a conflict between the rights of a mother and the life of an unborn baby," I say.

Destiny Grace gives a disbelieving shake of the head.

"How did you plan to keep your babies healthy?" asks Margaret.

Destiny Grace's eyes narrow. "I prayed to the Lord to save their lives and keep them healthy."

"Where does the Bible say an expectant mom shouldn't visit an ob-gyn?" I ask.

Destiny Grace grasps her Bible, as if to open it, but she doesn't need to. "Matthew 9:12: 'They that are whole have no need of a physician, but they that are sick'; James 5:15: 'And the prayer of faith shall save him that is sick'; Ecclesiastes 11:5: 'Thou knowest not what is the way of the wind, nor how the bones do grow in the womb of her that is with child.'"

"Christian organizations of all denominations have known of those passages from time immemorial, yet they don't reject conventional medical care," I say.

"Well, they're wrong, Mr. Henderson. A liberal lawyer like yourself should know the majority don't rule the truth."

"I'm a lawyer, not a *liberal* lawyer. I serve the interests of justice."

"If the majority decided what's true, you wouldn't be here, because I'd already be dead, wouldn't I?"

I glance at Margaret, who gives a wry smile. Despite her country-bumpkin demeanor, Destiny Grace Harper is neither stupid nor a pushover.

"Aruna Higgins tells us Reverend Jeremiah Tipple won't testify on your behalf," I say.

Destiny Grace presses her lips together as if recalling a bitter taste. "Why should he? I was an unwed mother. My mama went to medical doctors, and I drove her to her appointments. The news media, other religious leaders, even some of the pro-abortion people, are blaming the church for what happened to my babies. Reverend Tipple says my babies died because I lost faith. That it was my fault." Without warning, she breaks into heartrending sobs. Margaret goes over and wraps a long arm around the client. The younger woman prickles, but Margaret doesn't retreat, just leans over and whispers something in Destiny Grace's ear. Destiny Grace snuffles loudly and smiles. What magical words did Margaret whisper?

Once Destiny Grace calms down, Margaret asks, "What about the babies' father?"

"What about him?"

Margaret clasps her hands in front of her and leans forward. "Who is he? What does he think about all this?"

Destiny Grace retrieves a tissue from a box on the counter, blows her nose, and drops the tissue on the floor—no doubt a purposeful act of defiance. "If y'all talked to Aruna Higgins for more than two minutes, you know I ain't going to answer that question. He had nothing to do with birthing the babies. And why are *you* asking so many questions, ma'am, when Mr. Henderson's supposed to be my lawyer?"

"Margaret and I work as a team. Stop the bullshit. Why won't you reveal who the babies' daddy is?"

She uses an index finger to rub under her nose. "Like I told Aruna a hundred times, if I bring him into this, people will get hurt for no reason."

"Not a good enough explanation," I say. "We need a better one if we're going to save your life."

"Well, it's the best I got."

I stand up and pace around the conference room. An aimless exercise because I'm no less anxious when I get back in my chair. I look up at the perforated ceiling tiles, which are grimy and disintegrating. Easily removable. Have the authorities bugged the sacrosanct attorney conference room with cameras and recording equipment in the ceiling? Even if the room is bugged, the authorities won't learn anything, because the accused isn't sharing anything. "Destiny Grace, if you won't help yourself, we sure as hell can't help you. Let's try again—who fathered the twins?"

"Next subject, please."

I glance at Margaret, who gives a *move-on-to-something-else* shrug. She's right—never press too hard in the first interview. "A Lillian Wagers acted as your midwife before you fled the jurisdiction," I say. "Who helped you after you went into hiding?"

"Nobody."

Margaret glances at me sidelong.

"Y'all rolling your eyes at me now?" asks Destiny Grace. "I don't need a replay of Aruna Higgins. She's always doing that."

"We're trying to get to the truth," I say. "A concept you apparently dislike."

Margaret delivers a two-handed, palms-down gesture to encourage me to lower the temperature, but mine rises. "Ms. Harper, are you seriously telling us you planned to deliver two sick twins without help?"

"I planned to deliver my babies with the Lord God's help. But He decided to take them for His own."

"Let's put the Lord God aside. What was your plan for getting a flesh-and-blood human being to help birth your babies?"

Her shrug might as well be a confession of guilt.

"The medical examiner's report says that after the births, one of the babies was still alive," I say. "The DA claims that you abandoned her and went to the hospital alone for treatment. I don't believe you did something so heinous. But a jury might believe the prosecution's argument unless you tell us what really happened."

Destiny Grace springs up and shouts, "We're done!" She begins pounding on the locked door.

A young deputy sheriff, nametag reading *Maloney*, bursts in, his hand hovering over his firearm.

"Relax, son," I say. "Just some lively dialogue between attorney and client."

"Take me back to my cell," says Destiny Grace, almost hyperventilating. "They're leaving. Just take me back."

After shooting us an acid glance, Deputy Maloney escorts Destiny Grace out of the room.

Margaret gives a resigned headshake. "Here's my theory. In some warped, modern version of *The Scarlet Letter*, she's playing Hester Prynne, protecting some married asshole's reputation and family. Sacrificing herself for her so-called lover. The same pathetic old story. She's more vulnerable than a liar. Liars eventually tell the truth when they realize it's in their best interest. She'll never stand up to cross-examination."

"She won't have to. No way in hell we're calling her to the witness stand."

CHAPTER FOUR

Hazel Curnow's assistant, Anita, booked Margaret and me rooms at the Quartz Inn—the same hotel where Destiny Grace Harper once worked as a maid. The best hotel in town, according to the online rating services—although at two stars, that wasn't saying much. A cross between a convention hotel and a chain motor inn, with a cracked yellow stucco facade, the inn hadn't existed when I was a kid. The area had been fallow farmland, far more inviting.

"It's rustic; quaint—in a 1970s kind of way," says Margaret, swatting away a mosquito.

"I'm glad you like it. It's all yours."

"Who said I liked it?"

At check-in, an amiable man name-tagged *Thomas Styles* breaks with tradition and doesn't do a double take when he sees us. In his mid-thirties, he has a clean-cut, earnest look of a person seeking a promotion. His snaggletooth smile prevents him from achieving classic good looks. With the sugary enthusiasm typical of hotel employees, he identifies himself as the concierge. He pronounces the word *con-see-air*. He asks the rote, invasive questions that weary hotel guests never want to hear. *Ever stayed with us before?* Nope. *What brings y'all to Cole's Crossing?* Fly-fishing. *Two rooms, I see?* Yep. *You or the lady need help with your bags?* Not necessary, but thank you just the same.

At long last, he asks, "Two room keys each okay?"

Margaret nods.

"I won't be needing any room keys," I say.

Thomas rocks back at this one. "Excuse me, sir?"

"I'm not staying in the room." I point outside the lobby door. "I'll be sleeping in my van out in the hotel parking lot. My room fee should cover that privilege, yeah?" I slip him a twenty-dollar bill to close the deal.

He takes the bill without looking down and conceals it in his pants pocket. "I don't see why not. Can't guarantee the police won't hassle you. And room service is a no-go."

"Fine by me, son."

"You're sure you don't want to sleep in a clean bed, E?" says Margaret. "At least for a night or two? Change of pace? You've been on the road for months."

"Thank you for your concern, Margaret, but every day is a change of pace. My good old Ford Transit is stability."

Margaret and I agree to meet downstairs tomorrow morning at eight. She goes to the elevator. I exit the hotel and find my van, which has a shower, a toilet, a kitchen, a work area, a Wi-Fi hotspot, and a bed—all I need to work and live.

Despite my long drive from Laredo, Texas, to Coles Crossing, Alabama, I can't call it a night. I start up the van, drive out onto the main drag, and head north. About three miles down the road, past the warehouses and fast-food joints, the landscape becomes forested, with scattered homes and shacks. I pass a hovel with a huge Confederate flag draped in the front window followed by two much more elegant homes flying that detestable symbol of White supremacy. I recall that Pulaski, Tennessee, just thirty miles north of here, was the birthplace of the Ku Klux Klan.

After driving another half-mile up an incline into the foothills, I pull sharply into a graveled driveway and up to an isolated rectangular house with dull-green metallic walls. I can't see much in the darkness, but I grew up in this house, and I don't need my eyes to tell me it hasn't changed in a quarter century. In an early example of "green" planning, the house is made of two twenty-by-twenty-foot shipping containers, like you see on ships and freight trains and such. Other kids called my house the *Redneck Condo*. I didn't like that. They say when you return to your childhood home after a long absence, the place seems much smaller. But seeing the Redneck Condo through the front windshield of my current home, the place looks downright vast.

A beat-up old Jeep Wrangler is parked in the driveway, malignant rust making its way from the undercarriage to the army-green front passenger door.

A brass bell, green with tarnish and patina, hangs next to the doorframe. I grab the chain and ring the bell four or five times. The old flush of embarrassment returns—most kids in the 1980s had electric doorbells, even in Cole's Crossing.

"Who the hell is it?" The voice always sounded raspy but now, despite the loud volume, has a breathless quality. A dog barks and growls from behind the door.

"It's me," I shout. "Your nephew."

There's a combination groan and grumble. The old man opens the door, a can of Coors in one hand and a handgun in the other. A wonder he could turn the doorknob with both hands occupied, but my uncle, Buddy Holly Henderson, was always intrepid. Once a six-footer, time has stolen an inch or two. Two hundred and twenty pounds or more when I left, he couldn't weigh more than one-eighty now. I'm a couple of inches taller and about ten pounds heavier than him these days. He wears a blue work shirt and blue jeans, and they could be the same clothes he wore on the day I left—and every day before I left. The once reddish-brown whiskers have turned white, giving him an ashen look. He still has a shock of curly hair—gray-white now, but still impressive for a man in his seventies.

"Well, well, well, Elvis wants back into the building." He slams the door in my face.

I go back to my van, open my lockbox, and take out a set of keys I haven't touched in forever and a week, then open the pantry and pull out a Southern Pawz dog biscuit I bought at a pet supply store in Greenfield. I climb the porch, use the key to open the door, and step into the living area. My uncle sits in his old rattan chair, sipping the Coors while still holding his Smith & Wesson. The barking dog—looks like a border terrier with pit-bull jaws—runs up to me and growls.

"Sit, Rennie," I say.

The pooch obeys, and I reward him with the treat, which he takes to a far corner.

"How'd you know his name?" asks Buddy.

"You started naming your dogs after the Chicago Seven when we got Abbie. Before I left, you got Jerry. Figured you'd be on Rennie by now."

"Fuck me." He shakes his head. "You kept the house key all these years?"

"Weren't you the one who told me you never know what an old key might open? Still, might've thought you would've changed the lock after twenty-eight years."

"Didn't even use the lock until five years ago. Times have changed." He motions with the gun. "Have a seat, I guess."

"Do you have to hang onto that weapon?"

He sets it down on the end table.

He's my father's younger brother—or maybe *was* my father's younger brother. I don't know if my parents are alive. I have no desire to find out. The family was originally from Birmingham, but after Buddy got out of the service, my father convinced him to move to the utopia that was rural Alabama. When I was four, my parents departed utopia after concluding they had to save the planet, so they joined the Weather Underground or some other radical group so they could blow things up. A small child would interfere with those lofty goals. That's what Buddy told me when I was ten. By the time I turned fifteen, I'd figured out that no matter their excuses, my parents simply didn't want me. Neither did Buddy, but he nevertheless stayed here and raised me—through a marriage, an arrest for possession of an illegal drug with intent to distribute, and a divorce that left us hovering around the poverty line. All he wanted to do was find someplace where he could live the life of a man unencumbered. Such a scenario didn't make for the most harmonious of upbringings. Uncle Buddy did instill in me a progressive view of the world and a battling spirit, useful contributions to my personality that made my time in Quartz County a pleasurable torment. I liked to argue. I argued with my reactionary teachers and classmates. To his credit, he encouraged me to get out of town to improve my lot in life; to his discredit, he resented me when I took his advice. In fairness, no one anticipated that my hasty departure would be so dramatic. Buddy believed I left town out of cowardice—and, yes, I had been afraid. But I didn't leave because of the fear—I left because of the guilt.

"Cracking necks and adjusting spines these days?" I ask. Buddy became a chiropractor when I turned five, but he really functioned as a hippie healer—not only manipulating limbs but purveying natural and herbal remedies of all kinds, some of them quite illegal. His arrest harmed his business—most folks didn't want to hire a drug pusher. Certain religious groups believed his brand of healing was the devil's work.

"I retired, except to help some of the neighbors who're old as me and can't get around so well and can't afford a doctor." He sips some beer and then closes one eye to appraise me. "You're a lawyer? With your hair braided like Willie Nelson's?"

"I only braid it when it's unwashed, and it's only down to my shoulders, not almost to my waist like Willie's. It's an homage to the great William Kunstler—your favorite attorney back in the day. I'm in town for a case."

"I'm sure you're no William Kunstler." He shakes his head. "Good lord, Elvis, you're a craggy-faced, graying, middle-aged man. Still a decent-looking fellow, though. You take after your mother."

"How've you been getting along?"

"About the same as I have since you left. Except older, grouchier, and less able to tolerate alcohol. Get drunker faster, and the hangovers are worse. You have any interest in hearing how your parents are doing?"

I infer from his question that they're still living. "None whatsoever. If I did, I'd have googled them years ago. Can't be many Chuck Berry Hendersons in this world.

"You ever get married? Kids?"

"Married for a London minute. Hardly remember her name. No kids."

"Well, you must be here for a reason. What can I do for you, Elvis?"

"How about starting with, 'Welcome home, son'?"

"Welcome home. What can I do for you?"

"You're not going to offer me a beer?"

"No, I am not."

A blast from the window air-conditioning unit meets my sweaty skin and sends a chill through my torso. I grope for familiarity with this place but feel none. Oh, I know where everything is—not that there's much to know. Buddy's bedroom is to the left. Mine was to the right. I remember foraging in the refrigerator for something to eat and sneaking beers starting at age twelve until Buddy caught me and used his belt. An *object lesson*, he called it, although I knew corporal punishment was *not* an object lesson. None of these memories come with an emotional charge. I vowed to leave them behind when I got out of town. Looks like I succeeded.

"What do you know about my new client? Destiny Grace Harper."

He blows a soft whistle of surprise, perhaps appreciation. "The Harper girl? That's why you came back? She's not one you'd expect to be charged in a murder case."

"I heard she was pretty wild as a young teenager."

"I don't know anything about that. Most of the town hates her now after what she did to those babies—or, I guess, what she didn't do for them. The Harper girl's mother, LeAnn, she's better known. An accountant or bookkeeper for the Church of Our Lord's Rapture, but also does folks' taxes around here. I went to her for a couple of years, until she got sick. She saw doctors, against her religion."

"So her daughter told me. What about Destiny Grace's father?"

"Trent Harper. An auto mechanic. He died when the girl was a toddler. Medical malpractice—the anesthesiologist administered an overdose for simple oral surgery. That's how LeAnn Harper came to join the Church of Our Lord's Rapture. She lost faith in doctors. Can't say I blame her."

A tragedy, but a good fact supporting Destiny Grace's bona fides as a legitimate skeptic of medicine.

We sit in uncomfortable silence. I take a deep breath and slap my thighs with my hands. "I was wondering if you'd lend me one of your guns. Until I finish this trial and leave town again."

"No, sir. You know very well I believe the American public has too easy access to firearms."

I point a finger at his Smith & Wesson. "You exclude yourself from that theory?"

"Hypocrisy in the interest of self-preservation is no vice. I don't want to get mixed up in anything untoward you're likely to bring down on yourself."

"If anything untoward happens, I'll say I stole it from my intoxicated uncle. I'm worried I might need it, Buddy."

He picks up the gun and hands it to me. "That's exactly what you did. Stole it from your drunk uncle."

———

I pull into the Quartz Inn parking lot. I'm at the stage where the high-voltage electricity of fatigue will prevent me from sleeping. The van bounces hard over a pothole, the headlights rise and fall, and I catch a glimpse of a person standing near Margaret Booth's rental Dodge Charger. I park the van in two open spaces, retrieve Buddy's gun, and walk toward the Charger. The parking lot is lighted in theory, but the two commercial lampposts are far away, and their bulbs are dim—negligent maintenance waiting for a lawsuit over a crash, a fall, or a physical assault.

"May I help you?" I ask when I near the Charger.

The person turns slowly. "E?"

Whatever adrenaline I had in reserve deserts my body. "Jesus, Margaret, what the fuck?"

She beckons me over and holds up her smartphone, turns the flashlight on, and shines it on the passenger side. Spray-painted across the paneling in black letters are the words *tranny die*, punctuated by a swastika. She takes me to the other side: *tranny get out*.

I place my hand on Margaret's forearm. "Welcome to my hometown. I'm sorry about this."

"This shit doesn't only happen here. I saw hate stuff when I was a cop in California." Years ago, the Mar Vista, California, police department unlawfully ousted her when she decided to transition. Ms. Curnow won a hefty wrongful discharge settlement for her. Six months later, Margaret got her paralegal degree, and Curnow hired her.

"Most of the time, we blew this kind of stuff off," says Margaret. "Not that we liked ignoring it, but we didn't feel it was worth our time. In our minds, things like this didn't amount to real crimes, just harmless vandalism. I guess I see things differently now."

"Are you okay, Margaret?"

She gives an emphatic shake of her head *no*, crosses her arms, and looks up at the night sky, the stars far more intense but also more ominous than in Los Angeles. It's nine o'clock—no, ten o'clock—and the temperature must be seventy-five degrees or more. The air is dead still, the only sounds the occasional car passing on the highway and the buzz of mosquitos.

I'm puzzled. "What made you come down here this late?"

Even in the poor light, I notice her look of surprise. She taps her smartphone and displays a text message that says it's from me. *Meet me in parking lot, problem w/ the Charger.*

"I didn't send that." I inhale deeply. A dissonant chirping fills the night air—tree frogs. As a boy, I loved that chirping. Now, the sound conjures a biblical plague.

"Someone spoofed our phone numbers," I say.

She considers this. "Two possibilities for people who have our numbers down here. The hotel desk clerk or the cops."

Which is why I borrowed my uncle's Smith & Wesson.

CHAPTER FIVE

Shortly before eight the next morning, Margaret and I meet in the lobby. I didn't sleep, and the dark circles under her eyes tell me she didn't either. Thomas Styles, the desk clerk, called the police, arranged for a replacement rental car, and apologized profusely. He even comped our rooms for the night.

The sheriff's deputy who took the report acted with a solemnity that almost convinced me he wasn't silently snickering at the crime.

Margaret and I both wear dark suits, and we both pull litigation bags behind us. She hasn't asked where I went last night. She thinks I party too much, and I'll let her think I was out at a bar. No reason to discuss my family history.

We walk outside into the heat and humidity and stop in unison. Across the street, two dozen demonstrators have gathered. One carries a sign with a photo of a fetus and the words, *I'm a Child of God*. One man holds up a mocked-up wild-West wanted poster featuring the image of yours truly with a bull's-eye superimposed over my face, flanked by a similar image of Hazel Ruth Curnow. We're probably his targets not so much because of this case but because Ms. Curnow has traditionally fought for abortion rights. She filed a very persuasive amicus brief in *Roe v. Wade* that some believe influenced the Supreme Court's ruling. And now I'm associated with her. Is that bull's-eye with my image on it simply tasteless political commentary? No—far more ominous. Many years ago, the image of a Florida doctor who supposedly performed abortions appeared on a makeshift wanted poster like these. Soon after, an anti-abortion protester shot and killed the man. We live in a country where fanaticism is weaponized and justified by warped readings of the Holy Bible and the Second Amendment. Ms. Curnow likes to say that the enmity lawyers generate is directly proportional to their good works. Noble sentiment, but not much comfort when you imagine yourself in the sights of a sniper's rifle. Such people don't care about legal nuances between the abortion issue and Destiny Grace Harper's case.

Margaret and I arrive at the Quartz County courthouse with five minutes to spare. It's a neoclassical building made of buff-colored brick. A large portico supported by four columns rises to a pediment with a clock at the roofline. In this stately courthouse in 1949, an all-White jury convicted a Black World War II veteran of raping a White woman—although five witnesses swore under oath the defendant was drinking in a bar ten miles away at the time of the crime. In this courthouse in 1963, an all-White jury acquitted two Klansmen of murdering a civil rights worker from Illinois—even after the defendants bragged about the killing to at least a dozen people.

Despite its grisly history, when I was a kid this building was one of my favorite locations in town, inspiring awe and ambition. I admired lawyers, both fictional and real, and I aspired to become one of them. *Trial work is a meritocracy*, an occupation that values success, not connections and background—or so thought the callow Elvis Henderson. It only took a semester in law school for me to realize the law plays favorites just like most other institutions in life, beginning from the time we can string sentences together. But though trial work isn't a meritocracy, it is a primary battleground to fight bias and special interests, and that's something.

"Those are dogwood trees on the front lawn," I tell Margaret. "The best Alabama tree, if you ask me. They bloom in white or pink in the spring. I prefer the pink, but both are beautiful. On the West Coast there's something they call dogwood, but it's not the same. Scrubby little plant. The ones here are lush, beautiful."

Margaret looks at me as if surprised by my knowledge of Alabama flora—and perhaps by my willingness to compliment the state of my birth about something other than delectable pastries containing massive quantities of butter, salt, sugar, and lard.

After passing through security, we take the escalator up to the fifth floor, the office of the district attorney. The receptionist ushers us back into a conference room. A surprise: at the glass table sits Aruna Patel Higgins. Fired attorneys don't ordinarily show up at meetings between their replacement and their former adversaries. Higgins is dressed in a red cotton blouse and black skirt. She's young, in her early thirties. Our awkward *Hey*s and *Nice to meet you in person*s only underscore the situation's ungainliness.

Don't get me wrong, I do feel for Ms. Higgins. I believe she did a piss-poor job representing Harper, but I feel for her. How in the world did the judge appoint her as defense counsel in a capital murder case? She meets Alabama's technical requirements for defending a capital case—she's participated in four homicide trials. But she worked only as an associate on those cases, and all of them pled out. No trials to verdict, much less trials as lead counsel. I suspect the judge appointed her because Destiny Grace Harper rebuffed the liberal, pro–women's rights, public interest lawyers as a matter of principle, and the judge didn't want to dump an unpopular case on one of his cronies in the local defense bar.

When I commend Higgins for doing such a great job of "holding down the fort," she can't suppress an eye roll. She knows contrived flattery when she hears it.

"I didn't expect to see you here, Aruna," I say.

"Well, sir, as of this moment, I'm still Destiny Grace's lawyer. You aren't attorney of record. Not yet." She clasps her hands and lets them flop on the table. "You know, I wasn't just holding down the fort for y'all. The client is a damn headache. She's hiding the ball, and when I called her on it, she got pissed off and told her mother I wasn't competent."

"It's my understanding—"

"I'm not finished, sir." She holds up a hand, and I can imagine if I continue to interrupt, that hand will ball up into a fist and end up pounding the table. "Yeah, I suggested she consider pleading guilty to second-degree murder. I know you disagree with that strategy, but I was trying to save her life. Doing the job the court appointed me to do." She brushes a strand of dark hair away from her face, a gesture that accentuates her indignant brown eyes.

"I thought you might have welcomed the chance to disengage from this hot mess," I say.

"*Welcomed* isn't the right word. Was I relieved? Yeah, sort of. My husband is freaked out about the death threats. You work with Hazel Ruth Curnow, so I assume you're a good attorney. I know you've handled quite a few death penalty cases. If my life were at stake, *I'd* hire Curnow & Associates instead of me. So, yeah . . ." Higgins looks up at the ceiling.

Margaret has been standing with her back to us, gazing out the window. Maybe one reason she hasn't gotten her law degree is to avoid awkward encounters like this. "Is that the Tennessee River out there? So wide."

"The Elk River," says Higgins, not turning around. "The Tennessee is much wider."

"Our river in Los Angeles has concrete banks and hardly any water during droughts," says Margaret. "But people drown in it when the rains come."

"I'll be available twenty-four seven if you need my help getting up to speed," says Higgins to both of us and neither of us.

"We should talk about the judge," I say, an olive branch.

"I have thoughts about the judge and the jury venire both," says Higgins. "Local knowledge and such."

"I was born and raised right here in Cole's Crossing, you know."

"So I hear. That'll work against you. People around here will think you bailed on us."

"Tell us about the judge," says Margaret.

"Judge Merle Barraclough," says Higgins. "Before 2017, Alabama was the only state in the union where elected judges could overturn jury verdicts of life sentences and impose the death penalty instead. Barraclough was near the top of the list for doing that. The asshole bragged about it during his reelection campaigns. And it worked, of course. Judge Lethal Injection, we call him. He won't like you, E, and pardon me, Margaret, but he'll like you even less."

"Does he like *you*, Aruna?" asks Margaret.

"Doesn't hurt that I'm an attractive woman from Huntsville—or so my husband says. I'm not above wearing my skirts a little shorter in his courtroom."

"I wish women didn't have to do things like that," says Margaret. "You think times would've changed—even in this state."

"I do whatever I can to save my clients," says Higgins. "Destiny Grace Harper's life is worth far more than the sight of two extra inches of my legs."

Before we resolve the skirt-length debate, the door clicks open, and Quartz County District Attorney Kelsey Kerr walks in, followed by her associate Sabrina Graham. No polite knock. Just an arrogant invasion of our privacy. I exchange a look with Margaret, who nods an *On it, E.*

"Would you mind giving us a moment?" asks Margaret. "We're not done talking."

Kerr and Graham look surprised and go out the door again. I immediately stand, open the door, and say, "Thank you for your consideration. We're ready for you now." Maybe three seconds have passed.

Kerr half-frowns. Is Graham suppressing a smile? They come back inside.

Kerr is tall, in her early forties, with short brown hair, a long neck, and an impressive aquiline nose. According to Margaret's research and Higgins's intel, our adversary is originally from Athens, Georgia. She attended a fundamentalist Christian college in Orange County, California, then went to law school at the University of Alabama in Tuscaloosa. After a successful career as a big-firm trial lawyer in Atlanta, she moved to Cole's Crossing, opened her own shop, and got elected Quartz County district attorney. The media calls her a rising political star. One of her largest campaign contributors: Reverend Jeremiah Tipple. Not directly, because a religious organization loses its tax exemption if it becomes political. Tipple funneled campaign contributions through his two sons and his daughter and through numerous church congregants. So, Kerr has every reason to please Tipple, who won't stand up for his congregant Destiny Grace Harper and seems to want her convicted.

Assistant DA Sabrina Graham, the State's second chair, is a short, bespectacled young woman with laser-focused brown eyes. She went to law school with Higgins, who emailed us that Graham was number two in their class and a law review editor. Oh, and she's Black. I scold myself for being surprised at that. I have my own biases about the State of Alabama. I shouldn't. I spent some years in Los Angeles, and the day-to-day separation between the Black and the White residents is far more pronounced there than in this state. I've got to clear my brain of assumptions before I stand before a local jury.

There's a problem—four chairs for five people, and I'm the only male. If I relinquish my chair, I'll look sexist. If I don't, I'll feel rude. At heart, I'm still the Southern gentleman my Uncle Buddy never taught me to be, so I rise to greet my hosts and wait for them to sit, but they stay standing.

Kerr looks past Margaret and me. "Aruna, your last inquiry was about a plea to manslaughter and ten years in prison, so I assume that's still your position. That proposal still won't cut it. We'll agree to a guilty plea of two counts of second-degree murder and a sentence of forty-four years in prison. You'll save your client's life. The offer expires at five o'clock this evening."

I tuck my thumbs into my suspenders, Clarence Darrow style. "Your proposal—or should I say, your taunt—is rejected. Here's our counteroffer. The State of Alabama will drop all charges against Destiny Grace Harper. In exchange, our client will waive a public apology from the State and from you personally for making her a political prisoner. *That* would serve the interests of justice."

"This fella has no standing in this jurisdiction, Aruna," says Kerr. "You're counsel of record, not him. He may never be counsel of record."

"Are you threatening us, Ms. Kerr?" I ask.

Kerr behaves as if I'm a gnat unworthy of a swat.

Higgins hesitates a moment and then tilts her head toward me. "Mr. Henderson is Destiny Grace Harper's attorney. He said the offer is rejected, so consider it rejected."

"See you in court, Aruna," says Kerr. "Unless y'all change your mind and accept our generous offer by five o'clock this afternoon."

"Wait!" says Higgins.

"Don't wait," I say.

Higgins swivels toward Graham. "Didn't you once tell me Professor Karst was your favorite teacher, Sabrina? He taught respect for human rights, for women's rights. Didn't you win the book award in that class? If he were alive today, what would he think of what you're doing to Harper?"

"He'd think I'm serving justice by getting a murderer off the streets," snaps Graham. "How did you do in his class, Aruna?"

The prosecution team starts out of the room. Kerr pauses at the door and says, "Sheriff Coyle sends his regards, Mr. Henderson. Says you and he are old friends."

"We went to school together, but we hung out in different circles. Tell Dave hey—and to let Destiny Grace Harper out of his jail on her own recognizance." If Margaret asks me about Dave Coyle, I'll just tell her he was a rich kid from an influential family who could've become a criminal as easily as he became a cop. She doesn't need to know the rest.

Humorless Kerr abruptly turns and walks out. Although Graham has her back to us, she at least gives a little wave.

Once our side is alone, Higgins's shoulders slump. "I was hoping they'd be more reasonable. I mean if they'd just offer manslaughter and fewer than twenty years . . ."

I don't disagree, but there's no sense in wallowing in disappointment. "It's just as well," I say, and I mean it—attorneys can adopt both sides of any issue, even emotional ones. "Compromises are tepid, and nothing tepid ever tastes good or kills germs."

I get ready to leave, as does Margaret.

"A second before we leave?" Higgins says, and we sit down.

"There's something you should know about Kelsey Kerr," says Higgins. "And about me." She shuts her eyes and takes one, then another, deep breath. "Okay. So this is private, and I shouldn't be telling anyone, but Kelsey doesn't have any kids. Not by her choice. She's . . . she's had trouble getting pregnant, and when she did, she had at least three miscarriages. The last one was when the pregnancy was in its sixth month. So horrible. So this case is personal to her."

"You know this how?" I ask.

"Because my husband and I have also struggled to get pregnant. I'm going to a fertility clinic down in Birmingham, and one day who do I bump into in the waiting room but Kelsey? She's not like a *friend* friend, but we've confided in each other—before this case. No one explicitly said it was confidential information, but I'm sure we both feel it is."

"You said this case is personal for Kerr," I say. "Is it for you?"

"Yes, sir," says Higgins. "You want a baby so much, and then you see this woman who doesn't save hers? Terrible. Or at least that's where Kelsey's coming from. But there's something that's even more important to me. When a state tries to take control of a woman's body without her consent, that's also personal. I hate what Destiny Grace did, but I hate what Kerr's trying to do to her even more."

I point at Higgins. "Aruna, you are staying on as co-counsel in this case."

She looks at me in astonishment and then shakes her head. "Destiny Grace fired me."

"She'll listen to me if I tell her we need you on the team.

You were right about me. I'm no longer a hometown boy. I don't know this judge or this DA. I need . . . no, Harper needs your help."

She shakes her head again.

"Aruna, if you substitute out of the case, you'll regret the decision for the rest of your career. You'll be the lawyer who ran away from an important battle. Stay with us and fight."

Higgins folds her hands in front of her and straightens up. "When Destiny Grace told me that she'd hired you, she also said you criticized the way I was handling this case, sir."

"I've changed my mind about you."

"In the ten minutes we've been together? After Kerr and Graham walked all over me?"

"No, ma'am. After you stood up to the prosecutors with the story about your law school professor, and after I experienced the client's bullheadedness firsthand. After I realized your dedication."

That wasn't entirely untrue. But really, when Kerr mentioned Dave Coyle, I realized I need a backup trial lawyer in case I disappear.

CHAPTER SIX

Margaret drives us back to the Quartz Inn. The moment we exit the car, there's loud honking close by. Given Kerr's reference to David Coyle and last night's vandalism, I want to take cover behind the Dodge Charger.

Honk! Honk! Honk! Honk!

Margaret, braver than I, uses her hand as a sun visor and looks for the source of the noise.

Honk! Honk! Honk! Honk!

"Do you know anyone who drives a Jeep, E? A real old one?"

"You got to be kidding."

I step into the lane and wave. My uncle steps on the accelerator, drives up behind us, and hollers out the window. "Get in, Elvis. Just you."

"Margaret, meet my uncle," I shout. "Buddy Henderson, this is Margaret Booth."

An amused but also clearly concerned Margaret waves. Buddy gives a half-hearted wave back. "Get in, Elvis. Now!"

"I must've broken curfew," I say to Margaret. "I'll be back."

"You sure about this?" she asks.

"No." Still wearing my suit and carrying my coat, I get inside the Jeep. I start to roll up the window.

"Leave it open," says Buddy. "The air conditioner is broke."

Perfect. "Why don't you take down the top?"

"Same reason you're getting those wrinkles on your face. Too much sun. Skin cancer. With all your driving around the country, be careful of your left ear. Reconstructive ear surgery is no fun." He guns the engine, heads to the interstate, and exits a few miles south. He navigates around the curves and over the potholes defining Jessup Mountain Road, finally slowing near the summit in front of a luxurious Acadian-style residence. Arlette Coyle's house, long ago.

"What the fuck, dude?" I say.

"I heard what happened to your paralegal's car. We got to nip this in the bud."

"How did you—?"

"I hear things. From patients. From people."

"Wait, don't stop yet, Buddy. Let me think about this. Drive into the Preserve."

"The criminal returning to the scene of the crime?"

"Not within ten miles of being funny."

"None of this is a joke. We're stopping here and now."

The late Prather Coyle was a major real estate developer in the area. Prather hoped his son, David, would take over the business one day, but when Dave went into law enforcement and became sheriff, Prather sold out to a large regional company based in Atlanta. Then he promptly dropped dead of a heart attack while boating on Lake Guntersville. Buddy tells me Prather's widow, Gloria Coyle, lives alone in the big house.

Buddy and I climb the steep concrete steps. He's out of breath by the time we reach the top. He gapes at me, wrinkles his nose, and fans the air. "Jesus, you reek, Elvis."

"I've been wearing a wool suit and sitting in an un–air-conditioned Jeep," I say before my brain belatedly advises, *Don't engage him; you're not twelve.*

He rings the doorbell, which chimes a few bars from "*The Bells of St. Mary's.*" I expect a maid to answer—the house gives off that vibe—but Gloria Coyle opens the door. She must be in her mid-seventies, but she looks younger—blond hair, smooth complexion, firm jaw, neck pulled tight. It's elegant plastic surgery, a mask, with doleful eyes gazing out from behind. The unnerving part is that I can see the image of her daughter, Arlette.

She squints at us in confusion. "Buddy, it's Tuesday, I thought my next session wasn't until . . ." When her sad, surprised eyes catch mine, she mumbles, "Oh, my." Those eyes, the tone of voice, dash my hope that she wouldn't remember who the hell I am.

"Okay if we come in and talk, Gloria?" asks Buddy.

She considers this. "Just you, Buddy. Not him."

"I'll take a walk in the park," I say.

He nods, then goes inside. Gloria shuts the door hard.

I climb four blocks up the hill and into the Santee Mountain Nature Preserve, a forested area of trails and native foliage. A favorite of early rising birdwatchers; a place where small kids and seniors can hike safely. The exception to the gentle landscape is the Blaine waterfall and pit cave, where the entrance to the cave is vertical and deep—a natural elevator shaft where the slightest misstep can turn into a fatal fall.

I hike to the scene of the crime—or at least where the crime began. If I had any inkling, I would've changed into my Jack Purcell sneakers, or even the hiking boots I keep in the van's shoebox. I pass the rock formation we called the *dry waterfall*, a set of natural slate steps so smooth it seems like water must be flowing over them, even though they're dry. Yellow daffodils shoot up out of barren soil. I keep climbing to the vertical-shaft cave that plunges downward almost two hundred feet into an underground creek. I shudder. There's a six-foot-high chain-link fence surrounding the entrance. Back then, there was only a circular rock wall about three feet high. The rush of water from down below sounds like the hiss of a giant serpent. I look for cottonmouths lurking under the rocks.

One section of the barrier is a vestige of the old stone wall. I lean against it and remove a La Finca Nicaraguan cigar from my pocket. I rarely smoke—shouldn't smoke in the middle of a nature preserve, shouldn't smoke at all—but I'm distressed beyond measure.

At six-thirty sharp on a March morning twenty-eight years ago, Arlette Coyle was waiting for me at the cave entrance, where she knew no one would spot her.

When I got there, she sat shivering on the rock barrier above the vertical cave, leaning back all too far.

"Hey, Arlette," I said in soft voice.

She snapped her head around and greeted me with a sad wave and an embarrassed smile, as if I'd caught her in the middle of doing something embarrassing. I approached her as I might approach a frightened child, hands at my sides, and then I crouched down slowly so as not to intimidate.

"Do me a favor and take a slow step back to the earth," I said.

She looked down, and her eyes widened, as if the cave had appeared out of nowhere. Her eyes were jade green, and when she looked at me, they seemed as deep and scary the cave. She wore her honey blond hair in tousled waves just below her shoulders. On Friday and Saturday nights, Arlette would leave her house in a long blouse and baggy jeans, only to peel them off once she got inside the car. Magically, the blouse would become a minidress. But that day, she wore a pink Minnie Mouse T-shirt, a red hoodie, and white sweatpants. She had the hoodie pulled over her head even though it wasn't that cold.

I went over, gingerly took her hand, and led her down and away from the abyss.

"It'll be all right," I said.

She squeezed my hand.

I squeezed back. "You sure about this?"

She nodded but didn't move.

"Let's go, then, I guess."

She picked up her backpack, and we started back down the perilous trail, hoping no one saw us.

———

After a half hour in the preserve, I walk back down to the trailhead. Buddy's Jeep is parked in the lot. I hop up inside.

He strokes his chin as if pondering a dilemma. "Well, she says she'll try to convince Dave not to kill you. That's something."

CHAPTER SEVEN

On an hour's notice, Judge Merle Barraclough ordered us to appear in court. His courtroom clerk wouldn't tell Higgins why. Margaret and Aruna pass through courthouse security, but I set off the magnetometer—my sterling silver bolo tie, or perhaps the red suspenders. Once I've passed through, we make our way up the escalators to the judge's courtroom on the third floor.

A bailiff stands outside the door. He's burly, in his late forties, and bald except for a few reddish-gray strands. The aggressive puffed-out chest seems familiar. I glance at his name tag, which reads *Deputy E. Travis*. Ed Travis was the brawny left tackle on our high school football team.

"Well, well, well, Elvis is in the building!" he says.

I slap him on the shoulder. "Congratulations, Eddie. You're the ten-millionth person who's made that so-called joke."

Travis shakes his head in wonder. "I heard you was coming to town. Didn't believe it at first. Never thought I'd see you again."

Where would he have heard I was coming to town? "How the hell are you, dude?" I ask.

"Bald and fat but doing okay." He knits his brow when he looks at Margaret but then extends a hand with a smile as wide as the Tennessee River and introduces himself to her.

"Surprised to see you doing court duty, Eddie," I say in a low voice. "I figured you'd be sheriff by now."

He frowns. "So did I, E. The price of running for sheriff against the Coyle family machine and losing." He points to my neck. "Cool tie, man. A heads up—the judge won't like it. He won't like your pretty, long blond hair either. Not fond of male lawyers with long hair in his courtroom."

"If the jurors even notice; I don't give a damn what the judge thinks."

"What if the jurors don't like it either?"

"That, Deputy Travis, is irrelevant." And so it is. The greatest lawyers had flair to go along with preternatural talent. Darrow had his suspenders. Kunstler had his long hair. Gladys Towles Root had her hats. Hazel Curnow has—had—her retro frilly blouses and floral skirts, oxymoronic counterpoints to her ardent feminism. My flashy appearance is an homage to my predecessors. The preternatural-talent part—not for me to judge.

Before I can introduce Travis to Aruna Higgins, she and the bailiff greet each other on a first-name basis and chat amiably about former trials, mutual friends, and family. Higgins has appeared in this small-town courtroom many times. More than that, it seems Higgins's husband is the bailiff's wife's first cousin once removed or something.

Travis unlocks the door, and we file inside. The courtroom is as majestic as the building's exterior. The Stars and Stripes and the Alabama state flag flank the bench. The designer probably chose cherry wood for the walls and furniture to create a warm, welcoming ambience. The high ceilings and ornate detailing reflect a grandeur that can humble even the most powerful.

I walk to the defense table and close my eyes. When I enter a courtroom, I'm like a caged animal released back into the wild.

Assisting Judge Barraclough are a clerk and a court reporter. The clerk, Mildred Chilton, sits at a desk below the judge's bench. When I hand her my card, say hello, and flash a charming smile, her sallow cheeks droop, and she frowns inhospitably. Courtroom personnel, especially clerks, often reflect the attitudes of their judges, so Chilton's response is discouraging. So much for my charm.

The court reporter, a tattooed good old boy named Harold, sits stage left behind his steno machine. Kelsey Kerr and Sabrina Graham command the State's table.

Higgins and I take our places at the defense table, flanking Destiny Grace. Margaret sits on the wooden bench behind us. By rights, she should join us at the grown-ups' table, but the law embeds hierarchy into the system. Otherwise, why would the judge, the arbiter of fairness and justice, wear an intimidating black dress and look down upon us from on high?

A buzzer sounds. I flinch. Destiny Grace looks at me with concern. Certain elite athletes vomit before every game; I happen to flinch just before a judge walks in. I'm fine.

Judge Merle Barraclough comes through the door.

"All rise and face the flag," commands the clerk.

Everyone stands. Barraclough climbs the two steps to his bench, struggling a bit, even for a man in his early seventies. His most prominent feature is thick, snowy hair that sprouts from his scalp as if each strand has its own hidden agenda. His wrinkled face conjures scored leather. His bifocals perch precariously on a nose appearing too small to carry the weight of the lenses.

Then it strikes me who this Barraclough is—before he was a proud hanging judge, he was the assistant DA who prosecuted my Uncle Buddy for possession of marijuana with intent to sell. Why didn't I remember the name before this? Because I was nine years old when it happened, I suppose. Buddy was a man ahead of his time. He believed cannabis had medicinal uses, and he only sold the drug to his chiropractic patients. If he'd been convicted, he would've gone to prison for a long time, and I would've been placed into the system. A public interest lawyer from Atlanta got the case thrown out because the police illegally searched Buddy's car and lied about it. A witness saw the unlawful search and came forward. Still, Merle Barraclough had me a magnolia leaf away from becoming a ward of the state.

"All right, everyone sit," says the judge. "For the record, this is the case of *State of Alabama v. Destiny Grace Harper*, and that's case number 210-749368. Appearances, please."

"Good morning, Judge. Kelsey M. Kerr and Sabrina Sasha Graham for the State of Alabama."

I stand while fastening the top button of my suit jacket. "Good morning, Your Honor. Elvis Henderson, the law offices of Hazel Ruth Curnow & Associates, for the defendant, Destiny Grace Harper. With me is Ms. Aruna Patel Higgins."

Higgins stands and half-bows.

"Aruna, I thought this was going to be your show," says Barraclough.

"I had the chance to work with experienced co-counsel," says Higgins. "Couldn't pass that up, Judge."

"We'll see."

What does he mean, *We'll see*? I turn to Margaret, who stands. "Your Honor, this is our paralegal, Margaret Booth."

Barraclough gives her a long once-over, then shakes his head and says, "Is that Mr. Booth or Miss Booth?"

"You've got to be kidding me," I say, already violating my vow that I'll show respect for this judge no matter what.

Margaret compresses her jaw. I know she wants to answer

the judge back, but she can't. As a paralegal, she must leave the talking to the lawyers. I'm about to savage this decrepit son-of-a-bitch judge with language that would get me thrown into the county jail for contempt, but Higgins beats me to the lectern. "Judge Barraclough, I've been in your courtroom tons of times, and I've never once heard you make a racial or homophobic slur, but you just made a transphobic slur. I'm asking you to apologize to Ms. Booth, or I'll have to file a complaint with the Judicial Inquiry Commission. Don't wanna do it, sir, but I won't have a choice."

The judge's head snaps back. "Ms. Higgins, if you want to file some bogus complaint, have at it. I only got three months left on the bench. You have forty years of lawyering left."

Over on the prosecution side, Kerr revels in our early travails. Graham's face is expressionless as she pushes her eyeglasses back up her nose.

"Too bad you're not stepping up to the plate to say you're sorry, Judge," I say. "I understand you'll be retiring soon. I'd hate to have this inadvertent slip of the tongue tarnish your legacy. You do know the news media has for many years reported every word my colleague Hazel Ruth Curnow says. Every belch and cough." Ms. Curnow could make this case national news simply by dashing off a press release.

The judge stares down at the top of his bench and appeals to his clerk, who shuts her eyes, more of a long blink. I speculate that the blink means, *Judge Barraclough, remember you got a pension to protect.*

"*Ms.* Booth, I must've inadvertently misspoken," says Barraclough. "The Court meant no offense."

Margaret lowers, then raises, her head—acknowledging the judge's lukewarm apology but not accepting it.

The dull light in the judge's eyes intensifies to malevolent brightness. "Here's why I brought you down to court today. I learned through the grapevine that Mr. Henderson intends to substitute in as the defendant's lawyer."

Yeah. A grapevine by the name of Kelsey Kerr.

The judge strokes his jaw like a villain from a silent-movie melodrama. "I haven't seen a pro hac vice application for Mr. Henderson." *Pro hac vice* is Law Latin meaning "for this occasion." A lawyer from another state must get permission to appear before a local court. "Don't bother filing one, Aruna. I'm aware of your history, Mr. Henderson. You've represented a terrorist intent on attacking American soil; more than one. Not six weeks ago, you were incarcerated for contempt of court because you called a Lubbock, Texas, judge a racist."

Word travels fast. Thank you, internet.

I clasp my hands behind my back. "That Lubbock judge *is* a racist, and I was observing the trial as a private citizen, not as an attorney. In response to a reporter's question on the courthouse steps, I gave my opinion in exercise of my First Amendment right, just like the law experts do on the cable networks and internet."

Barraclough flicks his hand dismissively. "Under Alabama law, to practice in our courts, an attorney from another state must be a member in good standing of the bar in the state in which he practices. The granting or denial of an application for admission of foreign counsel rests in the sound discretion of the Court, and I don't think you're in good standing. Ms. Harper will have a fine advocate in Ms. Aruna Patel Higgins."

I've seen heavy-handed behavior like this from judges all too often—the burned-out, jaded judicial officer whose reserve of empathy ran out long ago but whose pleasure in wielding power always draws from a full tank. I stand and flash my best conciliatory smile. "I believe there's been a mix-up, Judge. We didn't file a pro hac vice application because I happen to be an active member in good standing of the Alabama Bar, and proud of it. I'm a native son, you know."

Barraclough removes his reading spectacles and rubs his eyes.

I retrieve my wallet and find my Alabama bar card, waving it like a magician proving he has nothing up his sleeve. Then I hand the card to the clerk, who takes it between her thumb and index finger as if I'd just pulled it out of a trailer park septic tank. She examines the card, examines it a second time, and then hands it back and shrugs at Barraclough. He doesn't ask for an explanation, but I give one anyway. "Judge Barraclough, the State Bar of Illinois has reciprocity with the State Bar of Alabama, and I passed the Illinois bar examination, so I automatically became a member of the Alabama bar, among others. The state that gave us the great Abraham Lincoln has reciprocity with many states. All credit to Ms. Hazel Curnow for coming up with the idea. Ms. Curnow frequently traveled into hostile territory, and she didn't want biased or corrupt local judges, prosecutors, and entrenched public officials using technicalities and sharp tactics to deprive our clients, the downtrodden and underprivileged, of their constitutional right to the attorneys of their choice." Curnow was very creative. Most lawyers are licensed to practice in a few states, at the most.

"Watch yourself!" says the judge.

"Oh, I didn't mean you, Your Honor. No, sir, perish the thought. As for the district attorney, however . . ." My exaggerated shrug draws laughter from the dozen spectators in the gallery—and from Eddie Travis, who laughs but covers his mouth when the judge's head turns sharply in his direction. Kerr is so irate I don't think she could respond if she tried.

"Thank you for the warm homecoming, Judge Barraclough," I say. "Any other reason you called us down here? If not, we have a case to prepare against the State of Alabama."

CHAPTER EIGHT

After a long day of trial preparation, I enter the hotel lobby and sidle up to the front desk, still staffed by Thomas Styles.

"Catch any fish today, Mr. Henderson?" he asks.

I laugh. It didn't take him long to figure out that tourists in town for fly-fishing don't wear wool suits on a scorching day, don't carry litigation bags, and don't attract protesters with signs threatening to shoot them.

"Fish aren't biting like I expected," I say.

He points to my black Austin City Limits cap I picked up on my recent travels through the Lone Star State. "Cool hat. I've always wanted to visit Austin. Love the music. Willie Nelson, Waylon Jennings. Maybe someday."

On impulse I take off the hat and offer it to him.

He backs away with hands up. "I couldn't, sir."

"Of course you can. It'll remind you to make your wishes come true. Besides, I have a red one in my van, so we're all good."

After a moment's hesitation and a grateful nod, he takes the cap and sets it on the counter.

I set my elbows on the desk and lean over. "Speaking of

which, I wonder if you can recommend a place where I might listen to some good local music?"

"Gypsy's Factory Lounge, sir. Walkable. Just take a right down Clinton, go to the second light, that's Jackson—you know it, of course, you grew up here. Take another right, then pass by a couple buildings and you'll find Gypsy's. Owner's a guy named Bubba."

"Still calling people Bubba here?"

"Come on, Mr. Henderson, it's the South." He motions for me to lean in. "I hate to say it, sir, but I don't think some of the crowd in there would be happy to see Ms. Booth."

"Margaret goes where she wants." Still, Margaret won't be joining me tonight; I need some alone time.

He thanks me again for the cap and puts it on.

I leave the hotel and walk into the Alabama evening. It's cooler and a little less humid tonight. I saunter down Clinton, turn onto Jackson, and find Gypsy's. I loiter at the entrance and listen. The band blasts out Stevie Ray Vaughan's "Love Struck Baby." The guitar player, bassist, and girl singer are mediocre. But, oh, the drummer—he's a young man in his twenties whose short-cropped haircut and square chin make me suspect he drove up from the Redstone Arsenal military base in Huntsville. His rhythms alone make listening to the band a pleasure.

A sign above the stage advertises free Thursday night bingo and a pint of Yuengling beer for $2.50—a tempting offer unless you prefer the stronger Southern Comfort the neighboring sign touts. After I sit down, a man with a scriptural beard and face piercings comes to take my order.

"A brew," I say. "Bartender's choice. And a side of pizza fries." Margaret would be appalled at my ordering french fries covered in mozzarella and pepperoni, but she isn't here.

The fellow leaves without a word and quickly returns with a basket of fries that could serve four and a bottle of Good People IPA, an Alabama craft beer. I hope it's a good omen—Destiny Grace Harper needs some good people on her jury.

The server walks away, and I people-watch and listen to music. A huge good old boy wearing an Auburn Tigers sweatshirt, Dockers, and a Ben Hogan driver's cap dances with a small woman dressed in a Roll Tide jersey and blue jeans. Across from me, two young women in tank tops and cutoffs sit on the same side of the booth, giggling and holding hands. Times have changed even in Quartz County, Alabama—it's a start. Not that I've forgotten the vandalism to Margaret's car.

A figure looms over me, and I think the waiter has come back, but I look up to see a woman. She's a few years younger than me, I'd guess. She has short, dark hair and a playful look in her brown eyes. She wears a glittery pink T-shirt and a short denim skirt. I can't help but glance at her tanned legs. While women still approach me from time to time, I'm no longer in my thirties—as Uncle Buddy so pointedly reminded me.

When she notices me looking at her legs, her faint smile broadens a bit. "I'm Callie. It's no fun to be a single woman in a bar . . . unless a hot guy invites her over to his table and asks her to dance."

"Care to dance, Callie?"

"I prefer you invite me over to your table." She ignores the empty chair across from me, comes to my side of the table, and sits next to me in the booth.

"I'm E." I hold out my hand.

She grasps my fingers and gives a dainty handshake. "Hey, there, E."

She doesn't ask what the *E* stands for. I like her already.

The server comes over, and Callie orders a Yuengling.

"That beer company's owner supported the demagogue who opposes every principle I hold dear," I say.

She lifts her glass. Her fingernails are long and painted with dark-maroon polish. "I try not to politicize friendships, and I definitely don't politicize beer. Cheers."

We tap glasses.

The band plays an Ozark Mountain Daredevils song—"If you wanna get to heaven, you got to raise a little hell."

"Are you fan of Southern rock?" I ask.

"I like all music. I wasn't always that way. Loved Alanis Morissette and Counting Crows when I was a kid, you know, the angsty stuff teenage girls of my era liked, but I hated country music—until I moved to Nashville and got a job covering the local music scene. That made me realize that talent is talent."

"You write articles about bands?"

"Yeah, among other topics."

I point to the stage. "If you like talent, you can't be here because of this band."

She shrugs. "Maybe they haven't hit their stride yet."

We each sip our beer and do the best we can to converse over the amplified music. She's the daughter of Brazilian immigrants—a college professor and a pediatrician. She grew up in Evanston, Illinois, got a degree in journalism, moved to New York, and ended up with her current gig in Nashville. She's divorced, with an eight-year-old son. The boy is with his father for the summer.

"What about you?" she asks.

"In town visiting a long-lost uncle. I'm based in Los Angeles."

She waits, likely hoping for more information but having the discretion not to push. She says she's only been to California once—San Diego.

"That's not the real California. Well, maybe there is no real

California anymore. So say the natives, anyway. The big cities are overcrowded, the forests are burning, and people are leaving by the droves. I've got a friend who sums it up—there used to be very few mosquitos in Southern California. Now we might as well be the Deep South when it comes to mosquitoes."

"You were born on the West Coast?"

I chuckle. "Born and raised in Cole's Crossing. I haven't been back for a while." I glance down at my beer, watching the bubbles rise to the surface. The ascending movement, the magical appearance of carbonation, gives the impression of life, even though I know it's a chemical process.

We chat about music and travel and college football and this and that, in the process each downing three more beers—I had planned on one. At some point, we're on the dance floor, a development so natural I'm not certain who asked whom. The band is covering "Ramblin' Man," a fast song, but Callie and I are pressed together dancing slow to our own melody. When the song ends, we separate and lock eyes—pleasurable and awkward at the same time.

I inhale deeply. "Callie, what do you say we—?"

"Good night, E," she says, giving me a quick hug. "Thanks for the company. Maybe we'll see each other again."

I give a gentlemanly nod and a friendly, platonic *So-long* smile. Before I can ask her to text me her info, she walks to the door, tapping at her smartphone to call a car that'll spirit her away.

CHAPTER NINE

Margaret and I walk up to the front porch, and I ring the bell. LeAnn Harper opens the door a crack and peeks out at us for a long moment. The resemblance between LeAnn and Destiny Grace is unmistakable. Except the mother's hair is thin and blond, not auburn. The chemo? LeAnn's pale cheeks droop into half jowls. Her deep-set eyes give her that distressed yet resigned look characteristic of the grieving and the gravely ill.

Margaret and I introduce ourselves. LeAnn's gaze lingers on Margaret, and she hesitates instead of inviting us in, as if trying to concoct a polite way of telling a peddler or proselytizer to get the hell off her property. When Margaret slaps at a mosquito, I finally ask permission to come inside. LeAnn snaps out of her trance and ushers us into the living room.

The room is well appointed—mahogany hardwood flooring, classic heavy drapes, and throwback Southern furniture. Expensive, especially for someone who had to declare bankruptcy.

"You have a lovely home, Ms. Harper," says Margaret.

LeAnn nods curtly and directs us to sit on the blue leather

sofa. She takes a seat in an armchair on the other side of the coffee table. She has a full glass of white wine in front of her. From the lipstick stain, I deduce it's been refilled at least once. Interesting—her former church frowned on drinking alcohol. She doesn't offer us anything to drink, a major breach of Southern decorum.

She takes a generous sip of wine. "You should know I don't agree with my daughter firing Aruna Higgins." Like her daughter's, her voice is high, but the tone is weary and unmelodic.

"Aruna is staying on as co-counsel," I say.

LeAnn raises her hand as if warding off an attack. "Only for appearance's sake, I'm sure. You're the number-one chair, and that worries me. Aruna wants to save Destiny Grace's life. I'm worried you and your famous boss care more about publicity or making law than you do about my daughter's survival."

I should listen, nod sympathetically, and wait until she calms down. I don't. "I'm confused. You were the one who reached out to Hazel Curnow's office."

"Because my daughter asked me to."

"E is a great trial lawyer," says Margaret. "He wins his cases."

LeAnn takes a deep breath. "Always?"

"Not always," I say. "Any attorney who claims never to have lost a case is either a liar or hasn't tried many cases. How about we get down to the business of defending Destiny Grace? Tell us how she got herself into this trouble."

LeAnn hesitates, as if still deciding whether to speak with us or toss us out on our rears. She lets out a long, raspy sigh. "Destiny Grace was a handful when she was younger, but she straightened herself out. When I got sick, she worked two jobs, and she took care of me. My little Florence Nightingale. Never thought she could manage it. Then, after I started feeling better, her weight ballooned. It happened so sudden. Before that, I always worried she was too skinny, but then it went in the other direction fast. She claimed she was eating too many chicken nuggets and nachos, but the truth got real obvious real soon. I finally confronted her, and when she admitted it, I asked her who the father was. She wouldn't tell me. I slapped her." LeAnn shakes her head in bewilderment. "I can't believe I slapped my grown child's face. Surely didn't slap any sense into her."

She lowers her eyes and finishes the rest of her wine. She excuses herself and comes back with the glass full. "I can't get that night out of my mind. Destiny Grace didn't cry, she didn't fight back, she didn't do nothing. She just nodded, as if she deserved it, which made me feel worse. Over the next few weeks, she inflated like some movie alien from another planet. One night, I noticed her hands were real swollen, so I called Lillian Wagers, the church midwife, who came over, took one look at my girl, and listened to her belly with the Pinard. She said Destiny Grace was having twins. Then Lillian took me aside and whispered that the swelling might mean that there was a problem with the babies. She begged me to convince Destiny Grace to see an ob-gyn. Lillian was breaking the church rules by suggesting this, so I knew it was bad. I'd already been kicked out of the church for seeing a doctor, so I had nothing to lose. I convinced Destiny Grace to see Dr. Ivy Woodruff in Huntsville by saying I'd get a relapse of the cancer if she refused. After her appointment, Destiny Grace lied, told me the doctor said everything was fine, that she was so big because she was carrying twins. Turns out Woodruff called the DA about the babies' condition. Next thing I know, Destiny Grace runs off, the babies die, and she's locked up in jail for murder." Before the tears start in earnest, LeAnn stands up and walks to the kitchen. When she returns a few minutes later, she sits down and says, "What else do you want to know?"

I ask about Destiny Grace's previous boyfriends.

"Aruna said the father probably didn't matter to Destiny Grace's defense. Aruna said it was more gossipy than relevant. I never understood that. And I don't come close to understanding why my daughter won't give me the name of the sumbitch. I'd like to come after him with my shotgun. He's the reason why Destiny Grace is in this mess."

"Despite what Aruna Higgins told you, information always matters in a trial," I say. "Just like stores of ammunition matter even if you never use them. And make no mistake—we're in a war. Any ideas about the father?"

"In high school, she was head over heels for Clayton Tipple, the reverend's younger son. You, of course, know about the Reverend Jeremiah Tipple, head of our . . . I mean, Destiny Grace's church?"

"I went to school with Jerry Tipple. Played football with him."

Her eyes widen in displeasure. "We knew you're from here, but I didn't know you and the reverend . . ."

"You were telling us about Destiny Grace and Clayton."

"Yeah. Sure. I thought they'd get married, hoped they'd get married, but then senior year of high school, he dumped her and got engaged to this snooty girl, Rebecca Townsend. I'm guessing it was Clayton's mother, Tamara, who broke them up. My daughter wasn't high class enough for the Tipples, although the irony is that Clayton's sister, Brandi, and Destiny Grace were best friends, and Destiny Grace helped get that poor girl through life." LeAnn leans in, as if trying to speak confidentially in a crowded room. "Anyway, maybe it was for the best. Tell you the truth, a lot of us in the congregation, well . . . we think Clayton is a closet homosexual, even though he's married. He's a pretty boy. No offense, Margaret."

I glance at Margaret, who rolls her eyes but also gives a slight shake of the head, urging me not to engage. I remind myself that LeAnn has a virulent form of cancer and a daughter who might end up on death row.

"Jeremiah and Tamara Tipple have three children?" asks Margaret.

"Hunter, Clayton, and Brandi," says LeAnn. "Anyway, the only other real boyfriend I know about was Wyatt Haines from Nashville. They met as counselors at a Christian summer camp. I was so hoping it would work out, because Destiny Grace only has a high school education and cleans toilets, and for her to marry an educated man with a future would've been . . . But Wyatt disapproved of the church because he hopes to become a medical doctor. So that ended that." LeAnn's tone is wistful. "I liked him. So anyway, lately, there was Thomas Styles from the hotel."

"The Quartz Inn desk clerk?" I ask.

"Destiny Grace says Thomas was just a work friend, but I think it was more. They went out on a couple dates I know of, once to Rosita's and once to a movie in Athens."

Rosita's Authentic Mexican Cantina was the only place Uncle Buddy would take me on the rare occasions we would eat out. He didn't believe in processed foods, but he made an exception for Rosita's Velveeta queso and canned refried beans.

We spend another twenty minutes asking LeAnn more questions, but we turn up nothing useful.

"You're on the prosecution's witness list," says Margaret. "Why?"

"I have no idea. I support my child. Aruna says Kelsey Kerr is a bitch who's listed everyone and their second cousin as a witness to make our side's preparation harder."

Margaret and I exchange a glance.

After I assure LeAnn that we'll win the case at trial, and if not, in the appellate courts—I don't know whether we'll win or not, but telling a person what they want to hear can be an act of mercy—it's time to leave. I ask LeAnn if I can use her bathroom, a request that clearly doesn't sit well with her. I pass through a dark hallway, past the bathroom, and into Destiny Grace's bedroom. The room is all pinks and pastels. A walnut cross hangs on the wall above the bed. On the particle-board desk are a laptop computer, unplugged and dusty; a smartphone with wired earbuds still attached; and a Bible. On the side wall, a poster reads, *For by grace you have been saved by faith.* There's another poster reading, *Jesus is my* ♥. On the wall are also pop music–megastar posters.

The Bible is open to a page on which a passage is highlighted in yellow marker. Before I can read the words, LeAnn appears at the doorway, startling me.

"What're you doing in here, sir?"

"Just trying to get to know my client."

"I told you all you need to know about my daughter. You don't belong in here."

"Ms. Harper, may I just look—?"

"Nothing in here concerns you or the case. Now, please." She glares at me, her arms wrapped around her ribcage. She's treating this room as a shrine, but it's too early for that. Destiny Grace Harper still lives, and I aim to keep it that way.

CHAPTER TEN

As Margaret and I leave the hotel on the way to a jailhouse meeting with our client, a group of news reporters and legal-industry bloggers approaches us. Destiny Grace Harper's unjust prosecution has become national news. Although Hazel Ruth Curnow made a living off her press conferences in her heyday, she's ordered me never to speak with the media. I don't follow that order—talking to reporters and bloggers and influencers is too much fun.

As the group gets closer, I stop and almost fall dead in the street. Among the circling media sharks is Callie, the woman I met and danced with at the Gypsy Lounge, and I'm quite unhappy about that. I knew she was a journalist, but I understood that she blogged about country and pop music. She didn't reveal that she's covering the *Harper* case. Did she set me up? Did I reveal confidential information? I can't recall talking shop, but . . . .. Ms. Curnow would probably fire me if she knew I'd fraternized with a reporter covering our case.

"I'm going over there to talk to the reporters," I tell Margaret.

"Don't do it, E," says Margaret.

I stop anyway and glare at Callie. Her cheeks flush, but she doesn't avert her eyes. She has lovely eyes.

Red Conley, a young reporter for an online legal news service, shoves a smartphone in my face. He's covered more than a few of my cases before, and he's considered a veteran journalist although he couldn't be over twenty-five. Like many of his generation, he believes he knows everything, a feat impossible for anyone older than him.

"Hey, Elvis, maybe not first-degree murder, but shouldn't your client be facing some form of punishment? Manslaughter? Child endangerment at least?"

Margaret grabs my arm hard and pulls. "No comment!"

I take a half step forward. Conley cringes, probably not prepared for me to take his bait. "Say, Red, did you ever know someone who's tumbled down a flight of stairs?"

Conley thinks about this, having no idea where I'm going. "Like, a year ago, my uncle Steve fell down his porch steps and broke his ankle."

"Did the police bust him for it? Lock him up in jail without bail?"

Conley snickers. "Of course not."

"I take it your uncle Steve wasn't pregnant at the time." This line draws laughter from some of the reporters, Callie included. She's writing with an actual pen on an actual notepad. I like that, despite my fervent wish to remain irritated with her.

"Red, there was an honest-to-God case in Idaho involving a pregnant woman who tumbled down a flight of stairs," I say. "She was arrested for trying to injure her unborn baby. It's not a crime in any state of the union to fall down the stairs—unless you're a pregnant woman. Now, take the case of Destiny Grace Harper. She merely prayed for the health of her unborn twins and decided not to visit a doctor. It's not a crime to pray for an unborn baby's health or to refrain from visiting a doctor—unless you're a pregnant woman, that is. Outrageous, unconstitutional, and cruel. My client is being tried for felony pregnancy."

Another reporter asks, "You don't have any children of your own, do you, Mr. Henderson? Is that why you devalue the lives of unborn babies? Is that why you and Hazel Curnow fight so hard for their murderers?"

Margaret shakes her head and tugs at my sleeve. "Let's go, Elvis."

"What's your name, ma'am?" I ask.

"Joanna Proctor of the *Southern Baptist Guardian*."

"Well, Joanna Proctor, I'm going to assume you're pro-life, devoutly religious, and hate when the government intrudes on a person's private business."

Proctor nods.

"Which makes you a hypocrite. Regarding the *Harper* case, you've taken the anti-religious position and the anti-privacy position. Ms. Harper put her faith in Jesus, and the State of Alabama sought a court order to cut into her body." Proctor wants to say something, but I keep talking. "I believe in the US Constitution, in the separation of church and state, and in the rule of law. I believe in the Declaration of Independence, which says we're endowed by our Creator with unalienable rights, which include life and liberty. The State of Alabama has deprived Destiny Grace Harper of her unalienable rights, endowed by her Creator. Which means *I'm* the one who's on God's side in this debate, not you. People who stand by and root for another human being's death play for Satan's team. Final question?"

Callie raises her hand. I should probably ignore her, but it's too tempting to hear her out.

"Calinda Rocha of the *Nashville Sentinel*," she says. "Doesn't your answer about the pregnant woman tumbling down the stairs beg the question? If a woman intentionally throws herself down the stairs carrying her newborn baby, and the baby gets hurt, shouldn't she be prosecuted? What if she was grossly negligent? By saying a pregnant woman who falls down the stairs shouldn't be prosecuted, aren't you really just arguing a fetus isn't a human being?"

Perceptive, I think, despite my wish that Rocha had posed a silly, mockable question. She is right. The words informing this argument are linguistic constructs, not verifiable facts. Yet each side fervently believes in the righteousness of its cause, and there's no way to bridge the gaping divide.

"That *isn't* the issue, Ms. Rocha," I say. "The *Harper* case doesn't involve a debate over the definition of human life. And Ms. Harper didn't take any affirmative action that would hurt her unborn twins, like taking drugs or attempting suicide. Ms. Harper exercised her right to practice her religion and to control her own body. It doesn't matter whether you consider a fetus a human being or not. Destiny Grace Harper *is* being charged for the crime of pregnancy."

"And for abandoning a baby that survived the birth," shouts Proctor.

"We're late for an appointment, so no further comment," says a livid Margaret, who grabs my sleeve and pulls, giving me time only to pick up my litigation bag. Rocha starts to give a little wave and catches herself. I give her the brightest Elvis Henderson smile I can muster.

———

Before Margaret and I reach the front desk in the jail's reception area, there's a loud shriek from behind a security door.

"Don't you touch me, cocksucker, don't you touch me! I'm gonna fuck you up!"

The metal door bangs open, and a burly corrections officer comes out, escorting a woman dressed in a lime-green jail jumpsuit. The inmate's hands are cuffed behind her back. When she spews additional profanities, the guard jerks the handcuffs hard, causing a high-pitched squeal of pain.

"Not so rough, ma'am!" I hear myself shouting to the aggressive deputy.

Margaret shushes me.

The jailer flashes a *Who-the-fuck-do-you-think-you-are* look at me and guides the inmate through a pair of doors across the room.

"You represent Shannon Blackwell too, Mr. Henderson?" asks Maloney, the deputy behind the desk.

"You know I don't."

"Then mind your own business."

I should mind my own business, but I don't like the guy's attitude. "A person's civil rights are everyone's business. Especially yours. So don't become the jerkweed who bankrupted the county coffers after that woman sues. You'll find yourself driving a long-haul truck back and forth from Peoria to Tuscaloosa."

"Anything else, sir?"

"Not at the moment. Take me to my client."

"Yes, sir, Mr. Henderson. The thing is, Destiny Grace is in the infirmary. Attacked by that same inmate you're so intent on protecting."

How can Margaret's hazel eyes so clearly communicate *I warned you to be quiet*?

Deputy Maloney escorts us to a small room more akin to a Navy ship supply closet than an infirmary. Destiny Grace lies in a hospital bed, reading her Bible. A large gauze bandage covers an area on her forehead above her left eye. She elevates her eyes over her Good Book.

Before I can ask if she's okay, she says, "I'm fine. Just an itty-bitty bump. Startled me, mostly. This girl, Shannon Blackwell, she comes up to me when I'm out walking during exercise time, hits me in the head with a bar of soap hidden inside her sock, and starts cussing and calling me a baby killer. Can't believe how much a bar of soap can hurt."

"You didn't do anything to provoke her?"

"Of course not. Been called a baby killer a lot. It was just a matter of time before someone did something about it."

Destiny Grace is too blasé about this assault. What's she hiding now?

"Show me the bump on your head," I say.

"I'm fine."

"Show me!"

She gingerly moves the gauze to reveal an ugly, swollen welt, already surrounded by a mottled bruise.

"My God, that's no little bump. That's a severe contusion. You might have a concussion. A doc needs to look at you."

Destiny Grace recoils. "You know very well I don't believe in doctors."

"You need to go to the hospital. If nothing else, you'll get a reprieve from this miserable jail and sleep in a clean bed."

"A hospital would be worse than jail."

Jeremiah Tipple's folderol coupled with bullheadedness—a toxic combination.

"Then at least let Margaret check you out," I say.

Destiny Grace looks at me as if I'm the one who got hit on the head. "No, I will not."

"She was a police officer. Had some training in trauma."

"Is that really true?"

Margaret nods. "Don't worry. I won't touch you." She proceeds to ask Destiny Grace where we are, what day it is, what she's charged with, and who her lawyers are. Destiny Grace follows an index finger and balances on one leg and then the other.

"Seems okay to me," says Margaret. "Of course, I'm a paralegal, so . . ."

Even Destiny Grace smiles at this.

We spend the next several minutes discussing the case. Destiny Grace previously told Aruna Higgins that she's never terminated a prior pregnancy, but I ask her again because I can't be sure that's true.

"Abortion is murder," says Destiny Grace. "I was never pregnant before Brooklyn and Lydia."

"How about a miscarriage?" asks Margaret.

"No, ma'am. Hear my words. I was never pregnant before Brooklyn and Lydia."

"We know you had some problems when you were younger," I say.

"But I didn't get pregnant, so I certainly didn't get no abortion. I would never." Her eyes glow impatiently. We leave the subject alone.

Because the trial starts in a few days, we discuss logistics. Destiny Grace's mother will bring her a dress to wear—a dress, not pants, because I want her to seem demure and, if possible, maternal. I talk about courtroom demeanor, stressing that she cannot lose her temper or engage in emotional outbursts.

As Margaret and I are about to leave, Destiny Grace says, "Speaking of sharing the facts, were y'all going to tell me someone trashed Margaret's car? Because of what she is?"

"I take it you mean *who* she is?" I say, my tone not gentle.

"Yeah, apologies, ma'am," she says. "Is it true, though?"

"Where did you hear that?" I ask.

"This is a police station, remember? Cops gossip like everybody else. Even to me."

"The car wasn't vandalized because of who Margaret is. The car was vandalized because there are some bad people in the world."

"Not sure it matters as far as my case is concerned."

"We're not revisiting Margaret's role in the trial."

"No, I don't expect we are." Destiny Grace thinks for a moment. "Margaret, okay if I ask you a question?"

"Go for it," says Margaret.

"Why'd you change from a man to a woman? Seems to me that men still control the world."

"Who you see is who I've always been," says Margaret. "I didn't just wake up one day and decide. It feels awesome to look in the mirror and see yourself as you should be."

"I wonder what that feels like," says Destiny Grace wistfully.

So do I.

Margaret and I say our goodbyes and leave the jail. We walk out into the main lobby, which seems uncharacteristically quiet. Ordinarily, there's a buzzing, a white noise of activity conveying that the machine is running as it should. Now, it's as if the machine has stopped.

The cause of this fraught silence intrudes on my line of sight: the sheriff is in town. Dave Coyle—Arlette's brother, and my old enemy. A tall man, probably six-four, he towers over his two subordinates, who stand at his side as he scans a document attached to a clipboard. He was always a stylish dresser, even as a kid, and now he wears a bespoke silk suit—lightweight for the summer season. There's an American flag pinned to his left lapel, but no indication he's the head of law enforcement for Quartz County. Makes sense—even as a kid, Coyle was a politician above all else.

Coyle's appearance in the lobby might be a coincidence. He does run this department. Maybe it's just my ego, but I think he's here to send me a message. He thinks he ran me out of town twenty-eight years ago. He wasn't the reason I left—at least not the only one—but if I don't approach him now, he'll think I fear him. I do, but I can't show it.

"Hang on, Margaret," I say. "I'm going to say hey to an old friend."

I walk three steps in Coyle's direction. The man doesn't look up, just takes a finger off the clipboard and flicks it in my direction, sending one of his minions toward me.

The deputy, a wiry young fellow, crosses his arms. "Sheriff Coyle doesn't speak to anyone without an appointment." The smirk in his tone matches the one on his lips. "Do you have an appointment, sir?"

"Yes, son, I do. I made it twenty-eight years ago. Tell Dave I'm here to keep it."

The deputy's eyes widen to the size of mini-donuts. He looks at me, at Margaret—who seems both amused and bemused—and goes back and whispers something into Sheriff Coyle's ear. Coyle replies at normal volume, but his words are unintelligible.

The deputy returns. "Sheriff Coyle says you have an appointment with something . . . but it ain't with him."

CHAPTER ELEVEN

I insist on taking the wheel of the Dodge Charger as a way of opening the safety valve on my internal pressure cooker. I drive onto I-65 and find out what the car can do. When the speedometer reaches ninety-one miles per hour, Margaret says, "Jesus Christ, slow down or you'll be back in a jail involuntarily—if we don't die a fiery death first."

I slow to eighty.

"Still too fast. Tell me what's bothering you. That crap with the sheriff?"

"Unresolved boyhood feud. He was a bully, and I didn't like to be bullied."

She considers this. "If you won't come clean, I'll have to let Hazel know there's something you're not telling us."

"You go right ahead, Maggie." She hates the name Maggie. "Then what? Does Ms. Curnow fly out here and try the case herself? The whole legal world and much of the news media would love to see that. *I'd* love to see that."

Margaret makes no reply.

"Or maybe Ms. Curnow orders us off the case, and we leave Harper's life in the hands of Aruna Higgins?"

"She's not a bad lawyer, Elvis."

"Is she experienced enough to try this case, Margaret?"

No reply to that one either.

"I own my past," I say. "Let's leave it."

"As long as it doesn't affect your focus."

"It won't." At least, I hope it won't.

"When do I get to meet your uncle again?"

"Won't happen."

"Transphobic?"

"Not at all. One of the most forward-thinking people I ever met, yet a hard-ass when it comes to everyday living. Let's say he's Elvis-phobic."

She points to the speedometer. "You're accelerating again."

I grumble but tap the brakes. Many passengers in my vehicles have told me to slow down over the years. Risky behavior thrills me—or did in my younger days. I left Cole's Crossing when I turned eighteen and joined the National Guard pararescue unit, stationed in Northern California, and jumped out of airplanes behind enemy lines to rescue and treat wounded soldiers. My team had three missions in Afghanistan and a sea rescue after a noncombat-related helicopter crash. I took enemy fire and shot a gun in Afghanistan but didn't kill anyone—as far as I know. Although I despise war, I don't regret my time in the service. I helped save some lives.

There's a risk I took back in the day that I *do* regret—a road trip with Arlette Coyle. Arlette was one of the few passengers who ever asked me to drive faster—which wasn't easy in my fifteen-year-old Buick LeSabre, a car Buddy had bought used seven years earlier and then sold to me at the upper range of the Kelley Blue Book price. I spent everything I'd saved working as a lifeguard at the county plunge and incinerating hamburgers at Woody's Grill & Shakes.

Arlette started acting weird in Hoover, about ninety minutes south of Cole's Crossing. We stopped at a service station so she could pee and buy some gummy bears and onion-and-sour-cream chips. Once back in the car, she tore open the potato chip package, the act so violent she spilled chips on the seat and floor—not that I minded much, because the car was already a pigsty. She gobbled down some potato chips, stuffed another handful in her mouth, and before swallowing those, opened the box of candy and consumed a handful. When she offered to share the snacks, I declined. Potato chips and sticky candy were not an appealing combination, and besides, I had no appetite because of what we intended to do. My refusal of her generosity annoyed her.

"Speed the fuck up, E. We're going to be late."

"We're fine. On track to make it an hour early. I'm going seventy, and if I go any faster, the Smokies will stop me, and then we really will be late. If I go over seventy-three, the car shimmies and shakes and might disintegrate. Not good."

"Just speed the fuck up," she repeated, then shifted her sullen eyes from me to the windshield. She sat gobbling snacks until she tossed the half-filled containers on the floor as if they were toxic (which they probably were).

"I told my family I was going with Tammy to visit Florida State and the Bible university in Tallahassee," said Arlette. "Told them Tammy would drive and that if I liked the school, I could stay overnight in the dorms for a day or two. Tammy said she'd cover for me. She's visiting the college for real. Hope they really believe that I went with her."

She'd already told me this a half dozen times. "It's all going to work out fine."

"Speed the fuck up, E," she said again, and I sped up and tried to keep the Buick from shimmying off the road.

"Slow down, E," says Margaret now.

How nice to have a person who can rescue you from your darkest memories.

CHAPTER TWELVE

On Saturday morning, two days before the trial starts, a larger group of demonstrators stands on a grassy knoll across from the Quartz Inn's passenger-loading zone, about fifty yards from the hotel entrance. The anti-Harper contingent comprises forty to fifty people chanting something incomprehensible. About fifteen people make up the "pro-Harper" contingent, which is chanting, "Protecting babies is a lie, they don't care if women die."

"This sucks," says Margaret as we scan the crowd from inside the hotel lobby. "No police presence. The groups should be separated on either side of the street. There should be barricades."

"Cole's Crossing isn't exactly a hotbed of protest."

"Anywhere there's a Wi-Fi connection can be a hotbed of protest. I'm worried it's going to get out of hand. It's hot out there."

The rhetoric does sound particularly violent today, and the actual temperature is in the nineties. The wanted poster with a bull's-eye over my face is back—except, now, the words *Dead or Alive* appear. There's a sign with Margaret's image under the

words *Homo Sex Is Sin*. A man carries doll replicas of two dead
fetuses hanging from a pole carrying the American flag overlaid
with a skull and crossbones; a young woman wears a blood-red
T-shirt reading *Abortion is murder, homosexuality is sin, evolution is a delusion, the vaccines are genocide*; a sign reads *Lethal
force to save an unborn child is justifiable homicide*; another sign
proclaims, *Planned Parenthood Sells Babies' Body Parts*; still another reads, *Bring her forth, and let her be burnt—Genesis 38:24*
over a scanned image of Destiny Grace's mug shot.

Reporter Calinda Rocha is among the crowd, asking questions. I focus on her, but she doesn't look my way. Members of
the pro–Destiny Grace group speak with her amiably. Not so
the anti–Destiny Grace folks. One fellow gets so close to her
that she takes two steps back. Someone at the left of the crowd
shouts *Fuck off*, and I take my eyes off Rocha and see two men
shoving each other, not yet a fistfight but close. A woman seems
to be egging on one of the men. This situation is escalating.
Where are the cops?

Someone jostles me from behind, and I turn aggressively,
but it's just a teenage girl who, along with her parents, is trying
to get a better look out the window.

Margaret bolts out of the lobby door and sprints across the
street toward a melee that started like a flash fire. The cacoph-
onous shouting is as loud as it is incoherent. I can make out
only the profanity.

I follow her out the door and across the street. "Come back
here, Margaret!"

Two large men face off against each other, one kicking at
the air and the other backing up and saying, "Come on, come
on." A woman, a member of the pro-Harper contingent, gets
in the middle and tries to break up the fight; another woman
shoves her to the ground.

Two guys kick another man who's lying prone on the concrete sidewalk. Margaret sprints over and shouts for the attackers to stop. A huge guy wearing a Confederate flag bandana swings at her and misses. Margaret's counterpunch hits its mark. With a look of shock, the assailant's sidekick runs away. I run over and grab the collar of the guy who swung at Margaret. He and I square off. Oh, how I want to knock this asshole from here to Tuscaloosa, but I don't get the chance. Police sirens blare, and the coward shrugs me off and runs away.

Police vehicles appear. Too late.

"Are you okay, Margaret?" I ask.

She nods. "You?"

"No. I'm pissed off."

She points. Calinda Rocha sits on the ground, blood streaming from a laceration over her right eye. In the hubbub, people are walking right past her.

"I'll try to find a paramedic," says Margaret and then jogs away.

I go over to Rocha and kneel. "You doing okay, Ms. Rocha?"

She looks up at me, clearly dazed. "I don't know." She turns her head a little. "Jesus, all I did was ask this guy why he was out here and what his sign meant. He shouted that I was part of the fake-news factory that stole elections and that I was a whore like Destiny Grace Harper. He punched me. He punched my face." She shakes her head in disbelief.

Margaret returns with a paramedic and Deputy Eddie Travis.

"No courthouse duty today, Eddie?" I ask.

"An all-hands emergency, Elvis," says Travis.

As the paramedic attends to Rocha, Travis asks what happened.

"Some asshole punched this lady—she's a reporter—and ran like a scared rat," says Margaret. "A White male in his twenties, flabby, brown hair, eyeglasses, medium height." She points to the sign on the ground near Rocha, the one calling for Destiny Grace to be burned. "He was carrying that shit."

Travis picks up the sign and displays it to the crowd. "Hey! Listen up! Any of y'all know the guy who was carrying this?"

An older fellow, one of the anti–Destiny Grace protesters, says, "No one on our side ever seen him before."

"You're not buying that horseshit, are you, Eddie?" I ask.

Travis turns and looks off into the distance. "How'd y'all become involved in a brawl in the first place, E?"

"We were watching from the entrance, and I saw the guy assault Ms. Rocha, so I came over to help," says Margaret.

"Word of advice. Y'all should've stayed in the hotel." To Margaret, he says, "As an ex-cop, you should've had better sense. Especially given your situation."

Margaret squares her shoulders. "My *situation*, deputy? Are you saying I can't exercise my constitutional and God-given right to walk on a public street? To protect people in harm's way?"

He raises his palms and takes a half step back. "Just saying y'all should walk away from confrontations rather than escalating them. You two are targets. You should've waited for us to arrive."

"You should've been here before the fighting started," says Margaret. "If you want to talk about good law enforcement protocol."

"You should be thanking Ms. Booth for doing your job, Eddie," I say.

He moves within whispering distance and changes the subject. His cop's eyes soften, and he's no more than an old pal. "You know, I've been thinking about the attack on Destiny Grace in the jail. Shannon Blackwell. It don't make sense. She's been incarcerated with Destiny Grace for months, and she's got her issues, but she always left Destiny Grace alone before the attack."

"What does Blackwell have to say for herself?"

"Just that she don't like baby killers." He shakes his head. "Don't make sense."

"Does Blackwell have friends in town? Family?"

"Not that I know of."

"Is your department checking it out?"

He looks around to make sure no one else is close. "Dave Coyle ain't so interested in helping the Harper girl."

"Because I'm her lawyer?"

"That don't help. But he arrested her for murder. He's close to Kelsey Kerr. He's also still friends with Jeremiah Tipple, who isn't piping up to help his congregant, as you well know. Coyle doesn't care all that much if Destiny Grace gets hurt. But if I was you, I'd pursue the Blackwell angle. It don't make sense." The cop gives a crisp nod, gestures for us to move along, and leaves.

Margaret looks at the crowd, her fists on her hips. Most people have dispersed, but some still mill around. "I want to talk to them. Call it jury research."

"Please be careful."

"Always."

As I keep my eyes on her in case there's more trouble, she approaches the anti–Destiny Grace protestors. I sense the tension from twenty feet away. When speaking with an antagonistic crowd, Margaret bends slightly forward at the waist to seem less imposing—a technique she once told me she used as a police officer to appear less intimidating. I can't quite hear her, but I can tell from her body language and my past history with her that she's asking simple, noncombative questions, listening to sometimes-hostile answers. She nods often, never interrupting. After a couple of minutes pass, I venture closer, just within earshot. Margaret has many of the demonstrators engaged in a heated yet civil discussion of the merits of

Alabama v. Destiny Grace Harper. Eventually, Margaret shakes hands with several of them.

Convinced that Margaret is no longer in danger, I go over to Calinda Rocha, who's now on her feet and speaking with the EMT.

"How are you doing, Ms. Rocha?"

"I passed the concussion protocol, but I need stitches. The police said they'll meet me at the ER and take a detailed police report." She shakes her head, a droplet of blood falling on her lavender T-shirt. "Jesus, that guy who hit me must think I use the blood of babies to make pizza sauce."

"Blame the internet. The crazies find each other and validate their insanity."

"Thank you for coming out here to help. Your paralegal is a tough woman. Thank her for me too." She pauses. "I'm . . . I didn't know who you were the other night. I heard Harper had a new lawyer, a guy named Elvis who lived in a van. But you were *E*, and you said you were visiting your uncle, didn't say anything about being a lawyer. I'm an ethical reporter. I wasn't planning on luring you in for information or anything. I never socialize with the subjects of my reporting."

If her explanation is just an excuse, it's a good one. We both have ethical responsibilities. "I get it, Callie."

She smiles, then groans in pain.

"How about I drive you to the emergency room?"

"No. I've called one of the other reporters. She's on her way. But thank you."

I feel a twinge of disappointment.

Rocha touches her face and frowns. "Oh my God, the stitches are going to leave a big scar. These small-town ER doctors don't know how to . . . I doubt I'll find a plastic surgeon. My God, I'm going to look hideous."

I pat her hand. "Trust me, that won't happen. And a lot of the doctors around here trained in the military. They know how to treat facial injuries as well as anyone."

She smiles through her discomfort. "Thank you. You're making me an Elvis fan."

CHAPTER THIRTEEN

The Church of Our Lord's Rapture might not believe in modern medicine, but it sure as hell believes in the internet. The church tweets; posts on Instagram, Facebook, and TikTok; and publishes a blog on its website each week with words of wisdom and a database of past sermons. It took Margaret hours to find a video in which Reverend Jeremiah Tipple refers to our case, although he never mentions Destiny Grace by name.

At least on a computer monitor, Tipple's platinum white hair, white goatee, and white skin have the paradoxical effect of making him look young, especially since his skin is wrinkle free. Stage makeup, perhaps. In the old days, some kids called him an albino—until he shut them up with fists he was happy to use. Now, his violet-blue eyes gleam with faith and lunacy as he preaches to his flock.

"Do not hesitate to trust God," he says in a stage whisper that likely could be heard in the last row even without the amplification system. And then he says in a booming voice, "We have no reason to doubt God. God lives. If you accept Jesus Christ as your Savior, say amen!"

A loud "Amen" from the congregation.

"Those who *know* in their hearts that Jesus Christ is a healer!"

Amen.

"Those who *know* in their hearts that Jesus Christ is their Savior!"

Amen.

"And though the hand of faith might tremble, it shall never wither."

He tells a story about a man who slipped from a hillside in the darkness but managed to grasp a plant so as not to fall to his death. Minutes passed. The man prayed for God's help, to no avail. Finally, the unfortunate soul's fingers gave out, and as he was about to fall, he cried out one last time, "God, you've got to help me!" He fell . . . five inches onto a plateau.

The congregation laughs, as does Tipple, who adds, "God always heals those with faith!"

"That's pretty funny," says Margaret.

"It is," I reply. "But Jerry Tipple never had a sense of humor. I'd wager he still doesn't. Which is probably why he lifted the story from a famous Los Angeles Depression-era evangelist." (I know this because Hazel Curnow once had lawsuit involving her heirs).

He goes on to spout some platitudes that are even more familiar: *good works without faith won't get you to heaven; faith is a key that unlocks heaven's door; those who lack faith in God are like fish thrown onto the shore with no hope that the rising tide will save them.*

"He's not bad at what he does," says Margaret.

"Depends on your definition of *bad.*"

After a choir sings, he calls several "afflicted" individuals to the altar, prays over them, and proclaims them healed. I can't be sure, but it sounds like some in the assembly are speaking in tongues. I hate to admit it, but I'm impressed by the racial diversity in his congregation.

Toward the end of the sermon, he said, "First Peter 3:15 calls every Christian to always be ready to make a defense to everyone who asks you to give an account for the hope that is in you."

Amen.

"I'm sure you all know about a fallen member of our congregation and how the godless media blames *our* church for the death of two innocent babes," he says. "Brothers and sisters, the blame lies not with our beliefs, not with our faith in the Lord. No, the blame lies with the sinner, a sinner who lost her faith, a fallen woman who ignored the teachings of Christ and became pregnant out of wedlock." Then he bellows, "I quote from Psalm 107. 'Fools, because of their transgression, and because of their iniquities, are afflicted.' Sickness and sin—two sides of the same coin. 'There is no soundness in my flesh because of thine indignation; neither is there any health in my bones because of my sin.' That is why first AIDS and then the monkeypox were inflicted upon men who sleep with men, why the hurricanes and the floods and the fire wreak havoc on the sinner and wipe out cities of sin. That is why the faithless and the lascivious suffer, and visit the suffering on their babies, while God heals those who have faith in Him. A righteous woman does not conceive the sick; the sinner who prays with true faith does not give birth to the dead."

He takes out a cloth handkerchief and wipes his brow, clichéd stage business that is still effective.

"Of this woman, of the attacks on our beliefs, of criminal prosecution, I shall say no more. She will answer for her sins on the day of judgment."

After five more minutes of praying and singing, a chyron

posts the web address and phone number where those with true faith can send their donations.

———

The church's main entrance is locked. I take a path around the building that leads to what I surmise are the administrative offices. The mosquitoes attack from their stronghold in the flower garden and dive-bomb my face and neck faster than I can swat them away. Light shines through a pull-down shade in a back window, revealing a silhouette working at a desk. I consider tapping at the window, but a thorny rosebush stands in my way; and besides, whoever it is probably won't let me in anyway. I go thirty feet farther and try the side door—success.

When I reach his office, Reverend Tipple has already swiveled in his chair as if he is expecting me. The man must've heard my footsteps on the linoleum. I used to walk with a cat's gait. I thought I still did. Or perhaps he's clairvoyant, as he implies to his followers. He looks as youthful in person as he did on the recording.

Our home state being Alabama, we knew each other through football. Tipple played quarterback at Quartz High School, and I played running back. I was fast and elusive. I rushed for quite a few yards, and I scored my share of touchdowns. I was also a good blocker, picking up blitzing linebackers when Tipple dropped back to pass. Keep your center of gravity low and inflict some pain, even if you absorb more—that's my technique, then in sports and now in the law. I didn't let Tipple get sacked often.

The minister slaps his right thigh in mock glee. "The prodigal Elvis Henderson appears—even though I've told you and that Indian lawyer I don't want to meet with you." The sermonizing preacher's voice, once a put-on, has become natural.

"Mind if I sit down, Jeremiah?"

"Would you leave if I said I did mind?"

"No, I would not."

Tipple gestures toward the one guest chair, made of hard, uncomfortable wood. The building isn't grand, but Tipple's brand of brimstone and righteousness deludes enough anti-medicine devotees to keep his church going, his mortgage paid, and his BMW serviced. He boasts that he's the Chief Physician's Assistant to Jesus. As Margaret keeps reminding me, the church isn't all bad, often helping the dispossessed—like the victims of the deadly 2011 tornadoes that struck Northern Alabama. Much of the church aid went to minorities. But good works don't make up for the distorted beliefs that caused Destiny Grace to shun a lifesaving procedure for her twins. His early anti-vax position resulted in the death of some of his members and some bad publicity, which seems to have put a strain on his finances, according to Margaret.

Tipple reaches behind his ear and retrieves a toothpick, which he uses to pick at his gums. He inspects the toothpick and tucks it back behind his ear, the way an old-fashioned bookkeeper carries a pencil.

"Your hygiene habits haven't improved since high school," I say.

"Poor man's dental floss. No need for bogus dentistry. Never had so much as a cavity."

So he says.

"You and I, we both claim to work for the poor, Elvis. But your service for the poor has made you rich."

"I was on the way to becoming rich back when I worked for the rich. I make almost nothing working for the poor. Seems to me that you aren't doing so badly exploiting the gullible and the desperate."

"Vow of poverty. Everything you see belongs to the Lord. Anyway, how can I help you?"

"Testify at Destiny Grace Harper's trial and tell the jury that by refusing the surgery, she was following the gospel of the Church of Our Lord's Rapture."

Tipple clasps his hands, throws his head back, and directs a guffaw at the heavens. "Like I already told your predecessor, that would be perjury. The Harper girl followed no gospel of mine. She's a heretic. She's promiscuous, and promiscuity is a sin. Not to mention she aided and abetted her mother in blasphemous behavior."

"Blasphemy as in consulting a doctor to treat ovarian cancer? Your gospel is nothing but a long confidence game."

Tipple pulls out his poor man's floss again and uses it with a ferocity that makes me want to look away. "The babies died because their mother lost faith, if she ever had it. If she'd had faith, they would've lived long and healthy lives. That girl turned her back on the Lord and now blames our church for the consequences so she can get out of a mess of her own making. The media is all over us, calling us a cult. We're no cult."

"You can't be suggesting Harper deserves to perish from the face of the earth because she got pregnant out of wedlock and you've gotten some bad publicity. You and I look at life differently, but I know your church teaches forgiveness. To execute a young woman for—"

"For all I know, she did want the babies to die, like the district attorney says. Maybe she deserves reciprocal justice. Eye for eye, tooth for tooth, life for life. You know that word *justice*, Elvis. It's what you say you're fighting for. Let a jury of her peers decide."

"That's ludicrous. If she wanted the babies to die, she'd—"

"Oh, yes, the stuff about how she would have had an abortion if she really didn't want the babies." He scoffs. "That girl always had her priorities mixed up. Besides, there's a difference between taking a gun and shooting a man and finding a wounded man on the side of the road and letting him die. Maybe in her misguided brain she thought abortion was like pulling the trigger but doing nothing was like leaving the babies by the side of the road. From what I read, the evidence is that she actually *did* leave one of the babies by the side of the road to die."

Tipple is parroting one of the prosecution's theories. I will not argue the merits of the case with him. "I won't hesitate to subpoena you, Jerry. Cross-examination on your anti-medical stance won't be pleasant for you."

"Just remember when we played ball together, you blocked for me and took the hits. *I* called the signals. Still do."

"When you're on the stand, I won't be protecting your sorry ass. Just the opposite."

Tipple laughs. "Always the sharp tongue, the last word. It's an art, man. Look, if you force me to testify, I'll say that Destiny Grace Harper was a sinner who lost faith and repudiated the teachings of our church even before she got pregnant out of wedlock. Which means she's lying about why she refused medical care. If I do that, your freedom of religion defense vanishes, and your client will look like the liar she is."

I get to my feet. "Thank you for your time, Reverend Tipple."

"A word of friendly advice? Reclaim some of your Southern attributes. In front of a local jury, your Yankee manner will lose the case after you say three words. Now, I got to review some scripture for my Sunday sermon. I'm preaching about loyalty to God and church."

"How about 2 Samuel 16:17? 'And Absalom said to Hushai, Is this thy kindness to thy friend? why wentest thou not with thy friend?'"

"I'm impressed. But we've never been friends. And one more thing—your predecessor, the Indian girl—"

"You're referring to my co-counsel. Her name is Ms. Aruna Higgins."

"She keeps harassing my family. That will stop."

"We need to talk to your daughter to do our job. She's on the prosecution's witness list." Just like almost everyone else in this town. The prosecutors listed so many prospective witnesses we can't possibly prepare for them all—a well-worn tactic by the more powerful side. "But I'll tell you what, Jerry. I might be able to reconsider your request if you give me a lead on the whereabouts of Lillian Wagers." Wagers is the church midwife who cared for Destiny Grace early in the pregnancy.

He points a long index finger at me. "Do *not* trouble my family. Understand what I'm saying?"

"Loud and clear, Jeremiah. Loud and clear."

CHAPTER FOURTEEN

I was a high school senior when last I visited the Tipple home, back when it was up on the bluffs at the end of Tatum Cove Road. That day, the Reverend Milton Tipple banished me—not because of political or religious differences, but because I missed a block in the Decatur game. Except I didn't miss the block. In the huddle, Jerry told me to flare out in the flat and said he'd throw to me in space, miles of open territory before me. When the opposing team's corner blitzed, Jerry panicked, held onto the ball, and took a devastating sack, which resulted in a torn ACL that ruined his football career. Jerry let me take the blame. I kept my mouth shut, protecting my quarterback to the end.

The irony was that the injury made Jeremiah's future. The surgeon botched the operation, resulting in a malpractice lawsuit. Jeremiah's pronounced limp was supposed to be permanent. He prayed, and the Lord healed—so Jeremiah claimed. Maybe he even believed it. He broke with his father's church, used his settlement money to buy some property, founded the Church of Our Lord's Rapture, and has raged against the medical establishment ever since.

Now, I park in a lavish circular driveway lined with brick, rosebushes, and magnolia trees. Since I left town, Jeremiah Tipple used his congregants' donations to build himself a Tudor-style mansion.

The door cracks open, and a young woman peers out. Brandi Tipple. She's a taller version of her mother. The sun reflects against her oversized, round glasses—*nerd frames*, we used to call them—so I can't see her eyes. When she gets a good look at me, she hop-steps back inside, as if I'm the trip wire on a land mine.

"Ms. Tipple, my name is Elvis Henderson, Destiny Grace Harper's—"

"I know who you are," she says in a whisper conjuring dry leaves skittering across concrete. "Please go away."

"I'm looking for Ms. Lillian Wagers."

Brandi makes herself stand upright. "She ain't here, and this is private property."

"I'd like to talk to you about your friend Destiny Grace. Your name appears on the prosecution's witness list."

"I can't. Please."

What does Tamara think of her daughter? In her youth, Tamara cared about fashion, clothes, status, money, and looks. Brandi might resemble her mother physically, but she lacks Tamara's self-confidence. A young Tamara Evans wouldn't shrink from a man like Elvis Henderson.

Nor would an older Tamara Evans Tipple, as it turns out.

"You're trespassing." Tamara's voice sneaks up from behind me as Brandi retreats back inside. She's accompanied by one of her sons. He's tall and fashion-model attractive. Clayton Tipple, judging from LeAnn's description. His left arm sports a very artistic brown, green, and red snake coiled around an automatic rifle with the words *Don't Tread on Me*—the insignia of the Gadsden flag, a favorite of some White supremacists. I'm more focused on the Mossberg Field 20-gauge semiautomatic shotgun he's aiming in my general direction. With that weapon, *general direction* is close enough to wreak carnage on my anatomy.

I raise my hands gingerly. Tamara probably won't let her son shoot me. *Probably.* I haven't seen her in over twenty-five years.

"Hello, Tamara. Long time. I didn't expect you'd greet me with an armed guard."

She uses a hand to shield her eyes from the sun. "Elvis Henderson?"

"You look good, Tammy."

Clayton tenses up again. "Her name is Tamara—Ms. Tipple."

"In fact, you look great," I say, ignoring him. I'm not just flattering her. She doesn't look eighteen, or twenty-five, but like her husband, she's aged well. Perhaps the Tipples' youthful appearances do evidence God's grace. Or maybe they hide monstrous portraits of themselves in their attic.

"You kind of look long in the tooth, Elvis," says Tamara. "Too much time in the California sun? Hard living and not enough prayer?"

"May I ask this strapping young man to lower his weapon so I can lower my soon-to-be aching arms?"

Tamara nods, but Clayton doesn't lower the gun.

Someone jogs up the hill. This man has Jeremiah's barley-blond hair, ultra-fair complexion, and blue eyes, and Tammy's diminutive physique. Hunter, the eldest child. He shakes his head at Clayton. "Put the gun down. Mr. Henderson is Daddy's friend."

"Hardly," says Tamara.

"Lower the gun anyway, Clayton," says Hunter.

Clayton lowers the shotgun. Once I'm out of immediate danger, I become aware of the day's heat, its unrelenting mugginess. I'm drenched in sweat. The Tipples look fresh, as if they just walked out of a meat locker.

"I'm sorry, sir," says Hunter. "I knew who you were before you came here, and I respect you, even though I disagree with you. I'm an attorney myself, and I know you're just doing your job." I listen for sarcasm, but he sounds sincere.

"Thank you for that, Hunter," I say. "I was hoping to speak with Lillian Wagers. I understand she works for the church as a healer and midwife."

"My father is the healer," says Clayton.

Tamara raises a hand. "Lillian cleanses the cut finger; she shepherds the wretched in from the cold and warms them. But the Lord heals."

With a hand, I wipe the sweat from the back of my neck. "LeAnn Harper says you know where to find Wagers."

"LeAnn Harper is wrong about so many things," says Tamara.

"Was she wrong when she told me Brandi was Destiny Grace's best friend? I'd very much like to talk to your daughter. Destiny Grace's mistake was to follow *your* teachings, and because of that, her life is at risk."

"Destiny Grace Harper is not who you think she is, sir," says Clayton.

Tamara shoots her son a sharp look.

"I've handled many a legal case where my client turns out to be someone different from who I thought they were," I say. "That's why I pursue the facts." Out of the corner of my eye, I see Brandi peeking through the slit between the window curtains. "You were close to Destiny Grace, Clayton. Kindly tell me who she really is."

The shotgun in Clayton's hand elevates, seemingly of its own accord. "Destiny Grace—"

Hunter glares at his brother.

"Hush up, Clayton," says Tamara. "As for you, Elvis, get off our property. Now."

Clayton points the barrel of the weapon toward my parked car and then back at me. "Listen to my mother and leave, sir."

I doubt young Tipple will shoot me, but the violent glint in his eyes says he might.

"May I walk you to your car sir?" asks Hunter, shooting his younger brother a look of disapproval.

"Not necessary," I say. "Y'all have a blessed day." I return to my campervan, willing Clayton Tipple to keep that gun pointed elsewhere.

CHAPTER FIFTEEN

Aruna Higgins, Margaret Booth, and I arrive at the courthouse early. I always arrive at the courthouse early. That way, the pores of my body have more time to absorb the elusive molecules of justice. We avoid the demonstrators and ignore the media. I do make eye contact with Callie Rocha. She has a small butterfly bandage on her forehead, not quite hidden behind the hair she's rearranged to conceal the wound. We exchange subtle nods.

Margaret and I follow Higgins through a door opposite the jury box and into a conference room, where Destiny Grace Harper sits at a large table. The client closes her omnipresent Bible. She wears the courtroom attire her mother brought her: a white cotton blouse, a blue skirt, a narrow belt (the Quartz County inmate handbook mandates the belt be *small*), and a pair of flats. The dress looks too big, even though LeAnn got it from her daughter's closet. Destiny Grace, already tiny, has lost fourteen pounds in jail, LeAnn says. I'm worried about her health. The bruise from the prison attack hasn't fully healed, so Margaret goes over, takes a bottle of Chanel concealer out of her handbag, applies it to Destiny Grace's forehead, and gives a thumbs-up. Throughout this mini makeover, our client looks too astonished to protest.

"How you doing?" Higgins asks her. "Ready to kick some butt?"

"Butt kicking is your job, Aruna," she replies. Her tone is dismissive, almost derisive. The rift between client and former lead counsel hasn't healed.

"Let's go over the ground rules one more time," I say.

"We done that a gazillion times, Mr. Henderson."

"Following the rules lowers anxiety and reduces the possibility of mistakes," I say. "Repeating the rules helps you follow them. You know who I learned that from? Hazel Ruth Curnow." That's not true; I learned it from my uncle, who worried I was a rule-breaker at a young age. But invoking the name Buddy Henderson won't have the same effect as mentioning Ms. Curnow.

"Whatever."

I try to play the dispassionate attorney and not the concerned human being, no matter how worried I am about her appearance. I go over the rules: never get angry; never stare at the jury; never look bored or yawn; never roll your eyes at a hostile witness; never, *ever* laugh or smile or otherwise hint to the jury that you don't take the proceedings seriously; and never speak aloud in court about anything. Some tears are okay during difficult testimony about the babies, but don't become hysterical. Sit straight but not stiffly. Take notes; pretend to take notes; look engaged in the defense.

"All these *nevers* and *shoulds* and *dos* and *don'ts* have not lowered my anxiety, sir. They just scare the shit out of me. Who can remember all these rules and still be themselves?"

Higgins turns her back and clasps her hands behind her.

Deputy Travis sticks his head in. "The judge is about to take the bench. He wants everyone in their places. Now."

"Knock next time, Eddie," I snap. "You've invaded the sanctified space occupied by attorney and client."

He glares at me for a moment, then holds up a hand. "You're right, Elvis. My apologies. I'm a better street cop than a bailiff."

We enter the courtroom. Destiny Grace clutches her Bible and walks with an unsteady gait. I have the urge to take her arm and support her, but she needs to stand on her own. The only empty seats in the room are in the first two rows, where the overflow prospective juror panel will sit. In the gallery are LeAnn Harper, sitting behind Destiny Grace just as I told her to; the media members; and a group of anti-Harper demonstrators.

Barraclough grunts, then says to Deputy Travis, "Eddie, round them up!" as if the prospective jurors are a herd of cattle.

Yesterday, the clerk's office furnished both sides with a list naming the prospective jury panel, along with a questionnaire each potential juror completed. Now, seventy-two jury panelists file into the courtroom and squeeze into the jury box and the two front rows of the gallery.

In the jury venire's presence, Barraclough transforms into a Southern gentleman hosting a weekend barbecue. He cogently summarizes the facts and issues in the case. He reminds the jurors that Destiny Grace is presumed innocent and doesn't have to take the stand in her own defense. Hard to tell whether Barraclough really believes these fundamental principles of justice or whether he's just repeating lines.

He asks the prospective jurors whether they'll suffer personal hardship if they're picked to serve on the jury. Of the fifteen people who plead hardship, he excuses two, a thrift-shop owner who's the sole support of her three children and her invalid mother and a septuagenarian retired railroad worker who travels back and forth to Huntsville twice a week for kidney dialysis.

Next, the judge asks the panelists questions intended to

ferret out biases and identify conflicts of interest. *Voir dire* is the legal term for this process—a term from the old Law French language and derived from the Latin *veritatem dicere*, meaning "say the truth." Once the judge finishes, we lawyers will get the chance to pose our own voir dire questions.

Barraclough asks the standard questions about bias, knowledge of the parties and attorneys, family background, hobbies, familiarity with the case, and whether any of the jurors morally oppose the death penalty such that they couldn't impose a sentence of death. *What kind of justice system excludes from the jury those opposed to killing in a trial intended to punish killing?* The handful of folks who answer yes are excused.

At the end of his questioning, Barraclough has winnowed down the jury panel by another sixteen.

"State of Alabama, do you have voir dire?" asks Barraclough. The judge pronounces the second word as in the phrase *dire circumstances*. California lawyers call the process voir *dear*— the proper French way—though we still pronounce the first word *vwar* instead of using the proper French pronunciation. Maybe that inconsistency explains why we became lawyers, not linguists.

Kerr stands and faces the panelists in the jury box, and then in the gallery, and introduces herself and Graham. "Fellow citizens of Quartz County, I want to thank y'all for your jury service. Will Ms. Annette Powell raise her hand?"

A woman sitting in the first two rows raises her hand. "I'm Annette."

"Insurance agent," whispers Margaret. "Forty-six, divorced, three kids. One of our A-listers." Margaret collated all the responses to the questionnaire and ranked the prospective jurors from most favorable to least favorable. Powell would make a good juror for us.

"Ma'am, you said in your questionnaire answers you believe a woman should have the right to abort her unborn baby, didn't you?" Kerr doesn't hesitate to humiliate innocent people. And to think Barraclough accused *me* of being the sharp practitioner.

"Objection!" I say. "Invades Ms. Powell's privacy rights. Such questioning should occur in judge's chambers, one prospective juror at a time, if at all. *Waller v. Georgia*, US Supreme Court, 1984. These good people shouldn't be forced to reveal their private views in open court."

"I already denied that very request from your co-counsel eight weeks ago," says Barraclough. "Read the court file, sir. Ms. Powell is excused for cause."

I suppress an urge to charge the bench. "Your Honor, this trial has nothing to do with abortion. The only evidence is that the defendant—"

"A juror who doesn't believe an unborn child is a human being or who thinks a mother has a right to kill an unborn human being can't render a fair verdict in this case," says Barraclough. "Proceed, Ms. Kerr."

"Absurd," I say. "The defense moves for a mistrial."

"Stop talking now, sir!" says Barraclough. "Ladies and gentlemen of the jury panel, you will ignore Mr. Henderson's diatribe. Mr. Henderson, there ain't—and this is not any Freudian slip; I mean to use that word—there ain't gonna be no mistrial. This young woman, Destiny Grace Harper, has languished in jail long enough without a trial."

Wait—this judge refused to release Destiny Grace on bail before trial, yet now pretends to worry she'll be in jail too long? "Set bail then."

"Not happening, either. Your motion is denied. That is my ruling. Do you understand me?"

"Very well, Your Honor," I say. *Very well, Your Honor.* The lawyer's way of telling a judge to fuck off without being held in contempt.

Hours of jury questioning follow. Kerr's ideal jurors are mothers or, better yet, would-be mothers who have fertility issues; religious, but not overly zealous; those who respect the judicial system or have been victims of a crime; and those who profess trust in the medical profession. Barraclough excuses for cause every juror who shows the slightest support for a woman's right to choose—because those people, while they might disapprove of what Destiny Grace did, will nevertheless more likely sympathize with a woman who claims that the government shouldn't control her body. His ruling devastates our strategy. Not only does it eliminate favorable potential jurors, but the prosecution doesn't have to use any of its precious peremptory strikes—the right to exclude no more than twelve prospective jurors without giving a reason.

After Kerr finishes, Barraclough adjourns for the day. Our team repairs to our conference room.

"I can't believe the judge kicked out everyone who was pro-choice," says Margaret. "Outrageous. At least we have reversible error."

Destiny Grace slams her Bible down on the table. "Is that what my case has come down to? I need murderers on my jury to get acquitted?"

"The judge excluded prospective jurors who'd approach this case with an open mind. He did us no favors."

"Abortion is murder in the eyes of God and under the laws of this state now."

"God is the concern of neither an Alabama circuit court nor a local jury," I say. "In fact, the First Amendment to the Constitution bars God from entering a courtroom."

"God is everywhere."

"Except in an American courtroom. To answer your question, yes, our dream jury was twelve people who favor a woman's right to choose and who are concerned about a woman's autonomy over her own body—even when those people might disagree with your decision not to have the surgery. Because of Barraclough's error, we're stuck with the backup plan." And a backup plan is never as good as the best plan.

CHAPTER SIXTEEN

Nights during a trial, I force down a light dinner and prepare for the next day, making sure I'm under the sheets by ten. I read Virginia Woolf. To my everlasting embarrassment as a feminist but gratitude as an insomniac, Woolf often transports me to the land of reveries.

Just as I settle into bed, someone knocks on my van door. I sit upright and retrieve Buddy's Smith & Wesson from under the pillow. *Careful, Elvis. If it's the cops and they see the gun, they'll shoot you.* But the cops would announce themselves, wouldn't they? Unless Dave Coyle told them not to so they could have an excuse to shoot me. "Who is it?"

"E, it's me."

I return the gun to its hideout, climb out of bed, put on a robe to cover up, open the door a crack, and find Tamara Evans Tipple waiting on the threshold. She flashes a seductive smile, bottom lip lightly pouty, eyes down. I remember that smile.

She enters, and I lock the door. While I have to bend down to walk in here—the interior height of my van is about five-eight, and I'm several inches taller than that—Tamara has plenty of head space. We stare at each other in amazement. She's wearing a light floral dress—yellow and pink roses on light fabric. Too youthful for her, too short, too tight, all of which nonetheless make the outfit more alluring. She wears Opium perfume, the same fragrance she wore in high school. So enticing that, over the years, when I have detected the fragrance on a woman, I can't stanch the flow of melancholic arousal. Where does her husband think she is tonight?

"Nice place you got here, E . . . considering."

"It ain't the Ritz. It's not even the Quartz Inn. But it's my home and my home away from home and my office all wrapped into one."

She takes a seat on the bed. "Might not be the Ritz, but it beats the crap out of the Quartz Inn. At least a half star better."

I sit next to her.

Her green eyes glisten. "How much do you hate me, E?"

"I don't hate you. Just never wanted to see you again."

"Sorry about the other day."

"Yeah, your son aiming a shotgun in the vicinity of my private parts was jarring. I still value the Henderson family jewels."

She chuckles. "I'm not sorry for that. We protect our property and ourselves. A lot of crazies don't like us much. We get our share of threats, especially lately. No, I'm sorry I called you an old man. Had to keep up appearances in front of my brood, know what I mean? You're not an old man. You're E."

"Better to be the young Elvis than the old one, huh?"

"Sorry about everything. Truly. I—"

My gaze quiets her. "It worked out for the best."

"Did it?"

Like the astute lawyer I hope I am, I avoid this dangerous line of inquiry. Tamara Evans was the love of my life, or so I once thought. A youthful romance? Sure. Also a painful emotional tattoo on my psyche, even now. We defied the laws of chemistry. Oil and water well blended. In the South of that era, adolescent love usually meant marriage. But Tamara's parents couldn't stand me. I was a poor boy, a liberal, a gadfly, the ward of a hippie uncle, and a budding heretic. The logical target of her affection was Jeremiah Tipple, the scion of a wealthier family, the star quarterback, a devout Christian. "I want *you*, E," she'd said. "We'll escape this shithole together." Then tragedy intervened. I decided to leave town, and Tamara wouldn't come with me. She announced her engagement to Jeremiah Tipple a week after I departed.

I don't ask why she's here. We'll get to that in due time. Rather, I ask about her life. She's fiercely proud of her church's good works and prouder of her sons. Like most mothers, she worries about all her children.

"Hunter, he's Jeremiah's right hand, and Clayton, well, he has his father's charisma." She boasts that Hunter was an excellent student who went to law school—the serious child, the problem-solver. But Clayton is clearly his mother's favorite. She raves about his athletic career. Like his daddy, he was a star quarterback in high school. Unlike his father, he had scholarship offers from some high major programs but decided to stay in the area and get a divinity degree. "Clayton will make a wonderful pastor someday, although Jeremiah thinks Hunter might be the better choice to take over the church because he works harder and is more stable." She says nothing complimentary about her daughter, Brandi.

"Clayton's tattoo doesn't exactly scream *man of God*," I say.

She looks out the window. "You can thank Destiny Grace for that. She has a wild streak; got into trouble with the law when she was younger. She got a tattoo, so he did, too, to impress her. The boy has struggled lately. She was a bad influence on him. She tried to worm her way back into his life. He's a married man. Or was. Because of her, Clayton and Becky are separated and might get divorced." She pauses. "Sorry. I know she's your client. To be fair, Destiny Grace was a good friend to Brandi, who's so shy. Destiny Grace gave her confidence, made her laugh." A sad shrug. "I probably took Brandi's confidence away. I was too harsh with her." She fidgets, using her fingers to brush at her hair. She did that as a girl. Her red lipstick has bled into the spider lines above her upper lips. None of it matters; she's captivating.

I talk about my failed marriage and about my career. Well, not everything. Some things you can't share. When she asks me why I decided to travel and work out of a van, I tell her what I tell everyone else—I got sick of Big Law and I'm a natural wanderer, so why not travel and do small law? True, as far as it goes, but incomplete.

As the minutes pass, conflicted feelings that have festered for over twenty-eight years recede to insignificance. Physical presence makes the past the past.

Tamara leans close, and I smell the perfume again.

"I came to ask a favor," she says. "I know you don't owe me, E. The opposite. I'll still ask. Leave my daughter out of your trial. She doesn't know anything about this, and she's fragile."

"Can't do it, Tamara. I can't jeopardize my client's case—her life. Brandi was Destiny Grace's best friend and Lillian Wagers's assistant. Wagers has vanished. Brandi can verify that Destiny Grace took care of her unborn babies in her own way, prayed for their good health. Brandi is also on the prosecution's list, and I can't control Kelsey Kerr."

"We'll deal with Kerr."

"Yes. The campaign contributions. More to come, I suspect."

She ignores the sarcasm and places a hand on my cheek. "Please, E. She's my daughter."

I gaze into her emerald eyes, which once gleamed with ambition and confidence but now convey weariness and resignation—and desire. When Tamara rests her hand on my upper thigh, then higher, I draw away, using every atom of willpower in this lonely man's mind and body. Some business is better left unfinished. "I can't," I say. "I won't trade Destiny Grace Harper's future for sex. Not to mention that you're a married woman."

Her cheeks redden in what? Anger? Embarrassment? She reaches back with her right arm, and before she can slap my face, I grab her wrist.

"You're still a coward; and an asshole," she says.

I release her arm, and she moves away. "I'll throw some clothes on and walk you to your car."

"Don't bother."

"It's dark outside, and the parking lot isn't well lit. It's not safe."

"This is small-town Alabama. I'm safe. The people here are friendly."

Yeah—so friendly they want to kill a woman because she had a problem pregnancy.

Without another word, she climbs out of the van.

CHAPTER SEVENTEEN

Entering the courthouse on the second morning of the trial, I'm bone-marrow weary. It takes extra effort for me to place one foot in front of the other, to unlace and retie my shoes at security, to balance the litigation bag while going up the escalator. In days gone by, the imminent completion of jury selection would propel me, amphetamine-like, toward opening statements, during which—so say the sociologists and jury consultants—most trials are won or lost. That's right, supposedly most juries decide which side wins before they hear a shred of evidence. Hardly the ideal way of doing justice.

It's not just last night's encounter with Tamara Tipple that's enervated me. The burden of this case weighs heavy. Whatever Destiny Grace Harper did or thought while carrying those babies, she does not deserve to die, and only our trial team stands between her and the executioner.

We take our places in the courtroom. Once the prospective jurors enter, Barraclough takes the bench. "Voir dire from the defense?"

I stand and smile at the prospective jurors. Not a broad

smile, which wouldn't be appropriate for a capital murder case, but a solemn smile that I hope conveys certitude in my cause's righteousness.

"Who believes the Bible is God's revelation to humanity and His word is the literal truth and historically accurate?" I ask.

Of the dozens in the jury pool, about 75 percent raise their hands.

"Keep your hand up if you know what Darwin's theory of evolution is."

All but three keep a hand up.

"How many of you still holding up a hand think the theory of evolution violates God's word?"

A good 60 percent leave their hands up.

"How many of you applaud the men and women who a few years back entered the Capitol Building in Washington while the House of Representatives and Senate decided whether to affirm the Electoral College vote for president?"

When only five or six hands go down, I have to restrain myself from shaking my head in disbelief.

"All right, feel free to lower your hands, ladies and gentle-men," I say. "Mr. Miller Holcomb, please give a shout."

A bespectacled man in his forties wearing a short-sleeve cotton shirt and khaki slacks raises his hand. This man has glared at me with unbridled contempt since he walked into the courtroom.

"Good morning to you, Mr. Holcomb," I say.

He grunts in reply.

"You're one of the folks who believes the theory of evolu-tion goes against God's word, am I right?"

He crosses his arms. "Absolutely."

"You also believe those who entered the Capitol Building did the right thing?"

His eyes shift defiantly. "Heroes trying to save democracy from people like yourself, sir."

"You have two boys, ages ten and seven?"

"That's right."

"Their names?"

"Brett and Mitchell."

"What do your sons do for fun?"

Holcomb bristles—although Kerr asked the jurors far more intrusive questions. "Brett plays youth football, and Mitchell plays the piano. My wife and I limit video games and the internet."

"Good for you, sir. Brett ain't a running back, I hope."

"Offensive line."

"Most people don't know this, but O-linemen are the most intelligent football players on a team, normally. Score highest on the NFL's Wonderlic intelligence test. I played running back at Quartz High in my day. I took far too many hits, as I'm sure y'all in attendance have figured out." The last line generates enough titters from the panel to make the joke worthwhile.

"I'll object to the personal details," says Kerr. "This is about the jury venire's backgrounds, not Mr. Henderson's."

"I was just asking about the witness's family, one local boy to another."

"Move on, sir," says Barraclough.

"Will do, Judge. Mr. Holcomb, your questionnaire says you like fly-fishing. You ever fished for trout in the Sipsey Fork branch of the Black Warrior River? It's the only place in Alabama that has trout." I turn toward the prosecution table. "For those of you who weren't born or raised in Alabama—I'm speaking to you, Ms. Kerr—the Sipsey Fork is about an hour southwest of here. Just take I-65 and turn off to State Highway 69 at Dodge City."

"You're as transparent as flat glass on a sunny day, Elvis," says Barraclough. "Move on."

"Never fished Sipsey Fork," says Holcomb. My insider's knowledge of Alabama fishing spots hasn't earned me one iota of warmth.

"You should take your boys. Let me ask you this. Do Brett and Mitchell attend a church school?"

"Jones Mountain Baptist."

"Would it be accurate to say one reason you send your children there is that the school doesn't teach children the theory of evolution?"

"Correct."

"Mr. Holcomb, what would you do if the government sought a court order to force Brett and Mitchell to attend a public school that teaches evolution?"

"I'd bar the door and get my gun." I can tell he's not exaggerating.

"No godless government is going to mess with your family, am I right, Mr. Holcomb?"

"You're right, sir."

"When I was a boy, I was rambunctious. I wanted to play sports all the time, watch TV shows, ride my bike. Homework came last. Any different today?"

"My wife and I make sure our boys do their homework. Not hard to do with Brett, the older one, but Mitchell, he's . . ."

"He's all boy?"

"Good way to describe it."

"What would you do, sir, if the State of Alabama sought a court order to force you to medicate Mitchell to get him to focus on his studies?"

"I'd get the best lawyer I could, and if that didn't work, I'd get my guns."

"You do realize this case is about the government trying to force medical care on my client's unborn children? About whether a parent has the right to resist government intrusion—just like you would?"

I spend the rest of the morning questioning the most conservative members of the jury panel, all with one goal—getting them to affirm their aversion to a government that might try to force them to violate their most closely held religious and political beliefs. Now that Barraclough has, on his own, banished every single prospective juror who supports a pregnant woman's right to control her body, everyone remaining in this group is *anti*-choice. I don't have enough peremptory challenges to get rid of them all. So although it might seem counterintuitive, I want the most conservative, fundamentalist, anti-government people I can find as jurors.

Just before lunch, we've picked a jury. Some are the conservatives I sought, and others are unknown quantities both sides accepted. Miller Holcomb, who works as a mechanic for an airport-based rental car company, made the cut. He's joined by a woman in her late sixties who hails from Iran and who, before retirement, taught physics at a local college; a female US postal worker, the only Black juror; a retired US Army officer who now runs his own security consulting firm; and a stay-at-home mom with a degree in communications. Also on the jury are a divorced woman in her late thirties who writes romance novels with Christian themes, an émigré from Vietnam who owns a seafood market and is a devout Catholic, a hospital orderly, two widows of engineers who worked for NASA (one is a retired schoolteacher and the other raised a family), a young construction worker, and a veterinary technician. Eight women and four men, six of whom reject the science of evolution.

Mildred Chilton, the courtroom clerk, directs the jury to stand and raise their right hands: "You do solemnly swear that you will well and truly try all issues joined between the defendant and the State of Alabama and render a true verdict thereon according to the law and evidence, so help you God." After the jurors mutter *I do*s, after all the gravitas, Barraclough orders us to lunch.

———

Although I have no appetite, Destiny Grace convinces me to share a nibble of her grilled cheese sandwich made with processed cheese and processed bread and a soggy, tasteless tomato. I almost gag trying to please her. The only grilled cheese "samwiches" I've ever liked were courtesy of my Uncle Buddy, made Southern style with pimento cheese.

Once we return to the courtroom and the parties are ensconced back at their respective battle stations, Barraclough takes the bench, and the jury walks from the deliberation room (where they'll ultimately decide Destiny Grace's fate) to the jury box. The judge swivels his large chair toward the jurors. "Ladies and gentlemen, before we get started, let me tell you a few things. First of all, don't discuss this case with anyone. There's an awful lot of people out there, including the news media. If anyone tries to talk to you about this case, let me know, and I will take care of it. Y'all with me?" He waits for all the jurors to nod or mumble a yes. "When you get home tonight after court, your husband, your wife, your boyfriend, girlfriend, son, daughter . . . somebody is going to ask 'Did you get selected on a jury?' Sure as my hair is white, the next question will be 'What's the case about?' And all you can reply is that 'The white-headed judge said I can't discuss it until the case is over.' Now, during breaks or before or after court, you might bump into the attorneys, and if they walk right past you or turn away, don't think they're being rude. They're doing what they're supposed to do, which is not trying to get in your good graces outside the courtroom. Understand?"

More nods.

The judge announces that the lawyers will give their opening statements, which aren't evidence but simply summaries of the evidence from the perspective of each side.

"The prosecution, which, I remind you, has the burden of proof beyond a reasonable doubt, will go first," says Barraclough.

Kelsey Kerr goes to the lectern to tell the State of Alabama's story.

CHAPTER EIGHTEEN

Kerr opens a black three-ring binder: "Judge Barraclough." A clipped nod toward us: "Counsel." A graceful turn to face the jurors: "Members of the jury. On November 17 of last year, Destiny Grace Harper learned that her unborn twins, Lydia and Brooklyn, suffered from a rare condition called twin-to-twin transfusion syndrome, commonly known as TTTS. Untreated, TTTS is a death sentence for babies. Destiny Harper knew this. The Good Lord offered her a mother's miracle—a simple, non-invasive procedure called fetoscopy. An almost invisible scar and a single dang night in the hospital."

Damned if Kerr doesn't get away with the *dang*. She has a forceful presence; she's conversational and articulate without bombast. Although sometimes a little bombast isn't a bad thing—or so says Hazel Ruth Curnow.

"Harper flat-out refused this miracle, ladies and gentlemen," she says. "Worse, when the State of Alabama took her to court to ask Judge Barraclough to order her to do the right thing, she turned tail and went into hiding. She didn't call anyone until *after* the babies were born, one already dead, the other alive until she abandoned her, too. Only *then* did she get medical help—for herself, after leaving a living, precious human being behind to die alone. Yes, you'll hear evidence that one of the twins lived up to twenty minutes and that their mother left at least five minutes before that. Destiny Harper committed double murder. She murdered Lydia; she murdered Brooklyn. She killed her own babies."

"Objection, improper argument," I say. Attorneys don't usually interrupt the opponent's opening statement. Doing so often signals inexperience and can backfire by underscoring the adversary's point. But Kerr has gone too far. Barraclough sustains my objection and advises the jury to disregard the argument, but Kerr doesn't care.

As she speaks, I regard her with indifference. Higgins keeps a poker face, and Margaret feigns boredom. A lawyer must never seem interested in what opposing counsel has to say. Meanwhile, anger spews from Destiny Grace's every pore. Good. She *should* be angry at the State's accusations.

Kerr smacks the lectern with an open palm, startling the courtroom when—inadvertently or intentionally—she also clips the microphone. "Double murder, after Harper falsely claimed to have accepted Jesus as her Lord and Savior; double murder, after she invoked the Lord's name as an excuse for not undergoing the lifesaving procedure. She abused those babies to death." All of these words are highly inflammatory, but I've already objected once, so I sit still.

In the jury box, Miller Holcomb leans so far forward his checkered sports shirt strains at the top buttons. The romance writer keeps glancing at our table, her eyes filled with contempt. The postal worker shakes her head over and over. The others follow Kerr's every word and gesture, rapt. Any hope Kelsey Kerr would botch her opening statement has vanished.

She proceeds to mock what she calls the defense's buzzword

excuses: *autonomy, women's rights, human rights.* "Her lawyers are gonna tell you that Destiny Harper had the right to refuse surgery because she's an 'autonomous human being.' We don't live in a fully autonomous society, members of the jury, meaning we don't get to do whatever the heck we want no matter who gets hurt. We live in a society where we care for each other. We live in a society where pregnant mothers take care of their unborn babies. By the way, there's no dispute Lydia and Brooklyn were human beings. Lydia was born alive. Brooklyn was a human being, too; was from conception. Even though the defendant's lawyer, Elvis Henderson, recently said in an interview that whether the babies were human or not didn't matter, that they could be killed either way."

That's not what I said to the media at all. I half stand to object, but Margaret whispers, "E, don't!" She's right. I can't make this case about my credibility.

"The jury will disregard the statement about what Mr. Henderson did or didn't say," says Barraclough, surprisingly coming to my rescue. "As I told you, an opening statement isn't evidence. Stick to the facts you intend to prove, Ms. Kerr."

After describing fetoscopic laser surgery as "safer than repairing torn cartilage in your knee," Kerr launches into a long and detailed discussion of the medical science behind TTTS and fetoscopy. Too much technical information; a momentum killer. The tedium disperses when Kerr tells the jury how no one attended the babies' birth. "What kind of mother tries to birth two sick babies with not another soul in the room, much less without doctors and nurses? A mother who hopes the babies will die, that's what kind.

"Now, the defense will undoubtedly tell you that the defendant couldn't have premeditated her babies' death; that if she really wanted to get rid of the twins, she would've run off to some liberal state and had an abortion. The evidence will show that her failure to get an abortion won't get her off the hook for premeditated murder. Harper could've thought abortion is a sin in the eyes of God—it is—but foolishly believed that letting the babies die wasn't. Or maybe Harper worried that if she had an abortion out of state, she'd be prosecuted when she returned to Alabama. The evidence will show that when the opportunity arose, Destiny Grace Harper refused to have a minor procedure to save her twins, and she ran from the law, and she hid from the law, and she abandoned the one baby that survived the birth, and she brought her well-planned scheme to murder her babies to a dreadful conclusion, and now she's trying to get off scot-free by falsely invoking the name of God."

Again, an entirely improper argument, but I let Kerr talk. I can't behave as if our side has something to hide.

Forty minutes after she first began, Kerr moves close to the jury box and clasps her hands like a supplicant. "Destiny Grace Harper, with malice aforethought, with premeditation, murdered her babies. At the end of this case, I will come back to you, members of the jury, and ask you to find Destiny Grace Harper guilty of two counts of first-degree murder. I will ask you to see that Brooklyn and Lydia Harper get the justice they deserve."

Kerr sits, grabs some tissue, and dabs at her eyes, and I'm thinking, *Good lord, these histrionics won't work, not even in Cole's Crossing, Alabama.* But the histrionics appear to work. And it occurs to me that maybe they're not histrionics at all, but the channeling of very real emotions surrounding Kerr's own torturous quest to become a mother.

Either way, the court reporter finishes transcribing Kerr's last words and sighs deeply. Mildred Chilton, the clerk, has tears in her eyes. So do several jurors.

———

I jump to my feet before Kerr sits down. Unlike her, I bring no notes to the lectern. I'm old school. Unlike Kerr, I ignore the lectern and inch as close to the jury box as I can get without invading the jurors' space. I fold an arm across my chest, rest my opposite elbow on that arm, grasp my chin, and nod my head. "Destiny Grace Harper, please stand."

We didn't plan this. It just feels right. Destiny Grace seems startled at this improvised request, but after a moment's hesitation, she rises. Her eyes are wide, shot through with blood from sleepless nights and weeping. She's a tiny woman and looks miniscule in this large room. She fidgets for a moment but then gives a solemn nod at the jurors. I walk over to her and place an avuncular hand on her shoulder. *Careful, Elvis; you want to humanize her, but this impromptu ploy could look insincere.* I don't leave the hand there for long.

I tell the jury Destiny Grace has followed her faith and worked two jobs to take care of an ill mother. A dramatic shake of the head and then a headlong dive into the problem area: "A year and a half ago, Destiny Grace became pregnant with twins. No, she didn't have a husband. That's no crime. These days, single parenting is common even among the devout. Jury members, I'd bet my house—well, my campervan, which is my house—that most or all of you know a devout person, a good person, who has found herself in similar circumstances. Destiny Grace did everything she could to take good care of her unborn babies."

Without employing as much medical jargon as Kerr used, I talk about the whys and the wherefores of TTTS. I describe the invasiveness of fetoscopy and the risks to both mother and unborn child of piercing the mother's abdomen and laser-burning the unborn fetuses. I summarize the beliefs of the Church of Our Lord's Rapture, never pretending to embrace them myself but giving them the respect that religious beliefs deserve under the US Constitution. "Destiny Grace Harper chose to pray and trust in the Lord's power to heal. When the long, authoritarian arm of the State of Alabama tried to force her to have invasive surgery, Destiny Grace appealed to God again and left town. In her own way, she protected her babies like any good mother would and should."

With hands clasped behind my back, I straighten my spine. The physical punctuation marks of oral advocacy are as crucial to understanding as the punctuation marks in a book. "There are unassailable fundamental truths at play here, members of the jury. First, a person who, like Destiny Grace Harper, acts according to deeply held religious beliefs and refuses medical treatment can't be found guilty of a crime. Cannot. Period. End of case."

I go to our counsel table and thumb through a blank yellow legal pad. Calculated silence becomes more effective when supplemented by action. "Secondly, the United States Constitution protects a person against forced medical procedures, even pregnant women. To paraphrase the Illinois Supreme Court, an unborn child, like no other being, depends exclusively on another for life itself. The pregnant woman's entire existence, awake and asleep, shapes the developing fetus. The circumstances in which each individual woman brings forth life are as varied as the circumstances of each woman's life. Which means there can be no objective legal standard by which to judge a woman's actions during pregnancy."

I pause and make eye contact with each juror in turn. "Sometimes what the prosecution doesn't say is as important as what it does say. Ms. Kerr said nary a word about motive. Because there will be no evidence of motive. Destiny Grace could've ended her pregnancy if that was truly her goal—if not here in Alabama, she could have terminated her pregnancy elsewhere. She did not. A five-hour and fifteen-minute drive to Greenville, South Carolina, where the procedure was legal when Destiny Grace was pregnant. A six-and-a-half-hour drive to Southern Illinois. So don't buy this malarkey about her waiting too long or being afraid to travel to another state."

"Objection," says Kerr. "That's argument."

Barraclough covers his mouth for a moment—to cover a smile at Kerr's hypocrisy? "Sustained," he says. "Confine yourself to the facts, Mr. Henderson."

"Instead of traveling to another state, close enough by car ride, Destiny Grace consulted a licensed midwife and then, when the midwife suspected complications, a respected obstetrician-gynecologist. You will hear testimony about Destiny Grace's great love and concern for her unborn babies, and about Destiny Grace's devotion as a mother. Women who want to end a pregnancy don't behave that way. There's no motive for murder because there were no murders."

This last statement arises partly out of our evidence and partly out of hope. The evidence: LeAnn Harper's testimony. Not ideal, because the defendant's mother is clearly biased. The hope: that Lillian Wagers, the midwife, somehow comes out of hiding and shows up at trial.

I hold up an index finger like an old-time evangelist pointing to the heavens. Why let Jeremiah Tipple monopolize the local pulpit? "Members of the jury, let's return to Judge Barraclough's preliminary instructions to you. His most important words: *reasonable doubt*. The burden of proof is on the prosecution. The prosecution will not come close to meeting its exceedingly heavy burden of proof."

As my words sink in, I walk over to Destiny Grace. "This young person suffered an unspeakable tragedy. She was an expectant mother whose beloved twins suffered from a rare disease.

Her decision not to have surgery will, and should, be adjudged only by her Maker—only by our merciful Lord. As for your duty as the earthly triers of fact, after you hear the testimony and weigh the evidence, I'm confident you'll return a verdict of not guilty." I nod, execute a quarter bow, and sit.

"State of Alabama, call your first witness," says Barraclough.

CHAPTER NINETEEN

Dr. Ivy Leigh Dobson Woodruff, a thin woman in her fifties with a hawkish face and short silver hair, has an admirable record of providing low-cost health care to underprivileged women of all races. She's antagonized the evangelical right because her clinics dispense birth control, and she's alienated the law-and-order faction because she's campaigned against the death penalty. But she also lobbies hard against any politician who supports a woman's right to choose. In other words, Woodruff is a rare independent thinker. Once she finishes cataloguing her professional accomplishments and her many accolades, Kerr asks about the doctor's encounter with Destiny Grace Harper.

Woodruff puts her glasses on—they're tethered to her neck with a silver chain—and speaks to the jury in a rich, resonant voice. "The patient presented with swollen limbs and an abdomen that was extremely distended for a woman who was eighteen weeks pregnant. She was anxious, and she expressed mistrust in doctors. She was terrified of the ultrasound procedure, so scared she almost left the office, until I persuaded her ultrasound is safe and noninvasive. She agreed to the procedure only after I offered to perform the ultrasound personally, which I rarely do. The sonogram confirmed the patient was carrying twins, monochorionic, meaning they shared a placenta. Very rare in itself. Three in a thousand pregnancies. Unfortunately, the ultrasound also showed high amniotic fluid in the amniotic sac of one of the twins and low amniotic fluid around the other twin, which indicates twin-to-twin transfusion syndrome—TTTS for short. This happens in three out of ten thousand births. Rarer than a double lightning strike."

I stare down at the table. Bad luck can wreak more havoc than Satan unchained.

Woodruff explains the effects of the condition—dehydration and anemia in the donor twin, high blood pressure and other complications in the recipient. "The death of one twin can affect the other twin's chances of surviving. Left untreated, the survival rate for twins with TTTS is 10 to 15 percent. The few babies who live face a higher likelihood of neurological problems, including cerebral palsy, vision loss, hearing loss, and intellectual disabilities." She goes on to talk about necrosis of cerebral white matter, hemorrhagic brain lesions, ischemia, cardiomegaly, biventricular hypertrophy, and atrioventricular valve regurgitation, technical terms that carry an ominous tone. Her statistics are bleaker than those Margaret uncovered in her research.

"I quickly reassured her by telling her about a relatively new procedure, fetoscopic laser surgery," Woodruff continues. "I informed her that the procedure would give her babies a 75 to 95 percent chance of survival. Flipped the odds. I told her how surgeons make a four-millimeter incision through the abdominal wall and uterus, allowing a laser to access the abnormal vascular connections and ablate them. In other words, the laser zaps away the blood vessels causing all the trouble. I let her know that the University of Alabama at Birmingham and

Vanderbilt University have world-renowned experts at their medical centers, and that both hospitals are just ninety-minute drives from Huntsville. I also told Ms. Harper that a woman usually receives only a local anesthetic and stays in the hospital for just one night. And that the state, or even one of my foundations, would defray the costs if she didn't have health insurance."

"How did the defendant respond to this?"

"She didn't seem to understand at first, just stared at me and shook her head. I repeated how her babies would be okay after the fetoscopic procedure. She became agitated. She shouted that I didn't know what I was talking about, said the Lord would take care of Brooklyn and Lydia. I told her I loved the names, and that the Lord *would* take care of them through the laser procedure. In response—and apologies for my language—she called me a "fucking bitch" and told me to "stay the fuck away from her and her babies." I could see there was no sense in arguing with her, so I left the room so she could get dressed and have some alone time to get ahold of herself. I worried she might become violent if I hung around."

Some of the jurors look at Destiny Grace in surprise. The faces of others register disgust.

"Were you certain of your diagnosis of TTTS, doctor?" asks Kerr.

She thinks for a moment, the hesitation adding to her credibility. "I had never seen a case of TTTS before Ms. Harper came in—that's how rare it is. Later that day, I asked a colleague at the University of Alabama at Birmingham medical center to look at the sonogram results. He specializes in complicated pregnancies. He confirmed the diagnosis. The Harper twins suffered from stage three twin-to-twin transfusion syndrome."

"Stage three out of . . . ?"

"Three out of five, according to what we call the Quintero scale. Stage three means the imbalance of blood has begun to impair the heart function in at least one of the babies. It was already serious."

"Stage four would mean?"

"Heart failure in one of the twins."

"Stage five?"

"One or both of the babies has died. Without the treatment, the Harper babies' condition worsened to stage five. It shouldn't have happened. A terrible, needless tragedy."

"Dr. Woodruff, does fetoscopy cause scarring for the mother?"

Woodruff holds up her thumb and forefinger, not quite touching. "Teeny-weeny."

"Did you tell this to Destiny Grace Harper?"

"Yes, ma'am. Loud and clear." Woodruff goes on to testify that, after consulting with an attorney, she alerted authorities that Destiny Grace was a neglectful mother who was recklessly or intentionally jeopardizing the life of her unborn babies.

Kerr tilts her head and gives Woodruff a puzzled look. "I don't understand, Dr. Woodruff. In 2016, didn't the American College of Obstetricians and Gynecologists Committee on Ethics issue an opinion advising doctors to respect a pregnant woman's refusal of surgical intervention, even if the surgery is needed to save a baby's life? Wasn't your decision to alert the authorities about the Harper twins inconsistent with that ethics opinion?" The question is the attorney version of a sheep in wolf's clothing.

"Yes, because I couldn't disagree more with the ACOG opinion. The opinion ignores the life of the unborn and assumes that the pregnant mother can do what she wants with her body. She can't. A pregnant mother has a moral obligation to care for her unborn babies. No one else in this wide world can do that for them. Destiny Grace Harper wasn't taking control over her body, she was being selfish at the expense of two innocent human beings. Those poor babies died agonizing deaths."

CHAPTER TWENTY

A trial is like a stage play, and on direct examination, the witness—who's usually on the interrogator's side—should play the starring role. Kelsey Kerr made Woodruff the star of the show. On cross-examination, the lawyer asking the questions must be the star. I'm ready for my close-up.

The jurors seem attentive—all except one of the NASA wives, who's looking down and knitting with imaginary needles and yarn.

"Do you believe in miracles, Dr. Woodruff?" I ask. The question is courtesy of Margaret Booth's research.

"You mean like Jesus performed in the Bible? Yes, sir."

"I mean modern-day medical miracles that could happen right here in downtown Cole's Crossing."

"Yes, I believe in modern-day miracles."

"Can you think of any you, personally, were involved in?"

Woodruff nods. "You're talking about JoEllen Doe. I wrote an article about her in the *Journal of Modern Christianity and Medicine.* The patient was diagnosed with a stage-three cancerous tumor, colorectal cancer, requiring chemotherapy. JoEllen

had a 72 percent chance of surviving the cancer if she underwent the treatment and a 93 percent chance of dying without
it. Because of past fertility issues, she decided not to have the
chemo, which would've interfered with her chance of ever
getting pregnant. Then she got pregnant. She gave birth, survived the cancer without the treatment, and is cancer free
today. A miracle."

"JoEllen Doe trusted in God and relied on prayer?"

"Yes."

"And Destiny Grace Harper likewise told you she believes
the Good Lord heals and would take care of her babies despite
the odds?"

"Yes."

"You had no reason to doubt her sincerity?"

I sense Margaret and Higgins have both stopped breathing mid-exhalation. A standard rule of trial advocacy is that
a cross-examiner should never ask a question he doesn't know
the answer to. That old saw teaches cowardice. I don't know the
answer to this question, and Woodruff could come up with any
number of reasons to cast doubt on Destiny Grace's sincerity,
but I'm no coward.

"The patient did seem to be sincere in her beliefs," says
Woodruff.

Margaret and Higgins recommence breathing.

"In fact, she even balked at a simple ultrasound because of
her religious views?"

"She did."

I crane my neck up to the ceiling. Another risky question
that depends on whether I believe what Destiny Grace has told
me. Why the hell not? "During your office visit with Destiny
Grace Harper, she never raised the issue of getting an abortion,
did she?"

A pause that makes my heart rate accelerate by the half second. Finally, "No, she did not. If she had, I would've told her that I believe in the right to life. I wouldn't have helped her."

"But you've had pregnant patients raise the issue before, haven't you?"

"That's confidential."

Kerr makes a tardy objection.

"I'm just asking generally," I say. "The answer couldn't possibly breach the confidentiality of any of Dr. Woodruff's thousands of patients over the years."

Barraclough puts his chin in his hands and finally nods. "You can answer yes or no, Dr. Woodruff."

The annoyed witness says, "Yes. But I've never given a patient information that would help her abort and always counseled against it."

"But Destiny Grace Harper, with two sick twins, was *not* one of the women who asked about abortion, was she?"

"Correct, as I've already testified to."

"At nineteen weeks, Ms. Harper could've legally gotten an abortion in Illinois, which permits them up to twenty-four weeks?"

"That's my understanding, yes."

Now I venture into another touchy area. "Dr. Woodruff, you've seen the babies' autopsy reports. Do you agree that Lydia, the twin who survived after her birth for a matter of minutes, would've died even if she had been born in a hospital?" I ask this because I don't want the jury to distinguish between the twins in deciding guilt or innocence. It would do no good if Destiny Grace were acquitted of Brooklyn's death but convicted of murdering Lydia.

"I'm not a neonatologist, but I do agree with that," says Woodruff. "The complications from the TTTS were devastating. Neither of those babies had a chance."

The judge holds up a hand. "I have a question of my own, doctor." Nothing is more exasperating than a judge who interrupts cross-examination and breaks a lawyer's rhythm—especially if the questions rehabilitate a flailing witness. Barraclough leans forward and slides to the edge of his seat, as if he and Woodruff are the only people in the room. "Suppose a six-month-old baby is suffering from continual undiagnosed vomiting. Suppose further the baby's mother refuses to allow the infant to undergo X-rays with heavy radiation. If the baby dies, would the mother be culpable? I'm not asking you about the law now. I'm talking about medical ethics."

"Other symptoms?" asks Woodruff.

Kerr squirms in her seat and confers with Graham, who shakes her head, likely advising her boss not to object to the presiding judge's question.

"Let's assume no other symptoms," says Barraclough. "A happy baby who just can't keep anything down."

What's this about? Is Barraclough looking for free medical advice?

Woodruff takes a long moment before answering. "As you describe the situation, my answer would be no, the mother wouldn't be culpable. X-rays can be very harmful to infants. Mother's decision."

"What if the child is losing weight?" asks the judge. "Vomiting and weight loss are signs of something amiss, true? The mother refuses X-rays and the baby dies."

"A terrible tragedy, but still the mother's choice," says Woodruff. "It's a different situation from our case, you see. X-rays have been proven harmful, especially to babies. Fetoscopy is very safe."

"The witness is all yours again, Elvis."

I hear Margaret typing quickly on her computer. To give her time, I say, "May I confer with my colleague, Judge?"

"Make it quick," he says.

I go over and look at the computer monitor over Margaret's shoulder. I have a sense of what she's looking for, but I can't process this type of information as quickly as she does.

"Proceed, counsel," says an impatient Barraclough.

I motion for Margaret to join me at the lectern. As Woodruff responds to each question, I listen to the answer and simultaneously absorb, and then ask, Margaret's next whispered question with any necessary modifications. I say with all humility that few lawyers can multitask this way. Maybe not with *all* humility—most people take credit for the gifts nature or nurture arbitrarily bestow upon them, and I'm no different. Margaret once compared me to a virtuoso jazz drummer playing a different rhythm with each limb. I think it's a kind of attention deficit disorder that works to my advantage in a court of law.

"Let's talk about the safety of fetoscopic laser surgery," I say, asking one of Margaret's whispered questions. "The word *fetoscopy* is a combination of the word *fetus* and the word *scope*, true?"

"That's true."

"In the procedure, the surgeon uses a laser to cut through the mother's flesh to get surgical access to the babies?"

"Yes."

"Until the 1990s, this kind of surgery wasn't done, as it was too dangerous?"

"That was before technology and smaller instruments made the procedure safe." I enjoy the harried edge in her voice.

"But, even today, the surgery isn't safe enough for a pregnant woman to have it done at her local hospital? Because not every ob-gyn has the expertise?"

"Just because a procedure is specialized doesn't mean—"

I point an accusatory index finger at Woodruff. "Do you know that, in the 1940s and '50s, the University of Michigan,

Mass General, and other esteemed medical institutions used harmful X-rays on babies diagnosed to have enlarged thymus glands? A condition medical science now knows doesn't even exist? Those know-it-all doctors irradiated those babies with between two hundred and four hundred rads, which we now know is an immense amount of radiation for a child but which the medical gurus of the era called *very safe*? Sound familiar, Dr. Woodruff?" My words echo throughout the courtroom, though I've stepped away from the microphone.

Barraclough overrules Kerr's litany of objections. He wants to hear this. Better yet, based on the jurors' attentive faces, so do they.

"You're right about the irradiation of the thymus, but you're referring to a completely different situation," says Woodruff. "Your client is an adult, and in the intervening years standards of testing—"

"Really, doctor? You just said it was called feto*scopy*, not adult*oscopy*."

Woodruff leans forward and glares at me. "Is that a question, sir?"

I make a slight turn to the jury and smile, one of those lip pressers where you don't show your teeth. I glance at the gallery; Calinda Rocha is smiling. That is affirming. Although the flippancy was effective, Hazel Curnow wouldn't approve. She isn't about snark or insults. They have short shelf lives, she says, and you're all too often stuck with the rancid leftovers.

"Dr. Woodruff, did you consider Destiny Grace Harper to be your patient when you examined her?" I ask.

"Of course. As her doctor, I wanted the best for her and her babies."

"You've heard of the Health Insurance Portability and Accountability Act of 1996, better known as HIPAA?"

"Yes. Patient confidentiality."

"But in reporting to the district attorney that Destiny Grace Harper refused a fetoscopy, you breached your duty of confidentiality to your patient?"

"No, I did not, sir. An important exception to HIPAA requires a health care professional to report child abuse to law enforcement. Destiny Harper's refusal to have a fetoscopic procedure was child abuse, pure and simple. It was my moral and legal obligation to report her behavior. My heavens, the babies ended up dead. Like I said before, I consulted my lawyer before we made the report."

This time, by asking a question I didn't know the answer to, I let Woodruff shove my question back up my ass, in the vernacular. Our short tenure as trial counsel, along with our own preconceived notions about the legality of Destiny Grace's actions, blinded us to the possibility that someone with Woodruff's beliefs would view our client as a mother who'd abused her living children.

Not easy to brush the answer off and sashay into my next question, but I try. "Doctor, one of your concerns as an ob-gyn is the high infant mortality rate in the state of Alabama, about seven deaths per thousand births?"

"That statistic is accurate, unfortunately."

"Do you agree that with better health care for pregnant mothers in Alabama, the seven deaths per thousand could drop to four deaths?"

"I've written that in my published articles."

"Should the Alabama legislators who vote against health care funds for poor pregnant women be charged with first-degree murder for the death of those three babies per thousand?"

Kerr's objection is sustained, but the jury has gotten the point.

I take a step forward and point at the witness. "You, your-self, think that sometimes it's fine and dandy to kill an unborn baby even though the mother is perfectly healthy, am I right?"

Woodruff crosses her arms indignantly and sits forward in her chair. "I resent the accusation, sir!" It takes a moment for her to grasp why I asked this question. Her arms uncross, and her back returns to its rightful place against the chair. She waits for the interrogative guillotine to drop.

"In fact, you believe the abortion laws should contain an exception for rape and incest. The innocent unborn baby dies, even though the physical trauma—and I am *not* discounting the horrid psychological trauma—but the *physical* trauma to the mother is over and done with. The baby could be born, and both mother and baby could be in excellent physical health. Yet, if you had your way, innocent babies would die to ease the mother's damaged psyche." Am I uncomfortable making an argument that contradicts what I truly believe? Not in the least—I'm an attorney.

Woodruff doesn't answer.

"Does the fact you've lobbied to allow innocent babies to be aborted when the mother's life isn't at risk make you an at-tempted murderer, Dr. Woodruff? Shouldn't you be the one on trial here?"

"Sanctimonious words coming from a man who defended his boss's socialite buddy, a pedophile-rapist," says Kerr.

Someone behind me in the gallery chortles so loudly that Barraclough slams his hand hard on his desktop, a technique far more effective than pounding the ceremonial gavel gathering dust at the far end of the bench. Bailiff Travis stands up. When the room falls silent, Travis sits back down.

Kerr is right about that—sort of. Two years ago, I repre-sented a very wealthy man in a sexual battery trial. The fellow donated a lot of money to progressive causes. He and Hazel Curnow had traveled in the same circles before Hazel withdrew from public life. The evidence against him expanded during the trial into strong proof my client had raped at least three minors. Said client was charged with rape and convicted, and justifiably so. Sometimes lawyers deserve to lose; sometimes—more than sometimes—you don't know who people really are. In any event, my involvement in that case didn't help my reputation as a defender of justice.

"I make no apology for the case the prosecution is referring to," I say. "The defendant received a rigorous defense from me, as the Constitution requires." Even saying this is too much—I took Kerr's bait. I calm down when Margaret puts a gentle yet firm hand on my shoulder.

"Now, y'all are going to stop this," says Barraclough. "The jury will disregard Mr. Henderson's questions about Dr. Woodruff committing murder. It's not evidence. It's nothing—puffed up words in the wind. Same with Ms. Kerr's accusation about representing pedophiles and such. Words in the wind, which will blow in and out of your minds, ladies and gentlemen. I instruct you to forget them, to give no weight to them. You got anything else, Mr. Henderson?"

"No further questions," I say, distressed that my cross-examination ended on this sour note.

"Redirect from the State of Alabama?"

"Only a couple questions, Judge," say Kerr. "Dr. Woodruff, you're aware of a pill that combines the drugs mifepristone and misoprostol, are you not?"

"I am. Commonly known as the abortion pill."

"And at the time that the defendant was pregnant, that pill was available by mail in all states because of federal law."

"I'm not a lawyer, but the post office had to deliver it."

"Up to how many weeks is the mail-order baby-killing pill effective?"

"Up to ten weeks."

"So when Ms. Harper saw you in your office, she was much too far along to use the abortion pill?"

"That's right. Eight or nine weeks too far."

"Nothing further. Thank you, doctor."

I have no idea why Kerr asked those questions, and on their face, they don't hurt our case. On the contrary, they seem to help because the pill is available and Destiny Grace didn't take it. But uncertainty as to the other side's motives always makes my gut clench.

"We're going to adjourn for the day," says Barraclough. "And, members of the jury, you be sure to remember what the white-haired judge told you."

CHAPTER TWENTY-ONE

Margaret and I stand at the Quartz Inn entrance, and I feel as if I'm carrying the weight of the entire sorry building on my shoulders. I walked right into Woodruff's allegation of child abuse, and the jury now knows I defended a billionaire lowlife. I can't blot out the image of Destiny Grace's fearful expression as the jailer was about to cart her back to her jail cell.

"Dinner at the café?" asks Margaret. It's an obligatory offer. I know she wants nothing more than to go up to her room and video-chat with her boyfriend, Gustave. He's a corporate lawyer at a Big Law firm in Century City.

"Thank you, no. I'll get something to go from the restaurant and prepare for tomorrow. Say hey to Gus."

She puts a hand on my shoulder. "It wasn't that bad, E. You did good. Better than good."

"Sure I did."

Once inside the campervan, I sit on the bed and wait for my adrenaline level to drop. It plummets, and I'm exhausted. Then the headache comes on, pickax chops pounding on my skull's interior. I check the van's pantry—no pain pills. I'm long overdue for a grocery and pharmacy stop. I call the front desk, get Thomas Styles (who else?), and ask if I can get a pain reliever in the hotel.

"I'm sorry you're feeling poorly, Mr. Henderson. No room service to the parking lot, and the gift shop is closed. Good news: I got some packets of Tylenol at the front desk."

"No ibuprofen? I'll even settle for aspirin."

"No, sir. Only Tylenol."

I thank him and hang up. I haven't taken a Tylenol since my journey with Arlette Coyle so many years ago. I will not take it now. *Arteries in my head, throb away.*

Throughout that drive to Florida, Arlette kept insisting I accelerate my shake-rattle-and-roll Buick to *Star Trek* speed. Then, after thirty minutes passed, she would demand we stop at a convenience store. The second time we stopped, she bought more chips and gummy bears, along with some Tylenol—the big bottle, extra strength.

"Do you keep going to the ladies' room to make yourself puke?" I asked.

She flashed me an irritated look, which wasn't exactly a no. "I have a headache."

How do you ask someone you don't really know if they have an eating disorder? I really didn't know Arlette. We had few classes together, but we never hung out. Yes, she was Tammy Evans's best friend, and, yes, Tammy and I had sort of a semi-public romance, and, yes, Arlette knew plenty about it. These facts amplified the distance between Arlette and me. Sad to say in hindsight, but I was indifferent to her. Don't get me wrong. She was attractive, even in her sweats, and she'd perfumed the car with her Gucci Rush, which wasn't a bad thing. As for her feelings toward me, I suspected she held me in some disdain.

I started to worry when she pulled her poetry anthology

from her knapsack and began reading Plath's "Lady Lazarus" aloud. *"Dying/ Is an art"? "My skin/ Bright as a Nazi lampshade"?* Not what you want to hear while barreling down I-65 in a death-trap vehicle. Then we stopped at another gas station in Montgomery to refuel, and she came out of the mini-mart with a box of SnackWell's Devil's Food Cookie Cakes, a bottle of water, and a second bottle of Tylenol.

"What's that about?" I asked. "You just bought a bottle."

"I told you, I have a bad headache."

I lay my left arm on the steering wheel and faced her. "Do you think because I was stupid enough to drive you, I'm stupid enough to believe that?"

She snapped her head in the opposite direction.

"Look at me, Arlette."

She didn't.

"Look at me!"

She met my gaze.

"We should turn back. That's what you really want."

Her faraway eyes rounded. "No. We have to keep going."

"Give me the Tylenol."

"I told you, my head—"

"Give it to me. Both bottles."

She reached in the bags and handed me the bottles, which I put in the side compartment of the driver's-side door.

As if nothing happened, she opened the box of cookies and pulled one out for herself.

"You want one?" she asked.

"Sure."

She tore a cookie out of the package and handed it to me. "Just get going," she said. "We're going to be late."

———

A knock on my campervan door relieves me from such thoughts. I don't bother to retrieve my uncle's gun. Irrational, but I hope my visitor is Callie Rocha.

"Yeah?" I call out.

"Mr. Henderson? It's Lillian Wagers."

The Church of Our Lord Rapture's midwife.

I reach out a hand and help her into the back of the van.

Before I can ask my first question, Wagers starts wringing her hands. A large, gray-haired woman in her sixties, she's dressed in a loose cotton blouse and baggy slacks. She has a round face, round haircut, and a round body. Her ruddy face is pinched with anxiety.

"I've been looking for you, Ms. Wagers," I say.

"I've been avoiding you, Mr. Henderson." She speaks with an elegant drawl characteristic of the Old Southern aristocracy. My bias against her church led me to assume that only the less-privileged economic classes would buy into Jeremiah Tipple's brand of religion. But gullibility and desperation don't honor class distinctions.

"What made you change your mind about talking with me?" I ask.

"Deuteronomy 31:6. 'Be strong and of a good courage, fear not, nor be afraid of them: for the LORD thy God, he it is that doth go with thee; he will not fail thee, nor forsake thee.' Well, Deuteronomy and Brandi Tipple, who quoted me that passage."

"*Brandi* Tipple?"

"Yes, you mustn't ever tell a soul. That poor girl has enough problems to deal with."

"Who are you afraid of, Ms. Wagers?"

"I received a visit from Clayton Tipple. That boy threatened me. I was working up at the compound, and Clayton came and told me Destiny Grace Harper was a sinner, and it's a sin to help a sinner. Then he said, 'The righteous shall rejoice when he seeth the vengeance; he shall wash his feet in the blood of the wicked.' I took that as a threat. Yesterday, Brandi called me said I should help Destiny Grace and tell the true story. When I told her what Clayton said, she quoted the passage from Deuteronomy."

"I assume when Clayton threatened you, he was doing his father's bidding?"

"You should assume no such thing, sir. How may I help Destiny Grace?"

I ask about my client's attitude toward her pregnancy.

"That girl wanted to have her babies, no doubt in my mind. She did everything I told her to do, took the vitamins, the herbs, prayed. Everything."

Wagers is intelligent and earnest. This testimony is exactly what we need. I try to contain my excitement.

"You saw her praying?" I ask.

"We prayed together," says Wagers. "Brandi Tipple could tell you the same thing. She was my doula, training to be a midwife. I'm sure she saw Destiny Grace take her vitamins and herbs. Those girls are very close."

"You sent Destiny Grace to a medical doctor in violation of your religious beliefs."

"It wasn't because I'd lost faith in the healing power of prayer. I sent Destiny Grace to a doctor because it's illegal in Alabama for a midwife to attend multiple or problem pregnancies. You're the lawyer; why am I telling you this? If I didn't get her to go to a medical doctor, I could've gone to prison. I should've been courageous and helped her no matter what. I'm a coward. And I violated the word of God by sending that girl to a doctor. My church, my friends will all disown me when I testify. So be it." She goes on to say that after the appointment,

Destiny Grace asked her for advice on treating the TTTS. In response, Wagers recommended protein drinks and horizontal bedrest, along with intense prayer.

"You aren't a coward, Lillian. It takes a lot of courage, coming forward like this."

She nods a skeptical thank-you.

My follow-up questions glean no more helpful evidence. Wagers doesn't know whether anyone attended the births of Destiny Grace's twins. If such a person exists, they could be charged with manslaughter, or even felony murder. If such a person exists, they could also save Destiny Grace's life by testifying that my client wanted the babies to survive and mourned their loss. Still, despite these gaps, Lillian Wagers might singlehandedly win the case for us. At this moment, she's my hero—she and Brandi Tipple.

Southern gentlemen that I am, I hurry around the front of the van and open the passenger door. The van has a high cabin. Wagers stumbles when she hops down to the asphalt. I bend down to steady her, but she rights herself and stands with unexpected agility.

A crack of thunder and another. Even in Alabama, how could there be lightning in a cloudless sky? There's a sound that could be a sharp sigh of resignation. Wagers slumps to the asphalt, blood oozing from her neck and chest, and I take cover behind the door of the van and avoid two more bullets that lodge in the passenger side of the Transit or ricochet off. In this war zone, I tend to Wagers the same way I tended to fallen soldiers in Afghanistan so many years ago. Even if the soldiers couldn't be saved, I had an obligation to go through the motions out of hope, respect, duty, habit. I feel the same obligation now even though Lillian Wagers can't be saved.

CHAPTER TWENTY-TWO

When I tell Destiny Grace about Wagers's murder, I expect her to break down. But though tears do fill her eyes, she simply whispers, "I loved that woman. She's dead because of what I did."

I press her on what she means by this, but she won't say anything more. Destiny Grace Harper never says anything more.

Two hours later, we stand in the courtroom, arguing for a three-week continuance of the trial plus bond for Destiny Grace. Because of my presence at the killing, I'm hardly dispassionate, so Higgins argues the motion.

"The murder of a key witness justifies an adjournment," says Higgins. "If Lillian Wagers was killed to prevent her testimony in this trial, the police should have time to investigate all leads. Proceeding without that investigation will prejudice the defendant."

Barraclough shakes his head. "Isn't law enforcement's working hypothesis that the bullet was meant for Elvis here? His face was on a wanted-dead-or-alive bull's-eye poster."

The police have indeed speculated that the shooter was a nut job who's upset at my politics or at Hazel's politics or at

Destiny Grace's actions—so says the detective in charge of the "investigation." *No leads.* The shots might've come from the woods adjacent to the parking lot, but inconclusive. *Forensics analysis ongoing.*

"The sheriff doesn't have a coherent theory or any leads," says Higgins. "That a key defense witness is dead justifies a continuance no matter what the reason."

I believe the bullet was meant for Wagers. People in this part of the world are usually good shots. But if someone did intend the bullet for me, my prime suspect would be none other than Sheriff Dave Coyle, the detective's boss. That's not a theory I can share.

"Wagers's death was a tragedy, but an adjournment won't bring your witness back," says Barraclough.

"Mr. Henderson was involved in a traumatic event," says Higgins. "He could've died, whoever the target of the shooting was. He needs some time."

"I gave him a day already," says Barraclough. "Are you traumatized, Elvis?"

"Of course I'm traumatized, Judge. You ever been shot at?"

He sits up defensively. "I served in Vietnam."

"Have you ever been shot at, Judge Barraclough?" I repeat. "Because putting aside the Wagers shooting, I have been under fire while serving in the military. And I know that not everyone in a war sees combat. Some people work clerical jobs at large air or army bases and never face gunfire." My venting at this jerk feels good, but it doesn't help my case.

"We're going to proceed with this trial," says Barraclough, the veins in his forehead popping out, and now I'm sorry I opened my big mouth.

"The defense requests permission to call yours truly to the stand to testify about what Lillian Wagers told me," I say.

"Which was that Destiny Grace Harper prayed and followed all the protocols for protecting the health of her twins."

"Denied. That would be inadmissible hearsay."

He's right, unfortunately.

Kelsey Kerr, until now enjoying the golden silence on her end, stands. "Judge, the State asks for an order barring the defense from mentioning Wagers's death in any way. It's irrelevant and unduly prejudicial."

"It's irrelevant that the defense's key witness was murdered just after she decided to come forward with exculpatory testimony?" I ask. "Of course it's relevant."

Barraclough considers the issue for a long time. "I agree with the prosecution. There's no reason to mention Ms. Wagers's death. It has nothing to do with whether the defendant intentionally withheld treatment from the babies to cause their deaths."

Ordinarily, I'd lose my temper, but I just sit down, exhausted. Yes, the shooting traumatized me. Yet here we are, back in trial as though nothing happened. Something *did* happen.

Once the jury assembles in the box, Sabrina Graham announces, "The State calls LeAnn Harper."

Destiny Grace gasps.

The State identified LeAnn on its witness list, but we on our team believed Kerr did this to harass and taunt, that she wouldn't dare call the defendant's own mother to the stand. LeAnn insisted she had no idea why the prosecution had listed her.

A shocked look submerges LeAnn's perpetually fatigued expression. She wears a solid blue dress over dark slacks. Drab. If we'd known, Margaret could've dressed her for the witness stand. She raises a trembling right hand and feebly swears to tell the truth. She won't look at our side of the table. Destiny Grace stares at her mother with a look of suspicion.

Higgins taps me on the shoulder. "My witness, Elvis." When I hesitate, she says, "She trusts me, not you. Besides, this calls for a woman's touch."

I glance at Margaret, who nods.

"She's all yours, Aruna," I say reluctantly.

"It's been a long time, LeAnn," says Barraclough.

"Sure has, Mr. Barraclough . . . I mean, Judge Barraclough."

Destiny Grace groans, and Higgins and Graham both start to inquire, and Barraclough says, "Don't get your panties in a wad, ladies. This is a small town. My son, Chuck, dated LeAnn in high school. Chuck took her to the prom, hired a limousine and such. We all thought they'd be married soon after graduation, but my idiot son left this lovely lady for a not-so-nice Chinese girl named Helen Han. Devious and manipulative, that Han girl was a dragon lady in the making. She broke Chuck's heart soon enough. I suppose he deserved it, LeAnn."

Why didn't LeAnn tell us she knew this loose-cannon, irreverent, no-filter judge?

Higgins says, "Judge Barraclough, I feel like I have to point out that the term *dragon lady* is not only derogatory, but it's a sexist term and also a racist term when describing an Asian woman."

"Your sensibilities demand political correctness, is that what you're saying, Aruna? I've never discriminated against you because your parents come from India, have I?"

Before a surprised Higgins can respond, Graham says from the prosecution's table, "The State of Alabama agrees with Ms. Higgins regarding the use of that term, Judge Barraclough, and also doesn't think the reference to Ms. Higgins's background was necessary"—an ethical move and smart trial tactics, so that Higgins alone won't occupy the high moral ground. Kerr glares at her.

"Well, I meant no offense," says Barraclough.

Higgins glances at me. There are no grounds to ask the judge to recuse himself because of his past relationship with LeAnn. Not after so many decades have passed since his son and LeAnn dated. And regardless, Barraclough wouldn't step down and declare a mistrial after we've gotten so deep into the trial. I shake my head at Higgins. Neither side objects to Barraclough proceeding.

LeAnn pretzels her thin body so she can look at the judge, her wan cheeks flushing scarlet. "I have a problem, Judge Barraclough. I shouldn't have to be up here. The prosecutors lied to me."

The judge's mood darkens.

"Ladies and gentlemen of the jury, you will disregard that statement," says Barraclough. "In fact, you will disregard the entire discussion between me and the witness about old times. You will judge the witness on her own merits. Now, I'm going to have Deputy Travis take you back to the jury room, ladies and gentlemen, while the attorneys and the witness and I talk over a few things."

Everyone stands as the jury files out of the courtroom. I don't interact with the jury when I'm not on stage performing. Too much can go wrong with a wink or a nod.

Once the jurors leave, Barraclough asks LeAnn to explain herself.

"Sir, it's not right to force me to testify against my own daughter when Sabrina Graham promised I wouldn't have to."

"I did no such thing, Judge," says Graham. "Ms. Harper approached us. She did say what she was telling us was confidential, but the State of Alabama never agreed to that. It takes two sides to make a bargain."

"Mama, what did you do?" says Destiny Grace.

Barraclough folds his arms on the bench, the puffy sleeves of his black robe overlapping and merging into one another. "Is Sabrina's statement accurate?"

From the pained expression on LeAnn's face, I know how this will turn out. "She doesn't have the right to trick me."

The judge frowns. "If you were an uneducated redneck, I might worry about you being tricked, but I know you have a college degree from Belmont University in Nashville. You been doing a lot of people's income taxes for years, and that's a tough job. You're smart."

LeAnn gives an embarrassed shrug.

"I'm going to allow the testimony," says Barraclough. "Eddie, bring 'em back."

It takes several torturous minutes for the jury to return to the courtroom.

Graham establishes that LeAnn is Destiny Grace's mother and a former member of the Church of Our Lord's Rapture, and that mother and daughter were living under the same roof when the events leading up to this trial occurred. While answering, LeAnn sits with her arms crossed tightly and her gaze down, as if someone is going to hit her.

"At some point, you learned your daughter was pregnant?" asks Graham.

"Yes, ma'am."

"Out of wedlock?"

Higgins's irrelevancy objection is overruled. She shouldn't have bothered. The objection merely underscores a fact everyone knows and we do not want emphasized. Damned inexperience.

"According to the teachings of your church, is sex out of wedlock a sin?"

"My former church. Yes, it's a sin."

I wish LeAnn would fight. Premarital sex is a sin in most

religions, but if it were a crime, most of the people in this country would be locked up behind bars.

"Did Destiny Grace tell you who the babies' father is?" asks Graham.

"No, ma'am."

Graham establishes that Destiny Grace hid the twins' TTTS from LeAnn, who only learned about the condition when a sheriff's deputy served Destiny Grace with the order to appear in court. After LeAnn insisted that they drive to Nashville for the procedure, Destiny Grace didn't come home from work that night.

Graham leaves the lectern and moves closer to her witness. "Two days after Destiny Grace fled the jurisdiction, you called the DA's office and talked to me, didn't you, Ms. Harper?"

"Judge Barraclough, I—"

"Answer the question," says Barraclough.

Graham takes another step forward, not aggressive but assertive. "Didn't you tell us you filed a missing person report with the police, but you believed Ms. Harper ran away to avoid the court hearing?"

Destiny Grace mumbles something under her breath. It takes a moment to register that she said "Fucking bitch." I don't know whether she means LeAnn, Graham, or both. Either way, more grist for those jurors with acute hearing.

"Just keep your mouth shut, girl!" says Higgins in a harsh whisper, earning a contrite look from Destiny Grace.

"That phone call was a long time ago, ma'am, so I don't quite remember it," says LeAnn. "I wasn't thinking straight."

Graham takes another two steps forward, and this time the approach *is* aggressive.

"Take a stroll back to the podium, Sabrina," says Barraclough.

Graham looks at Higgins as if Aruna is to blame and then goes back to the lectern. "Ms. Harper, did you or did you not call our office specifically to tell us Destiny Grace had skipped out on an order to appear in court?"

"If you say so."

Sometimes good lawyers must be sadists. Other times, they must be sociopaths. Graham regards her witness with a sociopath's detachment.

"I say so, Ms. Harper. And so do you, under penalty of perjury. True, ma'am?"

The witness nods once.

"You'll have to answer in words."

"Yes."

"And didn't you also tell us you feared Destiny Grace Harper wasn't in her right mind and didn't have the best interests of her babies at heart?"

"Y'all asked me a bunch of confusing questions."

"Confusing in spite of your college degree and your acumen with complex income tax issues?"

"I was worried and upset," says LeAnn.

"Answer my question, ma'am." Graham is a puppet master controlling a marionette despite tangled strings. This young lawyer is good.

"I might could've said something like that in the heat of the moment," mumbles LeAnn. "But sometimes mamas, all of us, we—"

"You've answered the question, Ms. Harper. And I have no more of them for you."

CHAPTER TWENTY-THREE

Aruna Higgins has the rare chance to cross-examine a friendly witness. By asking leading questions, she should be able to get LeAnn to testify to almost anything. At the same time, she can't look like she's putting words into LeAnn's mouth. Does Higgins have the chops to carry this off?

She pulls at her long black hair, sets her jaw, grabs both sides of the podium, and pauses for so long I fear she might faint. Finally, in a strong voice, she asks, "Ma'am, do you mind if I call you LeAnn?" Good move. This is Northern Alabama, and these two won't stand on formality. They'll have a conversation.

"Of course I don't mind, Aruna," says LeAnn. For the first time since taking the stand, the cords in LeAnn's neck relax, and her haggard face brightens.

"LeAnn, did you talk about baby names with Destiny Grace?"

"Yes, ma'am. When she thought there was only one, Brooklyn for a girl, Brooks for a boy. Then, after she learned she was having twin girls, Brooklyn and Lydia." LeAnn shoots a tentative glance toward her daughter. "I didn't like the name Brooklyn much until Destiny Grace explained this was the name of a model and actress she liked and not the borough in New York. Then the name grew on me."

"LeAnn, does a mother name her unborn babies if she wants them to die?"

"No mother I ever heard of."

Destiny Grace taps my arm and points to a box of tissue at the table's edge. I hand her the box, and she uses a tissue to wipe her eyes.

Higgins gets LeAnn to testify that Destiny Grace met with her midwife, Lillian Wagers, and went to church despite the not-always-silent censure of the other congregants. LeAnn confirms that she heard Destiny Grace praying for absolution and her babies' health. The expectant mother took all her vitamins and didn't drink a drop of alcohol or caffeine.

"You left the Church of Our Lord's Rapture, didn't you, LeAnn?"

"They kicked me out because I went to a doctor for my ovarian cancer and had surgery and chemo."

"How are you doing now?"

"You mean, aside from my daughter being wrongly tried for murder and some overambitious prosecutor who wants to be a senator forcing me to sit up here and testify? Other than that, fine and dandy."

Some of the spectators laugh. Barraclough admonishes LeAnn to stick to answering the question (although he can't hide his own amusement). Kerr appears livid at Graham, who likely convinced her boss that calling LeAnn to the stand could only help the prosecution's case.

Higgins looks down at the lectern, briefly at me, and then down at the lectern again. She starts to ask a question then stops. Her hesitation means she should *not* take the risk of asking what she has in mind. *Do not do it, Aruna. Sit down!*

"Since the time you left the Church of Our Lord's Rapture, you've acquired faith in the medical profession, am I right?"

"Faith? That's the wrong word. I have faith in God, not in doctors. But when I got so sick, I decided to do anything I could to save my life."

Sit down, Aruna!

"Do you disapprove of Destiny Grace's decision to forgo the laser surgery? After all, you were ready to take her to the medical center in Nashville. You phoned the district attorney's office and—pardon me for this term—ratted her out."

What's Higgins doing? If LeAnn botches the answer, Higgins will have destroyed the gains we've made through the earlier helpful testimony.

LeAnn puts her hands on her knees and leans forward. "You know, I've thought a lot about that, Aruna. Part of me thinks Destiny Grace made a mistake—she didn't commit a crime, mind you, but made a mistake. But, as time goes by, a big part of me wonders whether *I* was the one who made the mistake by seeing a doctor and not trusting in God's power to heal my cancer. God only knows how the chemotherapy affected me, will affect me. We on Earth don't know how He works, what matters to Him. I brought my daughter up to believe that prayer heals, that doctors interfere. Her father died a young man because those great doctors botched his surgery, and my daughter grew up without a father. She followed her beliefs when it came to her babies. Maybe I undermined *her* faith. Maybe *my* weakness set a bad example for my daughter and led to the deaths of Lydia and Brooklyn. If that's true, *I* should be the one sitting in the defendant's seat, not her."

Higgins passes the witness and sits down, a satisfied glimmer in her eye. I understand why she challenged LeAnn's beliefs. The mother had informed on her daughter, and LeAnn stood that fact on its head by taking the blame for doubting Destiny Grace. Still too risky to ask the question. What if LeAnn had said Destiny Grace should've had the procedure?

"That last part worked out okay," I whisper. "Never, *ever* do anything like that again."

She gives a slight nod and a wry smile and sits down. She's proud of herself despite my reprimand. And she must realize that I don't often follow my own advice.

Graham returns to the lectern for redirect, without notes this time. "You mentioned earlier that the defendant didn't identify Brooklyn and Lydia's father," she says. "You don't know if Destiny Grace would do anything to please the father, do you? Including letting the babies die if he ordered her to?"

Barraclough overrules Higgins's objection on the grounds of speculation, meaning LeAnn must answer—a clearly erroneous ruling. Not the first time a judge has made an egregious evidentiary error. Happens all too often.

"My daughter is stronger than that."

"And you don't know whether the unidentified father threatened to harm Destiny Grace unless she let the babies die?"

"I have no idea if someone threatened her, but I do know she wouldn't want her babies to die."

"It wouldn't be the first time your daughter let a man lead her into criminal activity, would it?" asks Graham.

Destiny Grace grabs my upper arm hard, digging her nails into my skin. Evidence of a defendant's prior criminal activity is mostly inadmissible in a trial. And, as far as I know, the only crimes Destiny Grace committed occurred when she was a juvenile—another reason for their inadmissibility. Even though Aruna Higgins is handling this witness, I can't stop myself from jumping up in tandem with her. When I see the rage and disgust on Higgins's face, I sit down.

"Object to the testimony as irrelevant and without foundation, and highly inappropriate," says Higgins.

Barraclough sustains the objection and directs the jury to draw no inferences from the question.

Up I stand. "That question alone is grounds for a mistrial, Judge. Which the defense requests."

"Denied."

"Does a defendant on trial for her life have zero rights in an Alabama court of law?"

"Watch it, sir!" says the judge.

"Sit down, E," whispers Margaret from behind me.

Showing genuine indignation to a jury isn't always a bad thing for a defense attorney to do. But it will do no good if I become unhinged. I sit.

Higgins faces Graham and says, "I can't believe you'd ask something like that, Sabrina."

"Confine your remarks to the Court, Ms. Higgins," says Barraclough.

Graham looks down at her notes, clearly abashed. I understand—Kelsey Kerr made her ask the question.

Graham suppresses whatever moral qualms she has about this line of questioning and asks, "Ms. Harper, is it possible that Destiny Grace slept with so many men that she doesn't know who the father is? That she wanted the babies to die because they were conceived due to her promiscuity?"

"Objection. No foundation! Calls for speculation!" Higgins almost shouts the words.

"Overruled," says Barraclough, another clearly erroneous ruling and more fodder for appeal that I hope we'll never have to use.

"She named the babies," says LeAnn. "She wanted to meet them."

"Maybe Destiny Grace doesn't believe in abortion but wanted the babies to die, and refusing the TTTS was a convenient way to make that happen?"

Objection overruled.

"My daughter loved her babies."

"And you have no way of knowing whether this unknown father said, 'Don't bother getting an abortion, just let them die'?"

Objection overruled.

Destiny Grace's shoulders droop.

"I don't even know what you're talking about," says LeAnn. "All you're doing is making stuff up."

Margaret mutters "This is such bullshit" under her breath.

"Did you say something, *Ms.* Booth?" asks the judge. Excellent hearing for a man his age.

"Just sighing," says Margaret. "Won't happen again."

"It better not."

The prosecution has no obligation to prove a motive in a case, but suggesting a motive usually helps persuade a jury to convict. People have an irresistible need to find reasons for bad conduct, even though bad conduct is often irrational. Now, Graham has given the jury a reason why Destiny Grace might've wanted her babies to die—the controlling lover trope.

Graham passes the witness.

Higgins gets up for redirect. "LeAnn, since you don't know who the twins' father is, you have no information that the father demanded anything of Destiny Grace."

"That's absolutely right, Aruna."

"So Ms. Graham's speculative questions about that issue are just a figment of her imagination?"

Barraclough won't let LeAnn answer, but it's a point for Higgins.

LeAnn makes her way down from the witness stand,

stumbling on the second step and almost falling—and providing an opportunity. I stand, hurry over to her, and give her my arm. Her defeated eyes widen when she sees me, but she takes my hand. I think she truly needs my support. As I walk her back to her seat in the gallery, I whisper to her, "Fetch Destiny Grace's Bible from her bedroom and bring it to me right away. It'll help make up for how badly you just damaged your daughter's case."

CHAPTER TWENTY-FOUR

As we wait in our courthouse conference room for Margaret to return with lunch, Destiny Grace walks over to a corner and stares at the wall. "Lord, I miss windows," she says. "Sometimes when I'm in the courtroom I look out those frosted windows near the judge's bench and lose my train of thought. I'm guessing the tree is a crepe myrtle and the bush is camellia. And decent food. So weird. This trial is about trying to put me to death, and the courtroom is the one place I can get some light and some fresh vegetables." A pause. "Y'all did a good job, Aruna. Mama's testimony didn't hurt us that bad."

"Yeah, it did," says Higgins. "The prosecution used her to argue to the jury that you let the babies die because your lover told you to."

"The jury won't believe such nonsense," says Destiny Grace.

"Oh, yeah, they might," says Higgins. "They were paying close attention. Searching hard for a motive. That asshole Barraclough put his stamp of approval on the prosecution's maneuver by overruling my objections. In a trial, the only person a jury trusts is the judge."

Destiny Grace slumps over and puts her head in her hands. "You're always so negative, Aruna."

The door opens, and Margaret walks in, carrying lunch. Destiny Grace finds her salad and tears into it. I eat only two saltine crackers.

"You should eat more to keep your strength up, Mr. Henderson," says Destiny Grace.

"Trial is my personal weight-loss program," I reply.

"You don't need to lose weight. You already look like an underfed king snake."

This afternoon's testimony won't be pleasant. All things considered, I want Destiny Grace in the courtroom at all times—a sign that she has confidence in her innocence, that she's not afraid to confront her accusers. But I don't want the jury to see her fall apart emotionally. She assures me she can handle it, so I let her come back into the courtroom with us.

———

Dr. Theodora Smith, the medical examiner from the Alabama Department of Forensic Sciences in Huntsville, testifies to the cause of death. "The recipient twin, whom the defendant chose postmortem to name Brooklyn, was stillborn. She died from heart failure as a result of the volume overload of blood. The heart muscle had thickened beyond repair. Her death caused Lydia, the donor twin, to lose a large amount of blood across the vessels connected to her sister, resulting in a drop in Lydia's blood pressure. Lydia suffered a fatal stroke *after* her birth."

The medical examiner brings photographs, which Kerr shows to the jury and hands to us. The photos depict two tiny babies. The pictures are worth a thousand sobs. *I* want to sob.

Dr. Smith points out that the stillborn recipient twin, Brooklyn, was 17 percent larger than Lydia, who'd given her life for her larger sister. The autopsy also revealed that both twins would likely have suffered severe neurological disorders had they lived.

"How long did little Lydia live after she was born?" asks Kerr.

"Anywhere from five to twenty minutes."

"So, if baby Lydia lived twenty minutes and it took the EMTs twenty-two minutes after the 911 call to arrive, and the defendant left even fifteen minutes after the call, the defendant would've abandoned a living child?"

As Barraclough sustains my objection, Destiny Grace lets out a doleful wail and bolts out of her chair. The jailer assigned to guard Destiny Grace reaches out to grab her arm hard, but Eddie Travis seizes the younger man with both hands and shoves him away. The two deputies square off and almost come to blows, but Margaret restores order by getting between them and maneuvering our distraught client into the defense war room.

Destiny Grace's crying was acceptable theater—the fleeing, not so much. My fault. I should've asked the judge to excuse her from the courtroom and to instruct the jury that she chose not to participate because of the graphic nature of the testimony. That might've generated sympathy among a few of the jurors. Now, these histrionics might make her seem like a remorseful killer.

Only after I begin my cross-examination does Margaret usher a red-eyed Destiny Grace back into the courtroom. Some of the jurors ignore her, but the stay-at-home mother and the romance writer look at her sideways. Some of the men seem sympathetic. An interesting, unscientific study in gender differences.

I can't discredit the medical examiner's testimony, so I use a cross-examination technique designed to convey that the witness failed to do a thorough job, even if they did. "In your findings as to cause of death, you saw no evidence of blunt trauma?"

"I did not."

"You found no evidence of suffocation?"

"I did not."

"You found no evidence of strangulation?"

"No, counselor."

"You found no stab wounds?"

I create some more fireless smoke, ruling out gunshot wounds, poisoning, electrocution, drowning, shaking, or any other form of physical abuse. All with the objective to make the witness become defensive. This technique works even with many experienced expert witnesses, especially when the cross-examiner's tone is accusatory—which mine is. But Smith answers in a straightforward, noncombative tone and never gets defensive.

Finally: "You do agree, Dr. Smith, that Lydia would've died even in a hospital with the best neonatological care in the world—a neonatologist being a doctor who treats newborns?"

Smith agrees.

I don't venture farther afield or probe any deeper. Sometimes, the facts are the facts—even in a court of law.

CHAPTER TWENTY-FIVE

When Kelsey Kerr calls Thomas Styles as her next witness, I pray that, when I look toward the courtroom entrance, I won't see the Quartz Inn "con-see-air," as he calls himself. Another prayer that goes unanswered. Worse, Styles is escorted into the courtroom in handcuffs!

When Kerr nods, Deputy Travis removes the cuffs.

Margaret reminds me the prosecution didn't include Styles on its witness list, a point I make to Barraclough.

"You want an adjournment until tomorrow to prepare for this witness, Mr. Henderson?" asks Barraclough.

"I want him excluded entirely."

"Not going to happen."

I look at Destiny Grace, whose cheeks have turned cadaver gray.

When I ask for a recess to consider whether we need the day-long adjournment, Barraclough gives us fifteen minutes.

———

"Yeah, so, like, I sold my body to earn money for Mama's medical care, and Thomas was, like, the one who found me the clients. I did it for two months and three days."

"Holy fuck!" says Higgins. Leaning against the wall, she lets her body slide down until it comes to a sitting position on the grimy floor, sullying her designer St. John suit. She puts her elbows on her knees and buries her face in her hands.

Destiny Grace lurches out of her chair, runs to the corner of our war room, and vomits into the wastebasket.

"I'm guessing your religion opposes psychological counseling, too, but you need some heavy-duty therapy, kiddo," says Margaret after Destiny Grace settles down and returns to the table.

"We need time to process this," says Higgins from her vantage point on the floor. "The adjournment until tomorrow. No, until next week. The DA now has another possible motive. Destiny Grace wanted the babies dead because the father is one of her . . . clients."

"Ain't true," says Destiny Grace. "I stopped long before I got pregnant."

"Then who's the father, God damn it?" asks Higgins. "We need to know so we can refute some of this upcoming testimony."

"You won't tell who the father is, will you?" I ask. "Even after all this rigmarole."

"No, sir, I will not." Early in my involvement in this case, I thought Higgins's inability to convince Destiny Grace to come clean about what happened resulted from the lawyer's youth, inexperience, and perhaps incompetence. I'd ride in on my oh-so-compelling white horse and save the day by straightaway convincing Destiny Grace to tell all. In the case of Destiny Grace Harper, my white horse is broken down and spavined.

"Did Thomas Styles know why you needed the money?" I ask.

"We talked a lot about how Mama was sick, that we was broke, that the medical bills were killing us. So one day, he said I could earn a lot of extra money, but it weren't legal or something I'd probably ever do. I wasn't as naive as he thought, and I already knew there was some weird things going on with some of the other housekeepers, although I didn't know for sure. So I said I'd hear him out. He told me a couple girls working at the hotel were using some of the empty rooms to earn extra money. I know the medical bills ain't an excuse. I stopped when I couldn't take no more, after I paid off the biggest bills. Whatever I earned went to the greedy doctors. You don't know how sick Mama was."

I give a resigned shrug. "Okay. Let's go back inside."

Higgins struggles to her feet. "E, we can't just go back into the courtroom and—"

"And what, Aruna? Our client won't name the father of her babies. Styles will say what he'll say, and we won't deny it as long as he approximates the truth. That won't change in a day or a week."

"I'll give LeAnn a heads-up," says Margaret. "That okay with you, Destiny Grace? So your mother isn't surprised?"

Destiny Grace looks as if she wants to vomit again but nods.

I kneel, fighting off a twinge in my knees, and take her hands. "You made a difficult choice for a noble reason."

"I broke the law and committed a horrible sin."

"If anything, *you* were exploited. And prostitution isn't a capital offense. Some believe it shouldn't be any kind of crime. Hazel Curnow herself fought to legalize sex work out in California. She even wanted to unionize the workers. Besides, if people didn't sin, we mortals would have no need for Jesus. I know you followed your church's teachings when it came to the twins. Let's go back inside and convince the jury of that." I stand and go to the door.

"I sure wish Hazel Curnow was here now," says Destiny Grace.

———

An ashen LeAnn again sits in the first row behind the defense table. When I pass by, she hands me a book. "Destiny Grace's Bible," she says in a hollow whisper. "Don't know if it matters now, but . . ."

I thank her, then riffle through the book. Scores of passages are highlighted. Which page did I see when I looked at the book at LeAnn Harper's house? More work for Margaret—as if she needs anything more to do.

Destiny Grace passes her mother without a glance. LeAnn reaches out to touch her but only pats air. The jury files in, and Thomas Styles gets back on the witness stand. He's still dressed up and clean cut as ever, but my perception of him has changed.

Kerr questions Styles about his criminal convictions, mostly misdemeanor charges for petty theft, confidence games, and pandering. He has no record of committing violent crimes (which I know doesn't mean he hasn't committed any—bad actors like Styles seldom draw such definite moral lines). Through his testimony, she establishes that he was using the hotel to run a prostitution ring. But about six weeks ago, a maid and part-time sex worker at the hotel, upset that Styles was taking too large a cut of her earnings, went to the police and reported him. She'd kept copies of incriminating text messages and smartphone videos of Styles taking payment for sex work disguised as tips. She also identified several other women at the Quartz Inn—*not* Destiny Grace—who were involved in Styles's sex ring. This information allowed DA Kerr to charge him with managing a prostitution business with two or more prostitutes—a felony punishable by up to ten years in prison under Alabama law.

When the police arrested Styles three weeks ago, he suggested that, in exchange for leniency, he could help in the prosecution of Destiny Grace. Perfect for Kelsey Kerr's trial-by-slander approach to advocacy and Judge Barraclough's willingness to let salacious evidence into the record. Kerr kept the arrest secret and even made sure Styles kept his job at the hotel so our side wouldn't suspect he was going to testify. A sharp practice, but perfectly legal, because Styles hadn't yet formally agreed to testify against Destiny Grace. Without such an agreement, he would've pled the Fifth and wasn't technically a witness. How convenient that Styles's attorney and the prosecutors only finalized the plea deal this morning so that Kerr could blindside us by keeping Styles off the witness list until now.

Styles, the unctuous son of a bitch who recommended dive bars, offered me Tylenol, and accepted my gift of an Austin City Limits cap and now threatens to sabotage our entire defense. How I'd like to get the hat back right now—with the asshole's head still in it.

"Was Destiny Grace Harper in your stable of prostitutes?" asks Kerr.

Throughout his previous testimony, Styles acted blasé—not happy to be on the stand but unconcerned. Now, he responds with a reluctant, "Yeah."

Those in the gallery who didn't anticipate this development gasp or murmur. Among the jurors, the construction worker and Miller Holcomb shake their heads in disgust.

"How did Ms. Harper become one of your prostitutes?"

"Objection," I say. "Irrelevant. Not to mention Ms. Kerr seems to enjoy getting down into the gutter."

"Overruled," says Barraclough, a weariness in his voice. "You know it's relevant to the defense of religious belief. As for the gibe targeted toward Ms. Kerr, sir, enough is enough."

For Destiny Grace's sake, I continue the battle and hope at least one of the jurors finds Kerr's approach as repugnant as I do. Not likely, but I have to try to persuade them. In the process of trying to persuade them, I lose my temper. "There should be an objection for being despicable," I say. "We can call it the Kelsey Kerr objection. Or maybe the Judge Merle Barraclough objection, because, Judge, you're letting this inadmissible tripe in and calling it evidence in a case involving exalted constitutional rights and a person's life. Reprehensible."

Barraclough swivels his chair and turns his back on me for a long time.

"Control yourself, E," whispers Higgins, probably envisioning a world in which I'm in jail and she's once again solely responsible for saving our client's life.

I stop talking. If nothing else, my diatribe signaled to the jury that Barraclough and Kerr can't intimidate us.

After the court reporter reads back the question—*how did Destiny Grace become one of his prostitutes*—Styles answers, "Me and Destiny Grace had some shifts that overlapped, and we became friends. Nothing romantic; we went for Mexican food, a movie once, but just as friends. I'd, like, have coffee with her or walk her to her car at night if she worked the late shift. I knew she needed money bad. She was working double shifts doing the maid work at the hotel and also teaching little kids at her church, and she was always tired. The housekeeping work at the hotel is exhausting by itself. I found out her mother was sick with cancer. One day, I asked her how it was going, and she said the medical bills was destroying them financially, that two collection agencies threatened to sue them. I saw desperation in her eyes, so I told her some of the other maids was making some extra money using the vacant rooms for entertaining some of the guests. She asked if I could help her make some money, too. I let her know what I wasn't talking about legal activities. I discouraged her, told her clearly what she'd be getting into, because I still wasn't sure she really understood. She made sure I knew she weren't naive, that she knew what she was getting into. I couldn't believe my ears because Destiny was this devout Christian girl. I thought she was a virgin, saving herself for marriage; told her so, but she laughed and said don't worry about that. I told her for a cut, I could arrange for her to use vacant hotel rooms so she wouldn't get caught. She ended up being one of my most popular girls. A good money-maker. Lots of fellas like the young-and-innocent look. Some women do, too."

This last observation was gratuitous. Does Styles want to hurt Destiny Grace, or does he just love to talk? Either way, I want to wring the creep's neck. Throughout the testimony, I make sure not to look at Destiny Grace. We can't have her running from the courtroom again or cussing out Thomas Styles in front of the jury.

I glance over my shoulder when someone behind me speaks. Deputy Eddie Travis is whispering in Margaret's ear.

"Do you think prostitution and Christianity go together, Mr. Styles?" asks Kerr.

Before I can object, Styles replies, "Well, there was Mary Magdalene, one of Jesus's most devoted disciples; and Mary of Bethany; and the sinful woman in, I think, the book of Luke. So I'd answer yes."

"I sustain my own objection to that last question," says

Barraclough. "The jury will disregard the last question and answer. Ms. Kerr, if you don't have another line of questioning to pursue, pass the witness."

An abashed Kerr sits.

Before I begin cross-examining Styles, Margaret relays what Travis whispered to her, and when I hear, I suppress a smile.

"You were brought into this courtroom in handcuffs, weren't you?" I ask.

"Yes, sir, Mr. Henderson," says Styles, again sounding like the accommodating hotel desk clerk.

"Were you in handcuffs coming from the jail to the court-house?"

"Objection, irrelevant!" says Kerr. The intensity of her tone makes some of the jurors' ears perk up.

Barraclough overrules the objection.

"No, Mr. Henderson. They cuffed me right outside the door. No idea why they did that. I'm not in jail. I made bail weeks ago, the day they busted me. I walked to court all by my lonesome today. I only live six blocks away. Quite a pretty day outside."

"Were you surprised when the sheriff's deputy cuffed you?"

He smirks. "Ain't never surprised by what the cops do. But I did ask Deputy Travis why he did it."

I turn toward the district attorney and pose the next question while looking at her. "What did Deputy Travis say in response?"

Kerr objects on hearsay grounds. How glad I am for the objection. "I agree the question calls for hearsay, Judge Barra-clough, so I'm prepared to cure the defect by calling Deputy Travis and Ms. Kerr as witnesses. Want me to play it that way, Ms. Kerr?"

Kerr shakes her head, her entire upper body moving along

with it. Her jaw descends but closes before she says a word. Sabrina Graham looks as puzzled as everyone else.

"I'll . . . Objection withdrawn," Kerr mutters.

"The deputy told me the district attorney wanted me in handcuffs so I'd look more like a criminal, so the jury would think Destiny Grace was an even worse person because she worked for me."

"How did the deputy know that?"

"He said that's what Ms. Kerr told him."

"The handcuffs were for show?"

"Seems like it."

Letting this testimony sink in, enjoying the rosy blotches on Kerr's cheeks, I probe deeper into Destiny Grace's desperate need for money.

"I met Ms. Harper, the mother, once during her illness," says Styles. "Don't mean any disrespect, but she looked like a bald zombie, barely anything left to save."

"And at some point, Destiny Grace stopped working for you?"

"Yes, sir. Came to me one day, said she couldn't do it no more."

"Why?"

"She said it was killing her, body and soul. Her exact words. She said she'd rather lose everything, even her house—except her mother."

"When was that?"

"Two years ago, June."

"So, since her babies were born the following May 17, they couldn't have been conceived while Destiny Grace was working for you?"

He pauses, calculating.

"Let me save you the math, Mr. Styles. Nine months prior to May 17 is August."

"Right. So the father couldn't of been any of my clientele."

I pass the witness, and Kerr stands for redirect.

"The defendant told you she would lose her house, yes?" asks Kerr.

"Yeah, her and her mother's house."

"Did you know neither Ms. Harper nor her mother own the house? The Church of Our Lord's Rapture holds title to the property."

Shit.

Styles pulls his brows together, tightly. "I didn't know that."

"So, if Harper and her mother don't hold title, Destiny Grace lied to you when she said she and her mother might lose their house?"

Styles shrugs.

I half stand, wishing I had an objection to quash this testimony, but I don't. I look at Destiny Grace—not a glance, a full-blown gaze, which does our case no good—and she whispers, "I can explain."

Kerr has nothing further.

On redirect, I confirm that Styles has no reason to believe that Destiny Grace was lying about the costs of medical care and her other debts. I also confirm that while she was employed as a sex worker, she continued also to work housekeeping at the hotel and her other job teaching. But the fact remains that the jury likely believes that Destiny Grace lied about losing the house. And if a jury thinks that a defendant lied about one point, no matter how trivial, they'll probably believe that she lied about more important things.

I end the redirect, and Styles walks out of the courtroom a free man.

Barraclough excuses the jury for the day but says, "I want the lawyers to stay put." Once the jury leaves, he says, "Mr.

Henderson, I find you in contempt of court for your insolence. *Tripe? The Merle Barraclough objection? Despicable? Reprehensible.* Those words will cost you some jail time. Deputy Travis, take him to . . . no, don't take him to the courthouse lockup. Take Mr. Henderson to the county detention center. Put him in the general lockup until I order otherwise."

CHAPTER TWENTY-SIX

Eddie Travis unlocks the handcuffs, and I stretch and move my wrists.

"Sorry about this, Elvis. If I know Judge Barraclough, you'll be out in twenty minutes. He's big on lessons but also on second chances."

Deputy Maloney at the processing desk completes the necessary paperwork and asks for my belt and tie. Good thing I'm wearing loafers. Removing shoelaces isn't hard but putting them back on is a bitch.

I catch Travis's eye.

"I'd prefer to keep the tie," I say. "Good luck charm."

Maloney shakes his head, but Travis says, "He won't be in here for long. You're not going to hang yourself, are you, Elvis?"

"Not while I still have a client to defend."

Maloney and Travis stare at each other for a long time.

Maloney shrugs. I have the feeling Eddie Travis carries more weight among his peers than an ordinary court bailiff might. Travis, a police officer with actual experience on the street, ran for sheriff, but lost to Coyle—a politician, not a true street cop. I bet the rank and file supported Eddie against Coyle.

I hand over my belt, then take the tie off and put it in my pocket.

I'm no stranger to contempt citations, which means I'm no stranger to jail cells. Often, I have amiable chats with my fellow inmates, most of whom welcome the chance to speak with an honest-to-goodness defense attorney. Maloney puts me in a large cell with white bars, gray flooring, and four bunk beds with thin, navy-blue mattresses—enough beds to accommodate eight people. The electronic sliding doors clank shut. I'm the only person in this cell. That's okay—there's security in being alone.

Fifteen minutes later, my sense of security vanishes. A deputy I've never seen before escorts another prisoner inside the room and into my cell. When the door slides shut again, ice crystals seize my spine. My new cellmate is at least six-four, with a linebacker's physique. He's a nightmarish caricature of the Southern bigot—goateed, with crudely inked White-power tattoos on his neck and a tattoo of a swastika and a skull and crossbones on his left arm. His skin is sun-parched brown, and his eyes lack any emotion save hatred. He smiles at me. His upper canines are gold.

I suspect he and I won't have an amiable chat about the law, the weather, or Wernher von Braun's controversial status as a Rocket City, Alabama, icon. Maloney and other deputies are nowhere to be seen.

Sheriff David Coyle suddenly appears outside my cell and regards me with his arms crossed. I knew if I ever came back to town . . . Has he shut off the video surveillance camera?

"Did you kill Lillian Wagers, Dave?" I call out. "A case of bad aim?"

His arms tighten around his chest. My cellmate glowers at me.

A long time ago, I parachuted out of airplanes into war zones. My mission: rescue trapped soldiers and treat wounded ones. We were special forces—which meant they trained us to kill. How much self-defense training do I remember? Not enough, I suspect. How has the transformation from an athletic, aggressive twenty-year-old to an itinerant, forty-something lawyer affected my ability to defend myself? A lot, I reckon.

Can Dave Coyle hear my heart pounding from his vantage point in the corridor? My heart drums deafening in my own ears. Now, I reconsider my request to keep my bolo tie. This goon could hang me with it and make it look like suicide.

Coyle leaves.

I put both hands in my pocket and assume a nonchalant pose that must make the fellow want to laugh. I can't be proactive because the video camera might still be operating. I can't let this guy claim he fought me in self-defense. I bide my time, trying not to quake in terror.

The fellow doesn't waste time with banter or taunts. He stalks me, rears back, and connects with a blow to the rib cage. I groan—not a fake groan, a genuine cry of pain, because the punch hurts like hell. I struggle not to double over. As the fellow winds up for a second blow, I remove the bolo tie from my pocket and whip the bear-clasp end hard at his left eye. He screams so loudly that I wonder whether I've half-blinded him. So many tough guys have never experienced true pain and can't handle it.

After composing himself, he reaches into his pocket and pulls out a knife, the blade tarnished and lethal. *Dave Coyle better upgrade his jail intake practices.* The goon flicks the knife toward my face, taunting. Then a more serious thrust of the blade. How odd he didn't attack the body. I manage to avoid the point and connect with a punch to his injured eye, and before he can gather himself and stab me in the gut, there's the sound of a shotgun cocking and the words, "Drop your weapons."

I drop my bolo tie, and to my everlasting relief, I hear the goon's knife hit the ground.

Who's holding the shotgun? None other than Eddie Travis.

"The judge released you, Elvis," says Travis. "I told you he would." To the other guy, he says, "You . . . Far corner of the cell."

Maloney and two other deputies walk in. The cell door slides open, and they come in and grab my erstwhile cellmate.

I pick up my tie and walk out of the cell, willing my gelatinous legs not to collapse.

"Thank you, Eddie."

He nods.

"Where's Coyle? He was here."

"I don't know what you're talking about," says Travis. It's a warning—let it go for now. "Just watch your mouth in court."

"Tell Coyle what I told him twenty-eight years ago: I had nothing to do with Arlette's death."

Not directly, anyway.

———

Because the law of the land has changed, the Panhandle Women's Free Clinic of Tallahassee, Florida, or any successor in interest, is no longer operational. In the twenty-eight years since Arlette and I drove there, so much has changed.

"I'm going to hell, Elvis," said Arlette as soon as we passed through the city limits. "For a lot of the shit I've done. We both are."

"I don't believe in that," I said. "But you don't have to do this, Arlette. We can turn around and go home."

"I thought you don't believe it's a sin."

"I don't. But it doesn't matter what I think. It's about what you *choose*."

"If I have the baby, will you change your mind?"

"I will not."

She shook her head hard, like a character in a sci-fi film trying to pry an alien attacker loose from her brain. "It's a sin. But I got to do it. Drive faster, damn it."

"We're almost there."

As I parked, Arlette wrapped her arms around her torso and began to shake. Not just shake—full-body tremors. I'd seen something like that only once before. When I was a lifeguard, a young boy was gleefully running on the pool deck. From my vantage point in the tower, I hollered through my megaphone for him to walk, not run. He looked up at me in surprise, slowed down, took three steps, and keeled over, shaking from limb to limb. He'd suffered an epileptic seizure, foaming at the mouth. Fortunately, he was fine, but I was scared. Arlette Coyle's shaking was just as violent.

I put the car key back in the ignition, started the car, and pulled away from the curb.

"What are you doing?" she asked.

"Honoring your right to choose and taking you back home."

Her eyes widened, and her jaw went slack. The shaking stopped. I waited for her to argue, but she reached below her seat and came up with two SnackWell's Devil's Food Cookie Cakes. She handed one to me, unwrapped the other, and took a big bite.

Not until we reached the town of Midway some time later did she lean over and kiss me on the cheek.

Not a day goes by when I don't wish that I'd ushered a quavering Arlette Coyle into that women's clinic and insisted that she go through with her plan to terminate her pregnancy.

CHAPTER TWENTY-SEVEN

Margaret wants to bring federal civil rights actions against Quartz County and David Coyle individually. A discussion for another time. I just hope Coyle doesn't come after me again. I asked Sabrina Graham about prosecuting the inmate who attacked me. Turns out he'd been "inadvertently" released from jail because of a clerical error—supposedly an incorrect court order indicating charges against him had been dropped. "Mistakes like this happen more often than you think," said Graham. "Not long ago, the same thing happened in Charlotte, North Carolina. Only, that guy was in jail for murder. He actually did the right thing and turned himself back in. Maybe your cellmate will do the same."

"We won't hold our collective breaths on that one, will we, Sabrina?" I replied.

She smirked in agreement.

Now, a pall has descended over the Quartz Inn lobby. An irascible woman with a no-nonsense frown and wary eyes staffs the front desk. Several media members, including Callie Rocha, approach me and fire questions, but Margaret fends them off. I discuss some logistical issues with Margaret, then escort her to the elevator and head back out of the hotel to my van. I take off my suit, dress in a muscle shirt and tennis shorts, go to the pantry, and pour myself a shot of Maker's Mark.

There's a loud knock at the door, and before I can get my gun, a man says, "Elvis, it's Jeremiah Tipple."

I slide the door open to find Jeremiah, accompanied by his son Hunter.

"Mind if we come in?" asks Jeremiah.

"Too cramped. I'll come out." I climb down into the parking lot, bringing my glass of bourbon. The slight breeze feels nice against my skin. The western sky is tinged scarlet. I give a mock toast to the Tipples. "I'd offer you a drink, but I know you don't imbibe. What are you doing here, Jeremiah?"

"I'm here because of what you and the jury learned about your client," says the reverend. "I'm in the business of saving people, and I might be able to save her. Also I want to get you out of harm's way sooner rather than later. Terrible what happened to Lillian Wagers. A huge blow to my congregation, to the county. I worry about our expectant mothers and their babies with Lillian gone. I also worry about you. Rumor has it that you were the real target." He shakes his head. "Oh, the havoc you brought to our quiet town—a crying shame."

"May I ask why you didn't come to discuss this alone?" I ask. "No offense, Hunter."

"None taken, sir," says the younger man.

"We'll be talking law, and Hunter is an attorney like you." The fatherly pride in his voice is evident. "General counsel for our church, our charitable foundations—an expert on the law of taxation and exemptions for religious organizations. Graduated summa cum laude from Stephen A. Webster School of Law."

I haven't heard of that law school. "Congratulations to you, Hunter. Especially for being smart enough to avoid the pressures of trial work and to pursue more cerebral areas. I barely passed my taxation class." The truth is I can't think of a more boring area of the law.

"My father is always bragging on me," says Hunter. "Webster isn't a tier-one law school like you went to, sir, but it was founded by the Pentecostals, which is what Daddy and I wanted."

"Many fine lawyers went to smaller schools," I say. "Many incompetent lawyers went to Harvard and Yale. Now, what can I do for you?"

"Heard you had a bad day in court today," says the reverend. "Kind of like that game we played against Cullman where you fumbled twice in the first quarter."

"I like a baseball analogy better. I became a big Dodgers fan after I moved to LA. We're in the top of the first inning, the opposing team has scored a few runs, but the home team hasn't yet come to bat. What're y'all doing here, Jeremiah?"

He reaches behind his ear and pulls out a toothpick, then picks at his teeth.

I see Hunter give a slight eye roll. I'd bet that Tamara doesn't approve of Jeremiah's toothpick habit. It disgusted her when we were kids. Seems like Hunter agrees with his mother.

"Please don't throw your toothpick on what I've come to consider my patio," I say. "I have a feeling after today's testimony, the hotel housekeeping staff might be depleted."

The reverend points the pick at me. "That's funny, Elvis. You always were funny." He puts the toothpick back behind his ear. "You thought I was yanking your chain when I told you the Harper girl was licentious. Now you know I was telling the truth. The jury learned of her sins, which is a major problem for you. But I'm a forgiving man, and she and her mother were devoted church members once. Although, I must say, sinning runs in the family." He motions toward his son.

Hunter's translucent blue eyes go from dull to bright, as if someone flipped on an internal light switch. "If Reverend Tipple intervenes, we're confident the district attorney would agree to a plea of voluntary manslaughter, two counts, for a term of twenty years total. Manslaughter is punishable for up to twenty years. Ten years for each baby would be a good deal for her." As if I don't know the law. "We could call the DA tonight," adds Hunter. He sounds like a child trying to impress a parent by reciting a poem from memory.

"Oh, you could, could you, Hunter?" I say, clenching and unclenching my fists.

"I know that expression, Elvis," says the reverend. "Hear us out before you blow an artery. First, I want to tell you why *we* can get this deal when you couldn't—and trust me, you couldn't. As you pointed out when we last met, Kelsey Kerr has political ambitions, and my church is not without political influence in Alabama. We can deliver quite a few voters. I know you think we're crazy evangelicals who tote guns and support neo-Nazis and reject doctors, but we were partially responsible for keeping that fellow who ran for senator a few years back out of office because of his alleged liaisons with underage girls."

"I doubt you supported his opponent, Jeremiah."

"No, but we encouraged our folks to write in another candidate, a God-fearing woman, which helped sway the election in the opponent's favor. Not ideal, but he only lasted a couple years. I'm quite sure Kerr will go along with our proposal if she wants to end up in Congress."

I don't dismiss Jeremiah's claim of influence over Kerr, but I don't quite buy that he can convince her to offer that deal—her obsession with convicting Destiny Grace arises out of personal reasons as well as political ambitions. "But if you do not forgive others their trespasses, neither will your Father forgive your trespasses," I say.

Hunter uncrosses his arms and straightens up, and the reverend looks puzzled.

"Matthew 6:15," I say. "I thought you, of all people, would recognize it. Your purported reason for helping Destiny Grace Harper."

"Purported?" says Hunter. "Remember when I talk about lawyers' weasel words, Daddy? That's one of them. We've come here—"

"You've come here because you're worried the jury will acquit Destiny Grace, and you want her locked up behind bars to stop that from happening. If the jury acquits, it likely means they concluded that she sincerely followed your church's teachings, but her prayers and her faith in you failed to heal the twins. Acquittal means the jury finds that your brand of prayer couldn't heal a hangnail."

The reverend knots his fingers together. "That's your ego talking, Elvis. Your client is losing, and we're trying to help."

"Not so, Jerry. Tell me the real reason you made this offer. Just between us. You can whisper, so I'll be the only one who'll know the truth. Like the audible you called in the Decatur game."

The reverend slaps his thighs and stands. "You know, when people abandon their hometowns and then come back years later, they assume nothing and no one has changed. Everything has changed, man. Yeah, you might've been one up on me when we were kids, but no longer. Not here."

"I was never one up on you. You beat me in our biggest competition of all."

Jeremiah scoffs. "Did I really now? Pass our proposal on to Destiny Grace before court begins tomorrow. If you don't take the deal, you'll both regret it."

CHAPTER TWENTY-EIGHT

I tell Aruna Higgins to "hush up." I haven't used that unfortunate command in at least twenty-five years, and I'm ashamed of myself. Sure, Aruna raised her voice, and yes, there are media everywhere, and yes, even the thickest walls are too thin, but I shouldn't have spoken to her that way.

Higgins wants to explore Reverend Tipple's proposed deal. Destiny Grace and I don't.

"Damn it, y'all don't get it," says Higgins, not hushing up. "This is Alabama, not California. And this jury is as conservative and anti–women's rights as they come. And our client looks like a guilty liar."

When Destiny Grace starts to reply, Higgins holds up a hand. "Girlfriend, I don't want to hear your denials anymore without facts to back them up. Just because you say something doesn't make it so."

A slack-jawed Destiny Grace glares at Higgins.

"The law is on our side, Aruna," I say. "The State shouldn't have filed this case in the first place. If there's no justice in this courtroom, we'll appeal the verdict. You can't appeal a plea bargain. Twenty years in prison for a crime Destiny Grace did not commit would be unjust."

"In twenty years, you'll only be forty-one, Destiny Grace," says Higgins. "I know it seems old now, but it's still young enough to have a life. With time served and a reduction in your sentence for good behavior, you'll be out before that." She appeals to Margaret. "You just gonna sit there?"

"I don't have an opinion," says Margaret.

"Fuck, Margaret, show some guts and give an opinion one way or another," Higgins says. "This is a life-and-death—"

"Let me finish," says Margaret. "I don't have an opinion, but Hazel Curnow does."

This surprises me. "How could you know that?"

Margaret sighs impatiently. "Because I texted her. And she says it's a bad deal and a worse idea to trust Tipple. It's time for *you* to show some guts, Aruna. Trust in the justice system and our skills—including your own. Fight for your client."

Higgins tilts her head upward and half rolls her eyes in disdain. She doesn't look down right away.

Destiny Grace gasps. "Oh my heavens, Aruna. You think I'm guilty."

Higgins shuts her eyes. "I don't want to see you sentenced to death."

"What Aruna thinks in her heart of hearts doesn't matter, Destiny Grace," I say. "Aruna could've withdrawn from the defense team, but she stayed. She's represented you to the best of her ability under tough circumstances, most of them of your own making. She'll continue to do that. Am I right, Aruna?"

"Yes, sir," says Higgins.

"Well, I'm grateful for your commitment to my case, Aruna, but I think in your heart of hearts you hate me, I truly do," says Destiny Grace. "I'm a mama who lost her babies, and you think it didn't have to happen. I'm a prostitute and a hypocrite. I'm a walking mistake at twenty-one. I despise myself. But I'm not a murderer. I dream at night of holding those babies in my arms, nursing them, and I wake up screaming and crying because the dream ain't real. You can ask the jailers if you don't believe me. Most important, I can't leave my sick mother alone, not for twenty minutes, much less twenty years. I have to walk out of here a free woman."

Before anyone can speak further, there are three loud knocks on the door leading to the courtroom—Bailiff Travis alerting us Barraclough is about to take the bench.

Higgins and Destiny Grace go into the courtroom, while I motion for Margaret to hang back.

"Did you really text Ms. Curnow?"

Margaret nods.

"You know she doesn't like to be consulted during a trial."

"She didn't like it this time either. She told me not to bother her. So I used my own judgment and put my words in her mouth. She always says we speak for her so . . ."

"Yeah. I just hope your version of Ms. Curnow is right."

———

Judge Barraclough and I regard each other with mild embarrassment. I should've controlled my temper. He should've controlled his. If he expects an apology, he won't get one. He could've made his point by sending me to the safe lockup on the fifth floor of this building. Instead, I got attacked in the county jail. Are he and Dave Coyle in cahoots?

Sabrina Graham calls Wyatt Haines, Destiny Grace's former boyfriend. Dressed in a navy-blue blazer, white shirt, and red-and-gray paisley tie, the pudgy, boyish Haines seems the model of the devout young adult. The aspiring physician who broke up with Destiny Grace because of her aversion to modern medicine. According to Destiny Grace, however, Haines is a scorned lover bent on revenge. She maintains *she* broke up with *him*, and that in his anger he grabbed her and shook her. He might've gotten even more violent if her knee hadn't connected with a strategic spot on his person. Afterward, he stalked her.

Margaret taps me hard on the shoulder.

"What is it?" I snap at her. Good lord. I rarely snap at Margaret.

"Oh my God, E. Haines is the same jerk who hit Calinda Rocha in the face."

"Are you sure, Margaret? You've gotta be absolutely sure."

"Totally. I'll testify to it."

I can't call Margaret to the stand. The last thing we need is a credibility contest between an apparently devout young Southerner and an ultra-liberal, transgender member of the California-based defense team. In this courtroom, before this jury, Margaret would lose hands down. I look out into the gallery. Rocha sits with her hand covering her mouth. I catch her eye, and she nods. I now have my cross-examination and corroborating witness.

In a nasally, confident voice, Haines swears to tell the truth, so help him God. He testifies he graduated from Independence Evangelical College with a degree in biology and that he's taking a year off to shadow a doctor at Vanderbilt medical center in Nashville and transcribe medical procedures. He works for a doctor named Nathan Arielo in the orthopedics department.

Graham asks Haines to talk about his relationship with the defendant. "We dated in the summer before my senior year, from May to August. So, like, three months."

"Was the relationship serious?"

"Destiny Grace wanted to get married."

"In his dreams," says Destiny Grace, too loudly.

"While you and Destiny Grace were dating, did the two of you ever discuss religion?"

"Lots of times."

"Did she ever discuss her belief in God?"

Haines leans forward in the witness box and places his hands on the railing. He's been waiting for this moment, because he answers a question that Graham hasn't asked yet. "Yes, ma'am. It's private, embarrassing, but I swore to tell the truth. Destiny Grace tried to entice me into having premarital sex with her. I was upset and disappointed, because I took a purity pledge, and before we started going out, she told me she took one, too."

"Objection to yet another scandalous, irrelevant intrusion into Ms. Harper's private life," I say.

"Overruled," says Barraclough. "I have the sense this is foundational."

"The foundation for a successful appeal for judicial error," I say.

"Then you know how to pursue your remedy, don't you, Mr. Henderson?" says Barraclough. "Still overruled."

"Just so the jury is clear, a purity pledge is also called a virginity pledge, meaning no sex before marriage?" asks Graham. As if anyone in the room doesn't know this already.

"Yes, ma'am. Exactly."

"What did the purity pledge have to do with your discussion about God?"

"I asked Destiny Grace why she'd be willing to break her sacred vow of chastity, and she told me she wasn't sure she believed in God anymore. She said sex was fun, so why not enjoy ourselves?"

Graham has no further questions.

After conferring with Destiny Grace, I go to the podium. "You testified, Mr. Haines, that you received a degree in biology.

My colleague, Ms. Booth, has searched the internet and has found a list of members of what you claim is your graduating class. You're not on it."

"Yeah, no, I, um . . . I had enough credits to graduate, but I was missing a microbiology class for my major. But I finished all four years with enough classes."

"No degree yet? No diploma?"

He clenches his fists. "Like I said, I'm going to take the last class at a community college and then go to med school."

"You said no such thing, son."

"Yeah, I sure did say that!" He appeals to the jury. "I said that, right?"

The jurors in his immediate line of sight, the romance writer and the seafood market owner, look away.

"Should I ask the court reporter to read back your testimony? The testimony you're giving under penalty of perjury?"

"Don't bother," says Barraclough. "Mr. Haines, you didn't say that before. You have now. Let's move on."

"You actually flunked microbiology, didn't you, Wyatt?" After the first semester of senior year, he called Destiny Grace and pleaded with her to give him another chance. He maintained he'd flunked the class because she'd broken his heart.

"The teacher was unfair," says Haines. "Everyone knew it. I stood up to her in class about her blasphemous reading of the Bible and God's creation of the universe. I reported her to the school administration for teaching evolution."

"You also claimed on direct examination you were shadowing a Dr. Nathan Arielo at Vanderbilt, transcribing patient examinations?"

"Yes, sir."

For show, I scratch my head and pretend to ponder. "Ms. Booth can't seem to find a Dr. Nathan Arielo at Vanderbilt in orthopedics or in any other department. The only Nathan Arielo she can find in the greater Nashville metropolitan region is a podiatrist. Are you shadowing a foot doctor, son?"

The witness gives an unconcerned shrug. "He's still a doctor." Pathological liars have a way of treating exposure of their falsehoods not as a personal flaws but as a weakness in the listener.

Several jurors shake their heads. Miller Holcomb, thus far a slab of stone, chortles.

"Let's turn to your discussion with Ms. Harper about believing in God. Are you familiar with the passage from the holy scripture found in the book of Mark, chapter 15, verse 34?"

"Yes, sir. 'At the ninth hour, Jesus cried with a loud voice, "My God, my God, why hast thou forsaken me?"' I left out the middle part, but that's the gist."

"Jesus was on the cross at the time?"

Graham starts to object, but Barraclough waves her away.

"Yes, he was. I'm impressed someone like you would know that."

"You'd be surprised what I do and don't know, sir. I also know, based on that verse, even Jesus himself could question His faith in God, His Father, am I right?"

"Yeah, but he was quoting from Psalm 22, which tells us eventually God will rescue us, despite our doubts."

"Destiny Grace Harper could've been expressing doubts but ultimately had her faith restored, per Psalm 22, don't you agree?"

"No, I just think she doesn't believe in God."

"You testified on direct that you broke up with Ms. Harper. Didn't she break up with you?"

"No way. I could never date someone who wasn't chaste."

"When she broke up with you, you grabbed her so violently she had to retaliate physically to escape?"

"I wouldn't hurt a woman."

"You're sure about that, Wyatt?"

"I wouldn't hurt a woman!"

"When you and Destiny Grace broke up, you were bitter, weren't you? You tried to get back with her several times? You said she broke your heart and made you fail microbiology?"

"No, sir."

"Several days ago, you were outside my hotel with a group of protesters, holding up a sign with her picture on it reading, *Bring her forth, and let her be burnt—Genesis 38:24*?"

There's a collective intake of air in the courtroom.

"I—"

"Do you deny you were carrying that sign, sir?"

"Destiny Grace killed her babies, and like everyone heard in court yesterday, she's a whore. That's what the Bible says to do with sinners like her."

"Did you not also throw a punch and strike a newspaper reporter named Calinda Rocha in the face? Requiring a doctor's visit and stitches?"

Graham gets her objection out this time, but Barraclough overrules it.

A splotchy-cheeked Haines shakes his head over and over. "No way would I hit a woman."

I turn to the gallery and nod at Rocha, who stands.

"I can call Ms. Rocha and ask if you hit her, Wyatt. I can also call Ms. Booth, who saw you do it. Shall I call them to the stand? And if we can adjourn for a few hours, I'm sure I can locate any number of protesters that day who saw what you did."

"Let's cut through this," says Barraclough. "Ma'am, did the witness hit you in the face?"

"He did, Your Honor," says Rocha.

Graham has the bad sense to say, "I still think this is all irrelevant, Judge. And the jury shouldn't be present for—"

Barraclough taps finger and thumb on the bench. "It's relevant to show the witness's bias, Sabrina. This is cross-examination. You didn't vet your witness. So we don't waste everyone's time calling yet two more witnesses or searching the town for others, you're going to stipulate that this witness, Mr. Haines, assaulted and battered Ms. Rocha. Unless you think you can cross-examine Ms. Rocha and undermine her credibility. Are you going to cross-examine Ms. Rocha?"

"No, sir," says an unhappy Graham.

"My question for you and Kelsey is whether you intend to prosecute this man for assault," the judge asks.

The attorneys for the State sit back in their chairs and hush up.

CHAPTER TWENTY-NINE

Tamara Evans Tipple lied to me. Kelsey Kerr has just called Brandi Tipple to the stand. The same Brandi who Tamara assured me would never testify unless I called her as a witness.

Tamara and her sons are here to support their sister. They all sit together on the prosecution's side of the room. Hunter wears a white shirt and blue blazer over his chinos, perfectly acceptable for court. Clayton is dressed in raggedy jeans and a NASCAR T-shirt that displays his muscles and his Gadsden tattoo for all to see. More than one California judge would've banished him from the courtroom for inappropriate attire. Barraclough ignores Clayton, even though he and his staff must notice. So much for Southern decorum.

When I look at Tamara, she averts her eyes. Was this development beyond her control? She assured me that she could handle Kelsey Kerr—just as her husband and son insisted that they control the DA.

Brandi Tipple marches to the witness stand like a tin soldier come to life. I imagine Tamara berating the tall, shy girl through the years, exhorting her to stand up straight, reminding her that pretty girls have good posture—resulting in this robotic gait. Brandi's large, round eyeglasses have slipped down her nose owing to the flop sweat already making her forehead glisten under the courtroom's unforgiving florescent lights.

She raises a trembling hand and takes the oath, her "I do" barely audible. As soon as she sits, her hand-wringing begins. In halting sentences, she identifies herself as the daughter and youngest child of the Reverend Jeremiah Tipple, pastor of the Church of Our Lord's Rapture. "The only international church founded in Quartz County, Alabama," she adds, as if she's memorized a recruitment brochure. She probably has memorized a recruitment brochure. "Reverend Tipple has disciples in all fifty states and in forty countries throughout the world."

What will the jury make of the fact that Brandi calls her father *Reverend Tipple*?

Kerr asks Brandi to explain the church's creed. In an anxious alto, Brandi says, "We believe Jesus Christ died for our sins, and, like, we . . . that he that hath pity upon the poor lendeth unto the Lord, and the . . . But the . . . you know, what gets people who don't know us, well, gets uninformed, narrow-minded people when they . . ." She pouts her lower lip and blows air upward, such that her breath rustles her bangs—an endearing, childlike mannerism, much to my chagrin. Then she glances toward her family. "Okay if I start over, Ms. Graham?"

"I'm not Ms. Graham. I'm Kelsey Kerr. You take your time, Brandi. I know this seems scary, but there's no reason to be scared."

During Wyatt Haines's testimony, Destiny Grace stared at Haines with a poisonous glare and a contemptuous frown. She doesn't show any disdain for this witness. No, she regards Brandi with a curious tilt of the head and a sympathetic gaze.

Brandi looks up at the ceiling, the way people do when they're fighting back tears. "Oh, my, I'm so, so . . . excuse me.

I was trying to say people who don't understand our church always talk about our beliefs on healing the sick. They try to make us sound crazy. We're not. We're the sane ones, the faithful ones. Like Reverend Tipple says, when someone gets sick, we don't call on a doctor, we call on God. That's not superstition or crazy; that's true faith in the Lord."

"You're employed by the Church of Our Lord's Rapture?" asks Kerr.

"Yes, ma'am, sort of. I'm learning to support the reverend in his good works, healing the sick. We have members whose job it is to shepherd the sick. 'Let him call for the elders of the church and let them pray over him, anointing him with oil in the name of the Lord.' That's James 5. Maybe James 6, I should know, but . . . Anyway, I want to be one of those elders someday."

"Have you known the defendant long?"

"You mean Destiny Grace?"

Kerr nods.

"Known her since church preschool when we was both four years old. We was best friends ever since, until she . . . changed." She glances over at her family again. Since Brandi took the stand, she hasn't once looked our way.

"How did Destiny Grace change?"

"Well, in high school, she got real wild, had a boyfriend who got her into drugs, but then my father let her into the church rehab program and straightened her out."

My jaw unhinges—this is totally inadmissible evidence—but there's no point in moving to strike. The jury has heard it. Some of the jurors squirm uncomfortably. Destiny Grace murmurs, "Oh my goodness." Higgins flashes me an angry look, clearly upset that I didn't object.

"But me and Destiny Grace was always good friends, even in her wild days," Brandi continues. "But then a couple years ago she started questioning the church tenets, even God's existence. When her mother got sick, Destiny Grace told me that maybe the sick should see doctors, and that the doctors were helping her mother. And then, of course, Destiny Grace got pregnant without a husband."

"Ms. Tipple, did you at some point learn that Destiny Grace Harper was carrying twins and that they were suffering from something called TTTS?"

"I did, yes, ma'am. First, I learned she was pregnant—well, I figured it out. She tried to hide it, said she was just getting fat, but . . . She finally admitted it, and I told her to pray for forgiveness, which she did. Asked her if she was going to marry the father, and she laughed. She wouldn't say who the father was, just said it was a mistake. Later, she got so big and went to a doctor, which shocked me again. Destiny Grace said the doctor told her the babies had to have an operation to survive and not be retarded or nothing. She said she weren't going to have the procedure, and I said, 'How wonderful you're trusting in God; prayer will heal,' but I also told her she had to have true faith and pray for forgiveness for all her sins.'"

I could object to the rambling answer, but that might just help out Kelsey Kerr if it made Brandi's testimony clearer and more concise.

"You had this conversation with Harper in person?" asks Kerr.

"No, ma'am. I called Destiny Grace to see how she was doing."

"Did the defendant say anything in response to your comment about trusting in God?"

Brandi looks toward her family yet again. "She said the Bible wasn't making her refuse the surgery. She said, 'I ain't gonna have no operation that's gonna scar my body and make me too ugly for any man to want. These damn babies are ruining my body as it is. They're like awful aliens that've taken over my body.' That's what she said."

The muttering in the gallery gets louder. Barraclough admonishes the spectators to quiet down.

Destiny Grace grabs my sleeve. "Oh lord, Mr. Henderson, she's lying."

Destiny Grace releases her grip and folds her hands in front of her. How odd—she still seems to harbor no ill will toward her former friend. Behind us, Margaret's computer keyboard clicks. What does she expect to find? You can't defuse a bomb that has already exploded.

Kerr uses silence to exploit Brandi's revelation for a while, then asks, "Did you say anything back?"

"Well, I about fell over, but you don't argue with Destiny Grace. She seems sweet until you cross her, and then she shrieks and cusses. I was just trying not to get mad at her or make her mad at me. Actually, I wondered if she went crazy. I did ask her if she was serious. I told her guys don't care about scars on pretty girls like her."

"What did she say?"

"She said guys hate scars, and what would I know about it, since I hadn't shown any guys my body? I told her I was sorry this was happening to her; I'd help her with prayer and such. I couldn't just abandon her. You don't abandon sinners; you try to save them."

"Do you think Destiny Grace was joking when she mentioned her fear of scarring as the reason why she didn't want the surgery?"

"No, ma'am."

"Why not?"

"Well, she didn't sound like she was joking, and it's not really something you joke about, is it? Especially if you're going to be a mother. I guess I get it now. Destiny Grace was selling herself, so she didn't want no scar. So anyway, I told her to pray, and we hung up the phone. I was so freaked out, I cried. I prayed for Destiny Grace and her babies every day. That was the last time I spoke with her before she ran off."

"Ms. Tipple, do you know if Ms. Harper ever tried to abort her babies?"

Before I can get the second syllable of the word *objection* out, Brandi says, "Lillian Wagers told me Destiny Grace had asked her how to get them horrible mail-order abortion pills—"

"Objection! Hearsay! Move to strike!"

"—and Ms. Wagers yelled at her for wanting to kill her babies, and said she was too far along anyway." This shrinking flower has turned into a steamroller. Someone coached her well on this answer.

"Ms. Kerr, you should not have asked that question," says the judge. "The objection is sustained, and the motion to strike is granted. The jury will disregard the witness's answer."

Yeah. Sure they will.

An anything-but-contrite Kerr asks, "At any time, did Ms. Harper say she didn't want to undergo the fetoscopy because of her religious faith?"

"No, ma'am. Never."

Kerr sends a triumphant look my way. "Your witness, sir."

"It just ain't true," whispers Destiny Grace.

"Which part?" I whisper back.

"I . . . Asking about them pills was a mistake. I wouldn't of took them even if I had them."

Whatever the truth, I will never raise this issue again. As far as this trial is concerned, there's no evidence whatsoever that Destiny Grace tried to abort.

When I'm halfway out of my seat, Destiny Grace takes my arm again. "Mr. Henderson, I got a huge scar from when I had my appendix taken out when I was fourteen. Huger than the little scar fetoscopic surgery would've left."

"Your mother took you to a—?"

"Yeah, yeah, she thought prayer wasn't working, so she told the elders I was better, just needed rest, then she rushed me in her truck to the hospital in Huntsville. I had peritonitis. It was bad. The surgery also almost killed me, because I got an infection from that, had to have an antibiotic stent for three weeks. I still wasn't big on doctors after that, still ain't. They don't cure everything. Kept it secret, but Brandi saw my scar. Dr. Woodruff did, too."

"Let's get moving, Elvis," says Barraclough.

I'd ordinarily use a light touch on an emotionally fragile woman like Brandi Tipple. Right now, I don't give a damn about light touches. "Do you believe a turncoat like you should have the guts to look her victim in the eye before sticking a knife in her back, Ms. Tipple?"

Brandi cringes.

"First question and he's already badgering the witness," says Kerr. "That's got to be a record."

"Overruled," says Barraclough. "This is cross-examination in a murder trial. Defense counsel gets latitude. But tone it down, Mr. Henderson."

"You don't have the guts to look your former best friend in the eye when you're trying to strap her to the executioner's gurney, do you?"

"I'm not—"

"Answer my question," I say.

"I am looking you in the eye, sir," says Brandi.

"No, you don't weasel out of this. Since you took the stand, you haven't looked in your former friend's direction once, much less made eye contact. Am I right?"

Brandi tries to steel herself, but she shrinks back in her seat when a slight rise of my shoulders and straightening of my spine reduces the space between us, even though I haven't moved forward an inch. Margaret often asks how I do this, and I reply that a magician never reveals his secrets. The truth is, I don't know how I do it; I just can.

"I haven't kept track, but if you say I ain't looked at Destiny Grace, okay then."

I next ask a series of risky questions about Destiny Grace's pregnancy, all of which Brandi answers favorably: Destiny Grace allowed Lillian Wagers to pray over her and anoint her with holy oil in Jesus's name; Brandi and Destiny Grace spent hours searching for baby names until Destiny Grace came up with Brooks and Brooklyn.

"Do you believe Destiny Grace Harper should've been forced by doctors and lawyers to have surgery?" I ask.

Another look at her family.

"Ms. Tipple, are you looking at your mother and brothers for help in answering your questions? You've looked their way many times before answering." I leave the lectern and walk to the row where the Tipples sit. I stand no more than three feet from Tamara, then hold out my hands like a circus ringmaster. "Just for the record, this is your mother, Tamara Evans Tipple, and your brothers, Hunter and Clayton. Am I right?"

The witness nods.

"You're an adult? Not a child?"

Kerr doesn't bother to stand. "That's offensive, sexist—"

"I'm a grown-up," says Brandi, finally taking umbrage.

"As an adult, do you need your family to help with your answers, Ms. Tipple?"

"No, sir."

I catch Tamara's eye and give her a look that says, *I'm just getting started*. She turns her head. I'm sure she wishes she had that shotgun Clayton pointed at me when I visited her family compound. But the betrayer has no cause for complaint.

I return to the lectern. "Now, you testified that followers of your church call on Jesus, not doctors, to cure the sick. Which means your friend Destiny Grace had every right to refuse the fetoscopic surgery and look to the Lord?"

I can tell Brandi wants to appeal to her family, but she resists. "Yes, sir. I believe God don't want doctors to cut into mothers and their babies. That cutting into mothers and babies is against the word of the Lord."

"If you'd been the one to become pregnant with twins suffering from TTTS, you would've done exactly what Destiny Grace did?"

A nod and a whispered, "Yeah, I would have."

"Even knowing what you know now about the tragic result?"

"I have faith in the Lord."

Margaret approaches the lectern and points to her laptop monitor, which I skim. Then I give a grateful nod to Margaret and say, "Brandi, let's discuss your testimony about Destiny Grace refusing the surgery because she didn't want a scar. Did anyone tell you about a criminal law case in Utah several years back where a woman who refused to have a cesarean section was charged with killing one of her twins, and the prosecution claimed she refused the surgery because she didn't want a scar?"

"No, sir. I was not aware."

"So it's a coincidence that Destiny Grace said the same thing?"

"I wouldn't know."

I raise my voice a half level. "Didn't the district attorney or a member of your family tell you to make up this story about Destiny Grace and the scar?"

Kerr shouts her objection.

"Sustained," says Barraclough, the ruling I hoped for, because despite Brandi Tipple's fragility, she likely won't implicate her family or herself in an act of perjury.

"Did you know Destiny Grace Harper had her appendix removed by a surgeon when she was fourteen years old?"

Brandi gasps and covers her mouth.

"You kept your friend's secret for years, even from your parents; do I have that right?"

She glances toward her mother.

"Look at me, Ms. Tipple, not at—"

Kerr objects to my partial command as argumentative and harassing.

"Just answer the question," I say.

Kerr says, "The witness has the right to look in any direction she—"

"And I have the right to call her out if anyone is coaching her or signaling her to—"

Barraclough pounds a fist on his desk. "Counsel, I want you both to wait until I—"

Harold, the court reporter, up until now calm during even the tensest moments, throws up his hands and says, "Please, y'all, I can't take down everyone talking at once."

Silence.

Even Barraclough seems embarrassed.

"My apologies, sir," I say to the reporter. "I'll repeat my question. Ms. Tipple, did you, or did you not, keep Destiny Grace's secret about her appendectomy?"

"Yes, sir, but Destiny Grace felt bad about the surgery, because her mama made her do it. I mean, she was a kid, fourteen.

We prayed for forgiveness together." Now, Brandi *avoids* looking her family's way.

"Did Destiny Grace show you her scar?"

Brandi blushes. "Yeah, when we were teenagers. And of course, when she was pregnant, I saw it, while I was applying the holy oil."

As much as I treat the courtroom as a stage, I don't like to rely on stunts. They so often go awry. A murderer's glove that doesn't fit a defendant's hand; a bag of drugs that supposedly can't be thrown farther than five feet flying Frisbee-like across a large courtroom; a computer crash during a demonstration designed to establish the software's efficacy. But now, I have no choice but to perform a stunt. "Destiny Grace, will you show us the scar from the appendectomy?"

The accused stands and uses one hand to lift her blouse and the other to lower the waistband of her skirt. She's exposing a lot of flesh. Like a model in some peculiar fashion show, she turns toward the judge, then the jury, then the gallery, and finally the jury again. She shows off a six-inch-long white, diagonal scar on the right side of her torso. The raised, lumpy scar is unsightly, even seven years after the surgery.

From the gallery, LeAnn utters a disapproving, "Good lord, girl."

Kerr objects. I buy more time by arguing against her objection. Destiny Grace continues to display the scar to the jury until Barraclough orders her to cover up. She waits a few more beats and finally complies.

I pause until a jittery silence falls over the room. "Ms. Tipple, were you in court when Dr. Ivy Woodruff testified a scar from fetoscopic surgery would be 'teeny-weeny'?" I articulate the last words in a falsetto voice and hold up my thumb and forefinger, the digits not quite touching, just as Dr. Woodruff did on direct examination.

"First time I been in court is today."

"Would you agree Destiny Grace's appendectomy scar is *not* teeny-weeny?"

"Objection," says Kerr. "The only thing I know that's not teeny-weeny is Mr. Henderson's ego."

"The objection is sustained, but the jury is admonished to disregard Ms. Kerr's inappropriate wisecrack," says Barraclough. "You done, Mr. Henderson?"

"Not quite, Judge. Ms. Tipple, do you know what the ninth commandment is?" I ask.

A brief hesitation. "They get numbered different, but in our church, it's 'Thou shalt not . . .'" She drops her head.

"Let me finish it for you. The ninth commandment is, 'Thou shalt not bear false witness against thy neighbor.' Isn't that what you've done on this stand with the fairy tale about the scar? Borne false witness against your lifelong best friend?"

"No, sir." Brandi's words are audible only because the courtroom has gone dime-drop silent. Her misty eyes signal that even *she* doesn't believe her answer.

Kerr says she has no redirect.

"Call your next witness," says Barraclough to the prosecutors after I shake my head in disdain and sit down.

CHAPTER THIRTY

Kerr announces that the prosecution will play Destiny Grace's 911 call on the day the babies were born and died. Graham projects a written transcript of the call on the screen so the jurors and spectators can follow along. The courtroom audio and visual systems click on.

DISPATCHER: 911, where's your emergency?

CALLER: I don't know, I'm in a house off I-65, my baby's coming, I . . . I need the paramedics.

DISPATCHER: Is there anyone there with you?

CALLER: (No response).

DISPATCHER: Ma'am?

CALLER: No, I'm all by myself.

DISPATCHER: Do you know where you are?

CALLER: In a house off I-65. Just off of exit 59. Then down the road a ways. It's the only . . . in a, a . . . (Pause, inaudible words). The only house on, it's . . . off Pioneer Lane, down to the end of the road and a little into the woods.

DISPATCHER: How old are you?

CALLER: (Inaudible) . . . one.

DISPATCHER: Thirty-one?

CALLER: Twenty . . . Oh lord, these babies are coming right now! (Inaudible words).

DISPATCHER: Have you had any children before?

CALLER: No. (Caller moans, inaudible words).

DISPATCHER: Okay, well, I've talked to them, and they're coming as quick as they can. You stay on the line.

CALLER: (Inaudible).

DISPATCHER: Ma'am, is anyone else there with you? Are you talking to someone else?

CALLER: I'm alone. I told you. Oh lord, one of the babies . . . she's here!

DISPATCHER: Is she breathing? Are you having twins?

CALLER: (Whimpers). No, she's not . . . So, big, poor thing. Oh, Brooklyn! (A scream). I have sinned.

DISPATCHER: Ma'am, are you there? Ma'am, please don't hang up; they'll be there soon.

(No further sound on audio).

Destiny Grace's anguished attempt to stave off hysteria during that call, her willingness to call for help—*medical* help—support innocence. Unless, that is, a jury believes she wanted the paramedics to help *her*, not the babies. Her parting words *I have sinned* counterbalance that conclusion. The unintelligible portions on the recording could be muffled conversations with another person. Or they could be panicked mumbles or pathetic pleas for the babies to survive. They could be entreaties to God.

There's something else about the recording—the words *Pioneer Lane* have seemed familiar to me, a memory fragment just out of reach. Margaret visited the place before the trial started and described it as just an old shack. I keep wondering whether I'm just imagining some connection to the words. I did a Google search, and maybe I'm thinking about a style of women's boots, or an album by the indie-folk duo The Watson Twins. (I stream a lot of different music while on the road.) I asked my uncle, but he said he knows nothing about the place.

The senior EMT who arrived on the scene describes how the paramedics found the babies' bodies. "Both were swaddled in blankets. The blankets had the babies' names on them. I've seen a lot of bad stuff over the years, but this was one of the first times I broke down crying. All three of us tough folks shed some tears. Hours later, I learned the mother checked into the Athens hospital emergency room. The police learned her identity, figured it out, arrested her. Still don't know why she didn't wait for us. How could she just leave them babies in an old log cabin?"

My body goes rigid. The words *log cabin* resurrect my memory of Pioneer Lane.

"The State of Alabama rests," says Kerr.

Not until the third time Barraclough asks me whether our side wants to cross-examine the witness do I regain enough composure to mumble, "No questions, Judge."

"We're going to break for lunch," says Barraclough. "Then the defense will tell its side of the story."

I pull Margaret aside and whisper, "We have to get a subpoena out. Today!"

"Who's the witness?"

When I tell her the name, she chortles in disbelief. When I tell her the reason, she stops laughing mid-chortle and gawps at me.

CHAPTER THIRTY-ONE

Eight days after Arlette Coyle and I drove to Tallahassee and then turned right around and went back to Alabama, two spelunkers discovered her battered corpse in the Santee Mountain Nature Preserve. She was lying on a jagged outcrop a little more than halfway to the bottom of the Blaine pit cave. She'd been missing for nineteen hours.

The *Quartz Star Journal* obituary didn't mention a cause of death. The official family line was a tragic accident: *Arlette loved walking in the nature preserve; the vertical cave had fascinated her since she was a small child; she stumbled, and the barriers weren't sufficient to prevent her fall.* The Coyles' lawyer threatened to sue the county for negligence and wrongful death, but he never did. The cops conducted only a cursory investigation, I suppose because the family wanted it that way. The police interviewed me, and I told them the truth about driving Arlette to Florida. I also told the truth about what had happened a couple of months before that between Arlette and me in the preserve. Yes, I might've been indifferent to Arlette, and yes, she might've held me in disdain, but those feelings hadn't stopped us from hooking up at a Friday night drunken party at the Preserve. A totally embarrassing, unsatisfying encounter during which she leaned against the trunk of an American smokewood tree, while I coupled behind her—a most impersonal way to perform that so-called intimate contact. At least we used protection, which was why I was skeptical when she told me that she was pregnant and that I was the father. Yeah, condoms break, but there was no evidence of that. Still, the timing added up.

She asked *me* to take her to Florida for an abortion, I told the authorities. I never insisted that she end the pregnancy. I also told the cops that I'd made it clear I wouldn't marry her even if I was the father. Hardly noble on my part, but sometimes nobility isn't all it's cracked up to be.

The cops didn't prosecute—no evidence of foul play. Arlette had a history of harming herself, and the family didn't want the shame that went along with suicide. Easiest to call her death accidental.

Arlette did kill herself. I knew she was suicidal because I saw her wrists. And she'd bought those the two bottles of Tylenol for her "headache." Arlette's brother, Dave, however, decided that I'd knocked up Arlette and murdered her after I'd failed to force her to have an abortion.

CHAPTER THIRTY-TWO

Our first witness, Gary Panman, MD, wears a too-large charcoal-gray suit and an extra-long red tie that goes halfway down the front of his zipper. His eyes are mere slits, so narrow that you got to wonder how he sees. His ears aren't large, but they stick out at a sharp angle. His long chin seems mismatched with the rest of his face. Perched on his head is a skullcap—in Yiddish, a *yarmulke*; in Hebrew, a *kippah*. Aruna Higgins couldn't find an expert; Margaret found Dr. Panman on only two weeks' notice. Panman looks like an oddball, especially in these parts, but if he performs well, the jury will never forget him. Diversity imprints into memory.

At the defense table, Destiny Grace confers with Higgins in hushed tones.

Before I can ask my first question, Barraclough says, "You know, there are some places named for famous Jews over in Huntsville. The Benson family have been in the town since the 1850s. Back in the 1930s, the family donated an athletic field to the city. And a wildlife sanctuary. Very philanthropic."

Yes. A generous and prominent family, and so they remain.

Never mind that the gift of the field was specifically designated for the enjoyment of *White* children.

"You ever hear of the Benson family, doctor?" asks Barraclough.

"I'm afraid not," says Panman in a clipped baritone.

There follows a moment of graceless calm. Finally, I ask Panman about his background.

The witness grew up in Borough Park, Brooklyn, New York. He attended a private Jewish religious school called Shalhevet. He graduated from Brandeis University in Massachusetts with a bachelor of science degree in biochemistry, and he received his MD from Vanderbilt University in Nashville. This last tidbit greatly improves the doctor's geographic credentials. So does the location of his internship and residency—Emory University in Atlanta. Panman goes on to testify he practiced as an ob-gyn until he developed an interest in genetics and medical ethics. He became affiliated with the College of Bioethics / Medical Ethics, specializing in complex genetic therapy for pediatric patients. He's conducted extensive research on court-ordered treatment of pregnant women and has thoroughly reviewed Destiny Grace Harper's file.

"Dr. Panman, have you formed an opinion about whether it was ethical for the State of Alabama to seek a court order forcing Destiny Grace Harper to undergo a fetoscopy?" I ask.

"It was *un*ethical, as well as medically contraindicated, for a court, a doctor, or anyone else to force such treatment on Destiny Grace Harper. I also believe this murder trial is unethical because it's just as coercive."

In response to my questions about the twins' condition, Panman agrees with Ivy Woodruff's description of TTTS, the dismal survival rates, and the medical benefits of fetoscopy.

"If fetoscopy is so safe and effective, why shouldn't a court have ordered Ms. Harper to have the procedure?" I ask.

He tugs at his ear. "First of all, fetoscopy can result in serious complications. One percent of the time, there's infection or placental abruption, and in 3 percent of the cases, pulmonary edema results. There can also be complications from the anesthetic. Secondly, forcing a pregnant mother to have a surgical procedure is not only ethically wrong but also medically unsound. The use of threats, not to mention physical force, can endanger the health of both mother and unborn child. If governments criminally prosecute pregnant moms for refusing an unwanted medical procedure, fearful women won't seek medical care in the first place." Panman turns to the jury. "Think about it—if Ms. Harper hadn't seen a doctor at all, she wouldn't be sitting here today, because she wouldn't have known the babies were sick. Doctors and patients shouldn't be adversaries. When they are, medical treatment suffers." Great testimony substantively, but the mechanical whirr of the courthouse air conditioner sounds livelier than Panman's monotone. There's more ear-tugging. The importance of presentation is the reason many dishonest charlatans get more experting gigs than true experts like Gary Panman.

"I also want to mention what we call prognostic uncertainty," adds Panman. "That simply means doctors, lawyers, and judges aren't gods or fortune tellers. One study of court-ordered obstetric interventions found that doctors and judges get it wrong about one out of three times. There's also the issue of selective pregnancy reduction. In cases of TTTS, there can be severe discordance in fetal growth between the twins; there can be fetal malformations. In those circumstances, selective reduction is an alternative therapy."

"In plain English, Dr. Panman?"

He grimaces. "It means when one twin is too sick to survive, you kill the sick one to save the strong one." He testifies that selective reduction is not unusual in cases of TTTS and that sometimes the mother must carry the dead baby to term. Selective reduction comes with possible complications, including internal bleeding, ruptured uterus, retained placenta, infection, and miscarriage of the other fetus.

"No further questions." I pirouette and return to my seat.

Kelsey Kerr's turn. "Sir, at the very beginning of your direct testimony, you gave some statistics about the survival rates associated with TTTS?"

"Yes."

"And you also gave some statistics about the risk to a pregnant woman from complications of a fetoscopy?"

"Yes." Panman tugs at his ear.

"Let's see if I have this right. *Without* a fetoscopy, nine times out of ten, babies like the Harper twins die; *with* a fetoscopy, one out of a hundred mothers might get an infection treatable with antibiotics."

"Your statistics are generally accurate."

"So Destiny Grace Harper's innocent babies deserved to die just so she wouldn't be the one woman in a hundred who had to swallow a couple pills?"

"Ms. Kerr, if you'd think your position through, you wouldn't be doing what you're doing. It's what—"

"Answer the question I asked you, sir," says Kerr.

"No, I want to hear this, and I want the jury to hear it," says Barraclough. "Assume you're answering the Court's question, Dr. Panman."

"It's what you judges and lawyers call the slippery-slope argument. If you successfully convict Ms. Harper and support the notion that the law can force pregnant women to have surgery, there will come a time when a prosecuting attorney with different political and religious views tries to force a woman to have an abortion because the fetus has Down syndrome. Or a prosecutor might bring murder charges against an unwilling transplant match for failing to donate a kidney to a dying patient. If that happens, we're on the path to forced abortions, to coerced organ harvesting. I know it's not what you intend, but that's where this trial leads us, Ms. Kerr."

"Doctor, you are a proponent of abortion, which you probably call a woman's right to choose, don't you?" says Kerr, trying to strike back by resorting to her security blanket—the jury's opposition to abortion rights. She pauses, waiting for me to object. No objection from me.

Back at the prosecution table, Graham futilely tries to get Kerr's attention. I've suspected Graham is a more astute—or at least a better prepared—attorney than her boss, and this incident confirms my suspicions.

"As an Orthodox Jew, I believe abortion is justified only when the mother's life is at stake," says Panman. "I know Dr. Ivy Woodruff testified for the State, and as it turns out, I'm a stricter opponent of abortion than she is. I don't believe abortion should be legal even in the case of rape or incest. And, no, I have no evidence or information that Ms. Harper wanted to abort."

"Let's move on to something else," mutters Kerr. "Are you aware of the publicized case involving the conjoined twins known as Mary and Jodie?"

"That case was different!"

Panman reacted defensively instead of calmly answering the question and waiting to see where Kerr would lead him. And that makes him look extremely evasive because he ran away from a neutral question. Not great.

I lean back and look at Margaret, who shrugs. Ah, well. No trial team can prepare for every obstacle, especially on just a few weeks' notice.

"Conjoined twins," says Barraclough. "Once called Siamese twins, though I believe that's yet another thing we're not supposed to say anymore."

"Rightly so," volunteers Panman.

I agree with Panman's sentiment but not with the good doctor's decision to express it at this juncture.

Kerr resumes her cross-examination, eliciting testimony that Jodie and Mary were the pseudonyms of conjoined twins from Malta. Unless surgically separated, they would've both died within three months. Surgical separation gave Jodie high odds of survival but would've killed Mary. Like Destiny Grace Harper, the twins' parents opposed the surgery on religious grounds. A court in the United Kingdom ordered the surgery, and Panman wrote an article agreeing with the court's decision. Jodie did live, and Mary did die. In fact, Jodie is living a normal life all these years later.

A floundering Panman says, "Ms. Kerr, I'd like to explain why—"

"You can explain if Mr. Henderson decides to question you on redirect, Dr. Panman. I'm finished with you."

I tug at my jacket sleeves and remain seated—a casual approach, because I want the jury to think I'm unconcerned (I'm *very* concerned). "Tell us why this case differs from the Jodie and Mary case, Dr. Panman."

"The Harper babies were still in the womb when they needed the surgery, so performing surgery to save them was also surgery on their mother. In the British case, the mother had already given birth when the court intervened. This will sound strange, but despite their youth, Jodie and Mary were autonomous from their mother in a way Brooklyn and Lydia Harper weren't. Jodie and Mary, as infants, couldn't make their own decisions, and their mother wasn't being forced to have surgery.

Therefore, a court had the right to intervene. From everything I've read and seen about this case, Destiny Grace Harper *is* decisionally capable and simply holds unusual religious beliefs. In a society that forces competent human beings to have surgery and prosecutes them if things go wrong, matters will not end well."

Not the clearest answer, but it'll have to do. I have no more questions, and the judge adjourns for the day. As the jury files out, Kelsey Kerr looks at the jurors, gloating.

CHAPTER THIRTY-THREE

Our legal team is working at the courthouse, getting ready for tomorrow's session. At 8:00 p.m., Higgins leaves for her Huntsville home, while Margaret drives me back to the hotel.

"By the way, E, I meant to tell you, I've been going through Destiny Grace's Bible when I can spare a second. I found something maybe interesting. Not sure what it means. I've emailed the passage to you."

"You know I hate reading documents electronically."

"Yeah, and I don't have time to print out a hard copy. Read the attachment."

I grumble my assent and open Margaret's email attachment. She included a highlighted passage from Deuteronomy chapter 22, verses 23 and 24: "If there be a damsel that is a virgin betrothed unto a husband, and a man find her in the city, and lie with her; then ye shall bring them both out unto the gate of that city, and ye shall stone them to death with stones; the damsel, because she cried not, being in the city; and the man, because he hath humbled his neighbor's wife: so thou shalt put away the evil from the midst of thee."

"What do you make of this?" I ask. "Did you research possible interpretations?"

"No time. But isn't the passage about adultery? You think Destiny Grace highlighted this passage because she believes she should die as punishment for her promiscuity?"

"If so, she's trying to commit suicide by murder trial." I study the passage and begin searching the internet for commentary. Before I can find anything helpful, we park in the hotel lot next to my campervan and decide to have a working dinner at the hotel restaurant.

As soon as we get out of the car, a tall figure emerges from the woods and blocks our way. He's dressed in jeans and a tight muscle shirt that shows off a Gadsden tattoo.

"You shouldn't have made my sister look like a liar, Henderson," he says through clenched teeth. "She's a good person. Sweet and kind."

I check his hands. No weapons. "You know, Clayton, right now you look like your daddy did when he was young and foolish. Jeremiah would wear that same silly scowl when he threatened to fight me. He never had the courage to go through with it, though. I guess that was wisdom of a sort."

"Let's go, E," says Margaret.

I'm too tired and too angry to take Margaret's sound advice. "As for your sister, she looked like a liar because she *is* a liar. Now, step aside, or I will report your impolite behavior to Ma and Pa Tipple." When I try to walk past Clayton, he slides over and once again blocks my path. Never mind that we outnumber him; never mind the laws against assault, occasionally enforced even in Cole's Crossing, Alabama; never mind the ubiquitous video surveillance cameras.

"Are you really this big a fool, Clayton?" I say.

"Dial down the insults, E," says Margaret. "Clayton, I'm going to ask nicely. Please walk away and let us pass."

"Fuck you, freak," he says, and then he spits on Margaret's boots. Oh, how I want to use the kid's face to wipe his saliva off those Tory Burches.

Margaret stays calm. She tries to walk around Clayton, but he blocks her way.

And then the gauze lifts, and I comprehend that Bible passage, and the truth comes into focus with cinematic clarity. I throw a left jab and then another, making sure to bloody Clayton's nose. I plow forward and apply a headlock, pulling his face to my body. When I've accomplished my purpose, I release him.

Blood pours from his nose.

"Y'all are fucking crazy," he replies, then darts back into the woods.

It's true—what I did was crazy. But insanity can make for a potent weapon.

Margaret glares at me with undisguised disappointment. Rivulets of sweat drench my shirt and tickle my armpits and rib cage. I shiver when a gust of wind blows through me. There's blood all over my shirt. I gingerly remove the shirt, careful not to touch the stain. "Remember the Ghilarducci case we had up in Ohio five, six years ago?"

"Of course." Her eyes enlarge. "You hit the kid to get a sample of his DNA?"

"Worth a try."

"You could go to jail if he presses charges. Probably should go to jail, to be honest."

"It's worth the risk."

"You could've injured him badly."

"Nah, I didn't hit him that hard. It's just a nosebleed."

She shakes her head in a kind of disapproving admiration. "Give me the shirt. Hazel won't like this."

"Then don't tell her, Margaret."

She starts to leave but stops. "There's blood on your face, E, and I think it's yours."

I touch my cheek. Damn. I am bleeding. Clayton must've scratched me during the scuffle. "Margaret, this is going to sound crazy, but—"

"Crazier than what you've already done?"

In a flash, I decide to answer a question that I've avoided for almost three decades. "I'm going to give you a sample of my DNA, too. Run my DNA against the unborn fetus of a woman named Arlette Coyle—if they kept a record of the baby's DNA. Arlette died twenty-eight years ago." There's certainly a chance that the fetus's DNA had been preserved. The authorities kept records even then, and Arlette died a violent death.

Margaret waits for an explanation. It takes only a look in my eyes for her to realize that none will be forthcoming.

"On it, but you owe me a dinner," she says.

———

Back in the van, I shower and change into blue jeans and a UCLA Bruins T-shirt. I try to prepare for tomorrow's session, but my mind jangles—from my calculated act of violence, from the anticipation of what Margaret's quest might reveal, from the knowledge we're losing the trial.

My phone rings.

"Hey, Elvis, it's Callie Rocha. I'm in the hotel restaurant. Do you have time to meet?"

"You don't seriously think I'll talk about what happened in court today."

"I have some information you'll be interested in. I'm in a back booth."

———

Compared to the rest of the Quartz Inn, the Clinton Bar & Grill is elegant—it's fairly clean, the Naugahyde seats aren't torn too badly, and the lighting is dim. I find Callie Rocha in the back, sipping a glass of red wine. I make a move to sit across from her, but she slides over and says, "Sit beside me. I have some documents to show you."

I point to her glass of wine. "Any good?"

"The best label in the house and pretty much undrinkable. But it has alcohol in it, which is good enough for me."

I summon the server and order a Maker's Mark.

Rocha takes a sip of wine. "Wild day in court. Your expert is knowledgeable, but has no charisma—unlike Ivy Woodruff. You scored some points on Brandi's cross-examination. You needed them. This case should've never been brought, and yet your client . . . Her life will be ruined even if she's acquitted, which with this jury . . ." She shakes her head. "Tough case. You're an outstanding lawyer, E."

She must have an ulterior motive for that compliment given that we're clearly losing, and it's all on me.

Rocha puts her elbow on the edge of the table and rests her chin on her fingers. "I've learned something that I think will help your client. What can we do for each other?"

"Always a quid pro quo with the media, huh?"

"I'm a journalist and you're a lawyer. Our professions invented quid pro quos."

"Fair enough. I've always admired the fourth estate. Let's say we reach an information-sharing arrangement on one condition,

Ms. Rocha. I'll give you some potentially blockbuster info. We won't know tomorrow if I'm right, but if I am, you'll have the opportunity to write the story in advance and get an exclusive. Again, if I'm right, you *will* be first to publish. In exchange, you'll tell me what you've learned."

When she turns to shake hands, her leg touches mine, and neither of us breaks the contact right away.

We share information. Then we both order another drink and some nachos smothered in genuine Velveeta, and we sit and chat until the restaurant closes. Before she leaves the hotel, she looks around to make sure no one's watching us and gives me a quick kiss on the lips. I take my own look around and give her a longer kiss.

CHAPTER THIRTY-FOUR

The humidity has broken. The daytime temperature will be in the midseventies. A perfect day for fly-fishing, a younger Buddy Henderson would've remarked. In those days, he and I would grab our gear and head to one of the many rivers or streams flowing through the Tennessee Valley. No fly-fishing today, though; not for this boy. The only breeze I feel will be from the courthouse air conditioner.

Margaret is wearing yesterday's wardrobe. She actually did pull an all-nighter.

"Results in an hour if we're lucky," she says, holding up crossed fingers.

Before speaking with Destiny Grace, I ask Margaret to make sure the conference room door is locked and no one is eavesdropping. The media hides in cracks and crannies.

"Destiny Grace, did you get pregnant with Brooklyn and Lydia as a result of being raped?" I ask.

"Whoa, E!" says Margaret.

Aruna Higgins gapes at me as if I've gone mad.

Destiny Grace? She doesn't look at me in shock; she doesn't

gasp in surprise or rebuke me. "Yes, sir," she says in a quavering voice. "I'm sorry."

Now I'm the one who's surprised. I expected her to avoid answering my question whether I was correct or not. On reflection, I shouldn't have. Eventually, some agony becomes so unbearable that the sufferer must cry out. I simply helped her find her voice.

"*I'm* so sorry this is happening to you," I say. "And you have nothing to apologize about."

"How did you figure it out, Mr. Henderson?"

"Your Bible—the one in your bedroom at home. You highlighted a passage from Deuteronomy. 'Ye shall stone them with stones that they die; the damsel, because she cried not, being in the city . . .' The older, sexist interpretations say the passage is about adultery, but the more recent commentators realize it's really about rape. You were raped, and you 'cried not.' The Bible is wrong on this one, Destiny Grace—it's not your fault."

Destiny Grace has behaved as many sexual assault victims do—she kept the attack secret and blamed herself. I suspect Clayton Tipple raped her. He threatened Lillian Wagers to stop her from testifying; he had no compunction about leveling a shotgun at me, an unarmed man who posed no threat to him or his family. He once dated Destiny Grace, who according to Tamara helped ruin his marriage. Most rape cases involve a person the woman knows—many of those committed by a current or former intimate partner. If I'm right about Clayton, in the grand tradition of powerful families from time immemorial, his family covered up the crime. If the truth comes out, not only will the son go to prison, but the church will likely collapse. The Tipples need a guilty verdict in our case. If Destiny Grace is convicted, she won't have an ounce of credibility. That's why Jeremiah wouldn't help her. That's why Brandi turned on her.

That's why Tamara betrayed me. That's why I punched Clayton in the nose and made sure I got his blood on my shirt—a DNA sample. Oh, no matter how the DNA results come out, am I glad that I clocked the creep. I wish I'd hit him harder.

As a human being, I'm appalled by Destiny Grace's plight. As a defense lawyer, I'm encouraged. Many who oppose abortion still believe the law should allow termination of pregnancies resulting from rape. Dr. Ivy Woodruff herself lobbied for a rape exception in the Alabama anti-abortion statute. Even if the jury concludes Destiny Grace wanted her babies to die, some of them might show mercy to a sexual assault victim.

"Oh my God, oh my God, oh my God," says Higgins. "Oh my God." She kneels next to Destiny Grace, puts an arm around her, and starts to cry.

"Please don't take the Lord's name in vain," says Destiny Grace, but she doesn't remove herself from Higgins's embrace. Rather, she rests her head on Aruna's shoulder. Then she straightens up and fixes a hard gaze on me. "Mr. Henderson, don't ask me who did it. He'll kill me and my mama if I tell. He can get to me. He proved it already."

"The attack in the jail?"

"That, and he killed Lillian Wagers. I didn't say a word to Lillian, but he must've worried I told her what happened. Or maybe after you came to town and started looking for her harder, he just wanted to get rid of the person who could help me most in court. Whatever, he did it."

Margaret and I exchange a glance. I have wondered whether the bullet was meant for me, because the motive to kill Wagers seemed flimsy. And I do have enemies in this town. But now, given what happened to Destiny Grace, there was a strong motive for murdering Wagers.

"He made me promise on the Bible I wouldn't tell," says

Destiny Grace. "While Shannon was hitting me, she said, 'Remember your promise. You swore it.' The beating would've been a lot worse if a guard hadn't-a run up and stopped it."

There are three loud knocks on the door.

"Destiny Grace, no one's going to harm you or your mother," I say. "You have no reason to fear this monster. He'll go to prison. When you take the stand, I'm going to ask you if you were raped, and you'll answer yes, and you'll describe the details and identify your attacker."

"I can't do it, Mr. Henderson. I can't. He'll kill Mama, I know he will. Anyway, who's gonna believe a whore like me?"

Should I tell her I suspect Clayton Tipple raped her? No. She'll deny it or ignore me and try to interfere with my plan. I'm fighting this battle with the prosecution *and* my client. I learned early in my legal career that the pleasure you feel after a victory is never as intense as the pain you feel after a defeat. It's taken me until now to understand that *victory* can cause the most excruciating pain of all. I'll win this battle with Destiny Grace, no matter how excruciating.

Ten minutes before we're due to start the trial again, Margaret leaves. A few minutes later, she returns and beckons me out into the hall. She's holding the precious lab report, which I skim.

Before we enter the courtroom, Margaret says, "There's something else. I texted Curnow about what's going on."

"Did she tell you not to bother her?"

"She says she wants to speak with you. Now."

———

After finding an empty conference room on an isolated floor two stories up, I punch in Ms. Curnow's phone number. She never answers her phone—it's always her assistant, Anita. Except this time.

"Do not put that girl on the stand," says Curnow. "Your jury already hates her. They'll find her guilty either way, but they might still sentence her to life imprisonment over capital punishment. We'll appeal and hope a higher court reverses and exonerates her. But if you put her on that stand, she'll only make it worse for herself. She might say something that makes a conviction appeal-proof. Do not turn an appealable case into a death sentence."

"The jury's still out on whether they hate her."

"Don't be glib at a time like this."

"Ma'am, I'm not being glib. I'm with these jurors every day. We can still win this case. How could you possibly know that the jury hates her? You're two thousand miles away."

"I've read the media reports and Margaret's updates. If that's not good enough for you, call it an old lawyer's intuition."

"Ma'am, didn't Margaret tell you Destiny Grace's pregnancy was the result of rape?"

"Of course she did. Which is exactly why you can't have her testify. The fact of rape gives the client a strong motivation for terminating her pregnancy." I hear a long inhalation and then a blowing sound, as if Ms. Curnow has taken a drag on a cigarette.

"Or evidence of rape garners sympathy from a jury you say hates her," I say. "It's worth the risk to keep our client out of prison entirely."

"*Not* worth the risk even if the jury believes her. And if they don't believe her, they'll recommend the death penalty."

Someone knocks on my door. Margaret sticks her head in. "The judge is coming back soon."

I make the *just a little bit longer* gesture with a thumb and forefinger, and she shuts the door.

"Ms. Curnow, no jury can find her guilty of premeditated murder. If she wanted to terminate the pregnancy, she would've gone to South Carolina for an abortion. It's a six-hour drive away."

"Please don't tell me what I already know. Elvis, you know as well as I that there are many reasons why she would want the babies dead even if she didn't abort. The prosecution has already mentioned them. She could've been in denial about the pregnancy and waited too long. A lot of rape victims are in denial about the rape itself, much less a resultant pregnancy. She might've believed that she'd be condemned to hell if she aborted but not if the babies died through inaction. She could've changed her mind about wanting the babies when she learned there were complications. You're insisting on rationality when rationality has little to do with this case. It was irrational for the DA to file in the first place. Let the higher courts do their work. Do *not* put that woman on the stand."

Margaret knocks again, very hard.

"I've got to go, ma'am."

"Elvis, please respect my opinion."

"I respect your opinion more than anything. But you're not here."

"Do *not* call Destiny Grace Harper to the witness stand! If you do there will be consequences."

"Ms. Curnow, if you don't like my decision, you can try the next case. I'll even lend you my van. Now, I got to go, ma'am. Court will be in session soon."

After ending the call, I hurry back to our war room, where our team is still waiting for me.

"Let's go, we're late," says Higgins. "Barraclough will be pissed."

I hold up a hand and turn to our client. "Destiny Grace, the time has come for you to save your own life."

CHAPTER THIRTY-FIVE

A brash iconoclast in high school, I made no secret of my support for *Roe v. Wade* and a woman's right to choose. I got into more than one fistfight over that issue. The principal suspended me during my junior year and would've expelled me if Uncle Buddy didn't have a friend at a Montgomery newspaper who threatened to expose the school and the entire district as anti–free speech.

Despite my views on abortion, when Arlette Coyle brought me out to the empty high school, maintained that I'd knocked her up, and asked me to drive her to Florida, I wavered— I doubted I was the father. I wavered because I knew Arlette abhorred the idea of terminating a pregnancy.

"Are you going to marry me if I keep it?" she asked.

"I'm sorry. I won't do that even if it's mine. We don't love each other. If the baby turns out to be mine, I'll support it, be a father to it as best I can—wherever I am."

She sneered. "With what money? Besides, I don't care about money. I care about being married when I have this baby."

"That won't happen. Sorry."

"Tammy said you're a nice guy. Guess she was wrong."

"Guess so. But I gotta be sure this is really what you want to do."

"E, if you don't take me, I'll kill myself. I've already tried before." She moved her thick gold bracelets up her arm and held out her wrists. On each, there was a scar an inch long.

I gave in. When I offered to pay for the procedure, she scoffed. "I'm gonna uses my weekly allowance. I'm sure you don't have that much in your whole savings."

After Arlette died, Dave Coyle and two of his buddies came to the Redneck Condo, accused me of pushing Arlette down the Blaine pit cave, and broke my jaw and three of my ribs. They might've killed me if my Uncle Buddy hadn't come home and chased them off with his Smith & Wesson.

When I came clean to Buddy about everything, he said we should insist on a paternity test—not easy to accomplish post-mortem on a fetus. I declined—guess I didn't want to know the truth. And I begged him to not inform the cops about the beating.

Nine days later, I left Cole's Crossing, Alabama, for good. Or so I thought.

CHAPTER THIRTY-SIX

I glance back at the courtroom spectators. Tamara, Hunter, and Clayton Tipple sit in the same seats as yesterday, joined by Brandi, who, now that she's testified, no longer has to sequester outside. I stand and announce, "The defense calls Destiny Grace Harper."

An incredulous Judge Barraclough gapes at me for a moment, looks down, and shakes his head slowly, the way judges do when faced with incompetent attorneys. Kerr and Graham exchange a glance and try to suppress derisive grins. The legal sophisticates in the gallery let out astonished whooshes and hums. Ms. Curnow isn't the only person who believes that Destiny Grace will make a terrible witness.

The jurors are the only people in this room whose reactions I care about. To a person, they lean forward. They want to hear Destiny Grace's side of the story, and that is reason for hope. If they'd written her off already, they wouldn't care what she has to say.

When Destiny Grace starts for the witness box, LeAnn leaves her seat in the gallery, hurries through the swinging door, and helps her frail daughter climb the two steps. I check the jurors. Some are moved, but others seem to find LeAnn's gesture of love contrived.

Clerk Mildred Chilton rises to administer the oath. The two women stand fifteen feet apart. The space between them crackles with high-voltage hostility. After Destiny Grace swears to tell the truth, so help her God, Chilton doesn't sit down right away, and neither does Destiny Grace. The pair resemble boxers staring at each other prefight while the referee recites the rules.

"You all right up there, Destiny Grace?" asks Barraclough, causing his clerk to blink first and sit down.

"Tired but happy to get to tell my side of the story, Judge." Excellent ad-lib.

"Proceed, Mr. Henderson."

I'd like to get to the bitter core of the matter, but that'll have to wait. So, after taking Destiny Grace through the facts leading up to Dr. Ivy Woodruff's diagnosis of TTTS, I ask why she refused to have the laser surgery.

"My father died when I was little, during what was supposed to be easy dentist's surgery. Killed by a doctor, an anesthesiologist. Mama sued, but the jury ruled against us. My mama brought me up to believe that the Lord, not arrogant medical doctors, heals the sick. I believed prayer would save my babies. The Bible says so. 'And the prayer of faith shall save him that is sick, and the Lord shall raise him up.' 'O Jehovah my God, I cried unto thee, and thou hast healed me.' With the lasering, it wasn't just about not wanting them to cut into me. This was surgery on my tiny, unborn babies, mostly on them, and they couldn't choose for themselves. I had to choose for them. How could I go against my beliefs and upbringing when it was their lives and souls at stake?"

"As a teenager, doctors removed your appendix. How does that jibe with your religious beliefs?"

"I was only fourteen. My *mother* made me have the appendectomy. She didn't think prayer was working, but how did she know it wouldn't in the end? I got a terrible infection from the operation; almost killed me. I was depressed for years keeping that secret."

"Didn't you support your mother when she had surgery and chemotherapy for her ovarian cancer? Drove her to her appointments? Sat with her during hours of chemo?"

"She's my mama, and I love her. I was following God's commandment to honor her." Despite an occasional quaver in her voice, Destiny Grace is doing just fine—mostly speaking to me but also looking at the jury at important times; talking in a measured yet confident tone; leaning forward in her chair.

I ask whether she consulted anyone after she received Dr. Woodruff's diagnosis.

"I talked to Reverend Jeremiah Tipple, our pastor."

"What did Reverend Tipple tell you?"

Destiny Grace closes her eyes and takes a long breath. "I told him I was having twins, that a medical doctor said the babies had a rare disease and would die or be disabled if I didn't have surgery. I told him about the prostitution, told him I made a horrible mistake. I was so stupid to tell him about that, but I thought he'd help me. I thought that if I confessed, I'd be washed in the blood of the Lamb. I said I didn't know what to do or where to turn. He called me a sinner for conceiving children out of wedlock, for selling my body, for seeing a doctor, for questioning the healing power of faith, but I never did question that. I said I was praying for forgiveness, for the health of my babies, and he said it didn't matter, because I was already lost, and I couldn't be in his church anymore."

"Wasn't there something else you wanted to tell him? About your babies' father?"

Destiny Grace goes rigid. "No, sir. I don't know what you're talking about." The answer is too adamant, too hostile. I'll approach this another way in a moment.

"Is it fair to say that Reverend Jeremiah Tipple forsook you?" I ask.

Destiny Grace shrugs. "Not for me to judge. But I knew the Lord didn't forsake me. I prayed He'd save my twins."

Over on the prosecution side, neither Kerr nor Graham look impressed with this testimony; nor do they look unimpressed. If I were them, I'd think that Destiny Grace is a better witness than expected but not so good as to torpedo their case. I'd still expect to decimate her on cross-examination.

"Destiny Grace, you left Cole's Crossing when you learned the government prosecutors wanted to take you to court and force you to have the fetoscopy. Why'd you do that?"

"'Cause Judge Barraclough was going to make me and my babies have the surgery."

"You never gave me a chance, did you?" says Barraclough. "You just assumed I'm a biased judge with no principles."

She looks up at the judge with wide eyes. "Sorry, sir, but that's what I believed. Still do. My heavens, the deputy who came to my house to serve me with papers, he said y'all considered locking me up in jail so I wouldn't run—for the crime of pregnancy. Now I've been in jail for months and months without bond—for the crime of pregnancy." She drops her hands from the railing to her lap. "No, sir. No way would I let you force me to do anything to my babies. I was protecting them." She goes on to testify that, during her pregnancy, she lay flat on her back for most of the day, stayed hydrated, drank gallons and gallons of protein drinks, and prayed. "Oh, how I prayed. The Lord had other plans for Lydia and Brooklyn, though. They got to be in His arms right away." Her eyes fill with tears.

"Let's talk about Thomas Styles," I say. "The part where you told him you wanted to work for him because you might lose your house."

"I actually said my mother might lose her house. Mama has dreamed of owning that house in her own name. It belongs to the church, and Mama worked for the church and got to live there. Surprised they haven't evicted us yet." She looks at the jury. "My mother wanted to buy it and leave it to me, and before she got sick, she was saving to buy if the church would sell. But all that money went for medical bills. Right, Mama?"

"No dialogue, Ms. Harper," says Barraclough.

"Destiny Grace, Brooklyn and Lydia were conceived as a result of someone raping you," I say. "Isn't that what happened?"

The only sounds louder than the gasps and murmurs among the gallery are LeAnn's shocked, "Oh, my poor baby," and Kelsey Kerr's chortled, "You must be joking!" The judge's sharp glance at the district attorney does nothing to diminish Kerr's mask of disbelief.

Destiny Grace doesn't respond.

"Answer the question," I say. "You swore to tell the truth, so help you God."

The courtroom falls silent. Destiny Grace looks at me with an odd combination of fear and anger. I've boxed her in. "Yeah. I was raped."

"Who's the father of your twins, Destiny Grace? Who raped you?"

Barraclough leans forward in his chair, and the prosecutors straighten up in tandem. Destiny Grace gives a barely perceptible shake of the head, twists her shoulders to the right, and returns to repose. She crosses her arms. How twig-like her arms have become in the few weeks since I came to town. "I can't talk about that. He'll kill my mother and me."

"Destiny Grace, I know you're scared. So I'll answer the question for you."

Her eyes widen in panic.

"No one will harm you." My tone is softer than at any time during the trial. "This is out in the open. You're safe." I wave the papers in the air and, impersonating an Old Testament prophet calling down God's wrath, call out, "Judge Barraclough, I hold in my hand a certified copy of the results of what's known as a rapid DNA test, performed early this morning by Dr. Marie Jones of the Department of Forensic Sciences in Huntsville. The test compared the DNA of Brooklyn and Lydia Harper—their samples were taken during their autopsies—with the DNA taken from a blood sample of a male. I obtained that sample last night during a fistfight I had in the parking lot of the Quartz Inn." The incredulous titters from the gallery don't deter me. "Ms. Margaret Booth, my paralegal, will, when called to the witness stand, testify to the chain of custody of that blood sample. This document proves the twins' father is Clayton Tipple." I whirl around and point to the gallery. "Clayton Tipple—the man who raped Destiny Grace Harper!"

Clayton hollers, "You're a damn liar!"

Kelsey Kerr objects to "this carnival sideshow" and asks for a recess.

Destiny Grace shrieks, "No, Mr. Henderson, no! Why did you say that? Why did you?" and then curls into a seated fetal position, hard sobs racking her diminutive body.

Amid this heartbreak and tragedy and chaos, I can't help feeling triumphant. Isn't that just like a lawyer? Our profession exists to make sporting competition out of other people's problems.

The jurors look at Clayton Tipple, then at each other, then at me, and then at the judge, hoping someone will sort things out. Destiny Grace gets to her feet and says through her tears, "No. Please. Clayton didn't. He would never do that. Never. He loves me." She points toward the gallery. "It was Hunter." She tries to speak but makes a gagging noise, then composes herself and says in an eerily soft voice, "Hunter Tipple raped me."

Brandi Tipple gets up and scurries out of the room.

CHAPTER THIRTY-SEVEN

I ask the judge to clear the courtroom of everyone but the jury, court personnel, the attorneys and staff, and the defendant and her mother. I'm going to ask for details, and Destiny Grace's privacy interests require a closed courtroom.

Callie Rocha stands up and introduces herself as a reporter for the *Nashville Sentinel*. "Judge Barraclough, the First Amendment guarantees open access to the courts. We members of the media object to being excluded from your courtroom. If you won't let us stay, at least give us a chance to contact our attorneys so they can file a motion to permit access."

Other reporters nod in agreement. Ordinarily, I'd agree with Rocha. I've represented the media against judges who want to keep records and court documents confidential. Open access to the courts is crucial in a free society. But now, a woman's right to privacy trumps the First Amendment.

"The media has all the information it needs," I say. "There is no free-speech interest in hearing the salacious, disgusting details of a rape." Indeed, Rocha already has the information she needs. Thanks to my side of our information-sharing quid pro quo, she's already written the story about the rape, although she will need to replace *Clayton* with *Hunter*.

Barraclough ruminates for a moment. "Two media members can stay, one from print and one from electronic. Those two will pool their information with the others. Y'all are also usually sensitive to victims of sexual assault. I expect that'll continue here."

Rocha confers with her colleagues, and she and her friend Joanna Proctor of the *Southern Baptist Guardian* remain inside, while the other reporters exit.

"Judge Barraclough, I ask you to order Hunter Tipple to stay in the courtroom," I say. "The defense will call him as our next witness."

"Deputy Travis will make sure Mr. Hunter Tipple does not leave this room. His family members may remain in the courtroom or leave at their option."

All this time, Hunter sits, not even a tiny splotch of emotion on his ice-white cheeks. Clayton has twisted in his seat so that he's turned his back on his brother. He nervously flexes his large biceps.

I jump right into what will be a testimonial cesspool. "Destiny Grace, tell us what Hunter Tipple did to you."

She looks at LeAnn and then lets out a super sigh. "It wasn't long after I quit working for Tommy Styles, you know, doing . . ." She closes her eyes for a long time. "Sorry. This ain't easy." In a halting voice, she testifies how, late one afternoon, Thomas Styles told her to reclean room 533 because the guest was dissatisfied. She knocked on the door, waited, knocked on the door again, and opened the door with her master key. A man was sitting on the bed, his back to her. She excused herself and said she'd leave. He turned around—it was Hunter Tipple.

Destiny Grace takes several slow, rasping breaths. "I seen his eyes many, many times, of course, but for the first time I noticed how empty they were." She shudders, tries to continue, but can't. "Possible to get a drink of water?"

Deputy Travis brings her water. Destiny Grace gives him a pathetic, grateful smile. She clears her throat once, twice. "Hunter says . . ." She clears her throat again. "Hunter says, 'Tommy Styles told me about you.' I said I didn't know what he meant, but Hunter knew I was lying. Then he said . . ." She takes a sharp breath. "'You look like a twelve-year-old, you pretty girl. I've always liked you.'" Before Destiny Grace chokes up again, she manages to say she'd left the door open so she could wheel the cleaning cart inside, and when she fled, she bumped into the cart and tripped. "When I fell down, Hunter laughed."

Several jurors glower at Hunter.

"Was that the day of the rape?" I ask.

"No, sir. About a month later, August 3, a Tuesday. He snuck up on me in the hotel parking lot with a gun and drove me to the bend in Flint Creek, and that's where he did it, in his car. That's what happened."

"Anything else you can add?" The question provides Destiny Grace her last chance to control her own testimony before I take over.

"Not really, Mr. Henderson."

I move away from the podium. I'll have to torture Destiny Grace to possibly save her. "I know this is excruciating for you, and I'm so sorry to say this, but you're going to have to share more details with us—from the time you were abducted until the time you were released. What happened on Tuesday, August 3?"

She appeals to Barraclough, who looks away, and then she reaches for her water with a herky-jerky groping motion, upsetting the glass from its perch but managing to catch it before it topples to the ground and shatters. Much of the water spills on the floor.

"Take your time," says the judge.

Bailiff Travis brings Destiny Grace another glass of water and wipes up the spill. Eddie's small act of kindness seems to buoy her courage.

"I had to start work in the hotel at six thirty in the morning, so when I got to the Quartz Inn, it was still dawn, a little dark. I parked in the back row of the parking lot, bordering the wooded area. We had to park there and walk across the lot to the hotel. It was deserted—"

"Please slow down a bit, ma'am," says the court reporter, his voice both firm and kind. Since Destiny Grace started this part of her narrative, she looks only at me, not even glancing at the court reporter when he spoke to her. I sense that, if she looks at anyone else, she'll disintegrate.

"Yeah, sorry. So, like it—the parking lot, I mean—was deserted so early in the morning. I was getting out of my car when I heard something running in the woods. Thought it was a deer." She takes a modulating breath. "Out of nowhere, he was at my car window. He had a gun aimed at me." Her fluty voice is steady now.

"He, meaning . . . ?"

In an act of colossal courage, she points. "I mean him. Hunter Tipple. He had the gun."

In the nearly empty courtroom, Hunter's derisive chuckle reverberates, drawing a scathing glare from Barraclough.

Her voice trembling, Destiny Grace describes how Hunter drove her to an overlook above Flint Creek and ordered her to strip naked. She tried to reason with him, then pleaded with him, then became hysterical. When she began fighting, he pointed the gun at her, disengaged the safety, and forced her to get into the back seat.

"He used a condom," says Destiny Grace through clenched

teeth. "Acted like he was a real considerate gentleman when he made me put it on him, but I knew the real reason why—that way he wouldn't leave no DNA." She shakes her head, incredulous. "Guess it didn't turn out that way. Anyways, he made me put that thing on him, and he raped me." Her lower lip quivers, and I consider asking for a recess, but Destiny Grace continues. "When it was happening, he was humming "I Stand Amazed in the Presence," one of my favorite hymns, and I tried to drift away—Lord knows I had a lot of practice doing that—but his humming wouldn't let me escape." She says he wore too much cologne, which smelled spicy. "When it was over—he still had the gun lying close to his hand—he thanked me." She shakes her head in disbelief. "So polite, he thanked me. He got mad when I didn't say 'You're welcome.' So I said it."

I glance behind me. Hunter still sits impassive, almost blasé. Does Clayton have tears in his eyes?

After, Hunter got dressed and ordered Destiny Grace into the front passenger seat. She made a move to get her maid's uniform, which lay crumpled up on the floorboard, but he shook his head. He drove to the banks of Flint Creek and told her to get out of the car.

"What did you do?" I ask.

"I got out of the car. I was sure he was going to kill me right then, so I started crying again. I was gonna run or fight back some more when he said, 'Hush, little girl. Don't do anything foolish. It'll be all right. Just keep quiet about this and you'll be okay. We understand each other?' I said I understood. He made me get in the creek, wash myself from head to toe. More getting rid of evidence, I suppose. Anyway, I got out of the water, stood on the bank, and started forward, but he made me stay put. He tossed me two packages, wrapped in clear plastic as tight as you please. One was a towel and the other contained a Quartz Inn hotel maid's uniform, panties, bra, and shoes. Everything just my size. I dried off and got dressed in the new uniform. Then, so weird—well, it was all so weird and horrible—he got out a Bible, made me put my hand on it, and made me swear not to tell anyone what he did to me. Then he put his hand on the Bible and swore he'd kill both me and my mama if he found out I told a single soul."

"When Hunter threatened you and your mother, did you believe him?"

"I could see in his eyes he was telling the truth. He would hurt us. And get away with it. The Tipples are powerful. They got that girl, Shannon—she's another inmate—to attack me in the jail; I know it because she warned me to remember my promise. Then he drove me back to the parking lot. Before I opened the car door, he handed me two one-hundred-dollar bills, which I shoved in my pocket. I just wanted to get out of there. But I did get out of the car, and he sped away. I just went back to my maid's job, pretending nothing happened. About a half an hour later, I reached into the uniform pocket for something and found the bills. I'd forgotten all about them, just like I was trying to forget everything else that happened. That's when I broke into a million pieces, tore the money up, and threw it in the dumpster. I screamed, and I cursed God. Mr. Henderson, I never, ever cursed God in my whole life, not even when Mama got so sick or when I did those awful things for money. But that day, I cursed God, and then I prayed."

CHAPTER THIRTY-EIGHT

Barraclough offers Kerr a recess.

"No need, Judge," she says, already standing and tapping her fingers on the lectern. No doubt Kerr believes Destiny Grace made up the rape story, just as she believes Destiny Grace is a murderer.

"Would *you* like a recess, Destiny Grace?" asks Barraclough.

"No, sir. I want to get this over with."

Kerr slaps both hands on the lectern.

"Why would your best friend, Brandi Tipple, a God-fearing woman, come into court and perjure herself?"

Well, good. Kerr has lost her composure. She's foolishly asked an open-ended *why* question on cross-examination, all to put forth an argument that she should reserve for closing argument.

Destiny Grace looks at the jury. "Reverend and Mrs. Tipple hate me for bringing all this negative publicity down on their church. Or maybe they know what Hunter did to me and are trying to protect him by getting rid of me. Brandi's scared of her parents; she thinks her father has the Lord's ear and speaks to Him directly. She's even more afraid of her mother, who says the girl can't do nothing right. Brandi will do whatever her mother and father tell her to, I guess including lying about me."

"When you made the 911 call while you were in labor, you admitted guilt, didn't you?"

"I mentioned sinning, but I was talking about prostituting myself and doubting our church's gospel. I thought what happened to my babies was punishment for those sins. I wanted them to live. They would've started me on the path to my redemption."

Kerr glances at the jury. "You say you love Jesus, you took a vow of chastity, but you've had sex out of wedlock with how many men?"

I object, citing a provision in the Alabama evidence code prohibiting an attorney from questioning a complaining witness in a rape trial about her prior sexual history. The problem: this isn't a rape trial, and Destiny Grace herself is the defendant. Barraclough overrules the objection.

Red blotches stain her cheeks. "I don't know how many, exactly. Twenty, maybe, when I worked for Tommy Styles. Before that, I slept with some guys I dated. Yeah, I had sex. So what? Jesus still loves me."

One of the jurors who hasn't shown much affect during the trial, the stay-at-home mother with the communications degree, looks as if she wants to spit on Destiny Grace. So much for being rewarded for candor.

Kerr asks ever-more-intrusive questions—*Did Destiny Grace sleep with married men? Did she sleep with more than one at a time? Did she have sexual encounters with women?* With each question and answer, the splotches on Destiny Grace's cheeks grow an ever-brighter crimson, but she doesn't shrink from answering.

"Stop this, E," pleads Higgins. "This is a follow-up assault."

"She has to tell the whole truth. No matter how obnoxious the questions."

"Let's talk about this fairy tale about you being raped," says Kerr.

"Ain't a fairy tale, ma'am," says Destiny Grace. "It's the God's honest truth."

Kerr fires off the expected questions, establishing that, after the rape—Kerr keeps saying *alleged* rape—Destiny Grace didn't file a police report, didn't go to a hospital or a trauma center, didn't preserve evidence, and didn't tell anyone about the alleged assault.

Our side can't prove through Destiny Grace's testimony that Hunter Tipple raped her. We'll prove that another way.

"When you were arrested for murder, you never told the police that you were raped?" asks Kerr.

"No."

"The very first time you made this claim was here on the witness stand today?"

"It's not a claim, it's the truth."

"Didn't you have consensual sexual intercourse with Hunter Tipple because you enjoy sex?"

Destiny Grace visibly shudders and wraps her arms around herself. "No, ma'am, absolutely not. And there was nothing enjoyable about it. It was sickening, violent, horrible."

"Didn't you have consensual sexual intercourse with Hunter Tipple because you're a prostitute, and he was paying you for your services?"

"No, no. I told you, I refused him, and I'd already stopped doing that. Tommy Styles testified I stopped."

Kerr gives a feline smile. Destiny Grace is a trapped bird about to be consumed. "Thomas Styles said you quit working for *him*. What proof do you have, Ms. Harper, that you didn't keep working as a prostitute, that you didn't just go into business for yourself?"

"I didn't."

"More profitable that way, right? You wouldn't have to share your earnings with a pimp. What proof do you have that you stopped, ma'am?"

Destiny Grace tightens her grip around her torso. "Just my word, so help me God."

"Well, that's not worth anything, is it, Ms. Harper?"

Before I can object, Kerr withdraws the "question" and passes the witness. The judge calls a recess.

———

LeAnn Harper waylays me before I can join the others in our conference room. I've concluded I don't like her. She raised Destiny Grace under a certain belief system but didn't show full support when her daughter acted according to those beliefs. She reported her own daughter to the authorities. My uncle and I fought with each other, ignored each other, carped at each other, but if any third party came after me—the school administration, an unreasonable boss, Arlette Coyle's family—Buddy fought for me. Out of unspoken affection, family pride, or contrariness, Buddy battled. LeAnn Harper did not do the same for Destiny Grace. When LeAnn got sick, Destiny Grace sacrificed her ideals and her dignity to help her mother, who didn't return the favor.

"What is it, LeAnn?"

Her face comes within four inches of mine. She looks around to check if anyone is close enough to hear. Of course people are close enough to hear. Reporters and spectators and

Mildred Chilton have supernatural aural powers when it comes to secrets. I take LeAnn's arm and usher her to the corner of the room nearest the door to the judge's chambers.

"Make it quick."

"You know I did the accounting for the church. Certain financial transactions . . ." She starts breathing hard, and her cheeks turn the color of a sunset during Southern California fire season. "We used church funds to pay off some women to keep quiet about . . . about one of the Tipple sons' bad behavior. Hunter handled the finances, so . . ."

"You think he was covering up his own crimes?"

She nods.

"You *mis*used funds."

She nods again.

The provenance of her house—owned by the church—and her lavish furniture is clear. "Let me guess. You received . . . let's call them bonuses for your noble efforts on behalf of a rapist? And the right to live in the house."

She lowers her eyes.

"Who else knew about these payments? Jeremiah?"

"Only Hunter, from what I know. I . . . I negotiated with the women."

"I need names."

She identifies four woman who received payoffs for their silence. "I'll take the witness stand right after the break if that'll help."

"Your testimony would be inadmissible, LeAnn. I can't bring in evidence of past crimes—not without knowing more about what Hunter did. The time to have revealed this was before you and your church engaged in the cover-up. At some point, the cops will talk to these women."

"I didn't—"

"Yes, you did."

As I start toward our war room, she grabs my sleeve. "Mr. Henderson . . . Elvis. Do you have to tell Destiny Grace what I just told you?"

I do not like LeAnn Harper.

CHAPTER THIRTY-NINE

Hunter Tipple stares down at me with vacant blue eyes. He sits on the stand round-shouldered and anxious, frowning remorsefully for the venial and quintessentially male sin of visiting a prostitute. Jeremiah and Tamara Tipple's psychopathic eldest child has assumed a victim's pose.

Before summoning the jury, Barraclough advises Hunter of his rights, cautioning the man that, considering the serious criminal charges Destiny Grace has leveled against him, he has the right to remain silent and to hire an attorney.

"I have nothing to hide, Judge, and I do understand these rights. I'm an attorney." Yes—a foolish one who should retain a good criminal lawyer, who would undoubtedly advise Hunter to keep his big mouth shut.

As we wait for the jurors to come back, I say to Destiny Grace, "Whatever you do, keep your eyes glued to his. Even when he tries to stare you down and intimidate you, which he will. Promise me you'll keep your eyes on him."

She nods, then looks up at Hunter, gritting her teeth.

Once the jury is seated, I sidle up to the witness stand and get in Hunter's face. It's improper to get so close, but no one stops me. "You abducted and raped Destiny Grace Harper on the morning of August 3 of last year."

"No, I did not. We had consensual sex. I paid her two hundred dollars for it. You want to prosecute me, prosecute me for soliciting a prostitute."

"You're the father of Destiny Grace's twins?"

"I don't know if I am or not. I doubt it. We used a condom."

"You question the accuracy of DNA testing?"

The courtroom doors open, and Brandi Tipple comes back inside. Her crimson-rimmed eyes suggest intense crying.

Hunter watches his sister for a long time. Then he looks at me and, with a twisted smile on his lips, says, "What was the question, sir?"

I appeal to the court reporter not for help so much as for time for the jury to notice Hunter's incriminating smile.

Harold, like most court reporters, rereads the testimony in a monotone, as though every word were its own sentence. "Question: Do. You. Doubt. The. Accuracy. Of. DNA. Testing."

"DNA testing was created by the so-called medical establishment, so . . ."

"Are you denying you had sexual relations with Ms. Harper approximately nine months before she gave birth to her twins?"

"As you admitted yourself to Judge Barraclough a little while ago, when family members are involved in issues of paternity, you need more testing. Heck, sir—just a little while ago, you accused my brother of being the father, and you acted like you were totally certain of that."

Jeremiah Tipple thinks he's smarter than he really is, but he also knows he has limitations. Hunter thinks he's smarter than he is, but he doesn't recognize that he has any limitations, and that makes him a fool. "Mr. Tipple, are you suggesting your brother, Clayton, had sexual intercourse with Destiny Grace Harper during the same time frame you did?"

"I don't know one way or another what Clayton did with that girl. They dated in high school, and she was hanging around him before she got pregnant, trying to break up his marriage. Which she did. Things got so bad, my sister-in-law Becky moved out of the house." Hunter sneers at Destiny Grace. "Plus I told Clayton about Destiny Grace being a hooker, so maybe he bought her services around the same time I did."

Jurors squirm. Destiny Grace's labored breathing is audible from twelve feet away. She doesn't stop looking at Hunter.

"Did your brother, Clayton, commit adultery?"

"I don't know what Clayton did or didn't do."

"You broke your own chastity vow to God."

"You weren't asking about me, and I'm not a married man."

"Hunter, if you believe your brother might be the twins' father, does that mean you also think Jeremiah Tipple might be the twins' father? After all, his DNA would also closely match the real father's DNA."

Hunter's shriek/giggle reminds me of the siren-whistle on that old Bob Dylan recording Uncle Buddy loves so much, the one about God and Abraham and killing a son.

"A proper DNA test would tell you that's nonsense," he says. "Not that it's important to this case, because I didn't do anything to Destiny Grace that she didn't want me to do. I paid her, and it didn't happen in the woods. It happened in the hotel room where she turned tricks. And besides, none of this is relevant to whether she let her babies die. A woman can't give birth and get away with killing her babies by crying rape. If Destiny Grace would've had faith, hadn't sinned, her babies wouldn't have gotten sick. If she'd prayed and meant it, the Lord would've healed them, and they would be alive today. So, anyway, the answer is no. I mean, no, you don't need to test my father. Or my brother. I'm pretty sure, when the tests are in, they'll show I'm . . . So, yeah."

The jurors look like they're being forced to watch a vivisection. But there is a problem—as Ms. Curnow so pointedly told me, the fact of the rape could backfire. I just hope my appeal to the jurors' emotions trumps the flaws in the argument.

I turn toward the gallery. Clayton glares at his brother. Tammy appears as if she's in the middle of an astonishing nightmare. Brandi raises her head, opens her eyes, separates her palms, and nods at me. I understand what she wants. I doubt I should give it to her, but not for the first time I act against my better judgment.

"With the Court's permission, I'd like to suspend Hunter Tipple's examination so the defense can call another witness. We might not even need to recall him—unless the State wants to cross-examine him."

Kerr gives a sweeping shoulder-to-shoulder turn of the head, the better half of a headshake, but before she can object, Sabrina Graham says, "The State has no objection. We'll decide about cross-examining him later. Judge Barraclough, can you remind the witness that he's not to leave the courtroom?"

"You on board, Ms. Kerr?" asks Barraclough, a show of respect for the district attorney whose employee has just undercut her.

After a beat, a resigned Kerr says, "Why not?"

Destiny Grace regards me with a trusting expression, as if I have some grand plan. I do not.

CHAPTER FORTY

Hunter leaves the witness stand and takes an empty seat in the back of the room, on the aisle near the exit, which causes Bailiff Travis to go outside and bring in another deputy to guard the door.

"The defense calls Brandi Tipple," I say.

Tamara mouths a surprised "Wait" and grabs after her daughter, who shakes her off.

Brandi marches to the witness stand. I don't know what she'll say. Have I fallen for another trick? I hesitate, not sure how to approach her testimony.

Brandi rescues me. "Mr. Henderson, a little while ago, I . . ." She flinches and makes a noise that sounds like a cross between a squeak and a hiccup. "I'm sorry, I'm just so nervous, I was wondering . . ." She points toward the defense table. "Destiny Grace, could I borrow your Bible?"

Destiny Grace hands the Bible to Bailiff Travis, who gives it to the witness. Brandi clutches the book with both hands, like a child holding onto a safety bar during a roller-coaster ride. "When Destiny Grace testified about what Hunter did to her,

I had to leave the room. I thought of the Gospel of John. 'For the law was given through Moses; grace and truth came through Jesus Christ.' Jesus wants me to tell the truth."

I, myself, believe grace and truth come through the laws of mortals—but only if mortals apply those laws equitably and mercifully. Maybe Brandi and I will reach the same end point by taking different paths.

"I was lying when I testified against Destiny Grace. Hunter forced me to make up the story about her not wanting a scar. Destiny Grace was telling the truth when she said Hunter raped her."

"Everyone knows my sister is mentally challenged," shouts Hunter. "She lives in a fantasy world."

Deputy Travis struts over to Hunter and puts his hand on his holster. Hunter raises his hands in compliance.

"How do you know your brother raped Destiny Grace Harper?" I ask.

"Because Hunter once tried to do the same to me. I was fifteen. I screamed, and my brother Clayton came in and stopped him, beat him badly, said he'd tell my father if it happened again."

Kerr objects, arguing Brandi has improperly testified to Hunter's past bad acts. Barraclough overrules the objection. "The testimony goes to Hunter Tipple's motive for manufacturing evidence," he rules.

"Did Destiny Grace know what Hunter tried to do to you?"

"No, sir. No one else knew but . . ." Brandi kneads her fingers together and inhales. "Clayton said not to tell anyone. Said he'd handle Hunter. No reason to upset our parents."

"Ms. Tipple, did you deliver fifteen hundred dollars in cash to someone named Clara Blackwell?" This question results from Callie Rocha's investigation of the Blackwell family and the information she provided me as part of our quid pro quo arrangement. An intrepid reporter is Callie Rocha.

"Clara Blackwell is a church member, going through hard times. She needed grocery money. We take care of our own. I brought her some money to help her out."

"Did you know she bought a big-screen TV the day after you gave her the money?"

"No, but it don't matter to us what she bought. Reverend Tipple says we don't put strings on charity."

"Did you know that three days after you brought the money to Clara Blackwell, her cousin Shannon—an inmate in the Quartz County jail—attacked Destiny Grace Harper with a makeshift blackjack?"

Brandi's hand flies to her mouth. "Oh my goodness. Of course not. I don't know the cousin."

"Who asked you to bring the money to Clara Blackwell?"

"My brother Hunter Tipple." Brandi half-raises a hand. "Also, I want to say, Mr. Henderson, like . . . I helped Destiny Grace run off, and I did some midwifing."

"Miss Tipple, stop talking!" commands Barraclough. "What you say on this topic might subject you to criminal prosecution." A second Tipple sibling is informed of their Miranda rights.

"I understand what you're saying, Judge, but I know what Jesus has asked me to do," says Brandi. "If I go to jail because I tried to help Destiny Grace and the babies, so be it. We went to an abandoned cabin hidden in the woods not far from the Tennessee state line. I don't think anyone owns it. Destiny Grace found it. I tended to Destiny Grace as much as I could. At least two, three times a week, I brought her food, supplies, those protein drinks, and sports drinks. I saw her drink them with my own eyes, and I cleaned up the empty cans and bottles and bought more. She drank so much I thought she'd bust like an overfilled water balloon. Destiny Grace laid in the bed on her back until she almost went crazy. We prayed."

"But you weren't there when the babies were born, were you?"

"No, sir. The babies came early. I don't know what happened. It was the Lord's will that those babies died."

No, it wasn't God's will the babies died—it was the product of foolishness and superstition. But democracy and the Constitution protect the foolish and the superstitious. Such protection is the essence of democracy, Hazel Curnow once observed.

"I'm so sorry, Destiny Grace," says Brandi.

I pass the witness; Kerr has no questions. The judge calls a recess, and the jurors file out. Once the door leading to the jury deliberation room closes, Sabrina Graham gestures at Bailiff Travis. The sheriff's deputies handcuff Hunter Tipple, who looks at the cops the way a belligerent child looks at a reproachful parent.

CHAPTER FORTY-ONE

Before I left town back in the day, my uncle called me a coward. Now, the proverbial shoe is on the other foot—he is the coward. He didn't come forward on his own.

"The defense calls as its next witness Buddy Holly Henderson," I say.

Destiny Grace tries to get my attention. I ignore her. Margaret goes out into the corridor and escorts my uncle into the courtroom. Buddy is dressed for court in a blue work shirt and blue jeans. They're a bit crisper than usual, so he must've washed and ironed them in deference to the gravity of the occasion. He scowls at me, which doesn't mean he objects to being here—a scowl is his face in neutral gear.

Kerr objects on the grounds Buddy isn't on our witness list. Barraclough will have none of it.

"Sir, what do you do for a living?" I ask.

"I'm a retired chiropractor. I'm a holistic healer, mostly retired. I'm also a licensed midwife in the state of Alabama."

"Before I can ask my next question, Destiny Grace hands a Post-it note to Higgins, who in turn leans over and hands the paper to me.

"DON'T DO THIS!!!" reads the note.

I nod, fold the piece of paper, stick it in my pocket, and ask, "Mr. Henderson, we're related by blood, yes?"

"I'm under oath, so I have to admit to it, like it or not. You're my brother's son."

"You raised me from a pup after my parents left town without me?"

"You raised yourself, Elvis. I just made sure you didn't piss on fire hydrants and shit on the neighbor's lawn."

"Watch your language, sir," says Barraclough. Does the judge recall his bungled prosecutorial attempt to throw Buddy in prison for conduct now legal in many states and largely tolerated everywhere else?

"Strike the word *shit* and replace with the word *poop*, Harold," says Buddy to the court reporter.

Barraclough doesn't appreciate the laughter. I'm not sure Buddy does either.

"How did you become a licensed—is it midhusband?"

"It is not. I'm a midwife. Not so unusual. It's a caring approach and good practices that matter for most expectant mothers, not the caregiver's gender. Some people, many women, might think what I do is creepy, but in the end my patients don't."

I ask about the requirements for becoming a licensed midwife in Alabama.

"You gotta be over twenty-one years old. That was an easy one for me. A citizen of the United States. Born in Alabama, and I served in the illegal Vietnam War. Then you need a Certified Professional Midwife credential, which I earned five years ago."

I hesitate for a moment, deciding how to formulate my next question. Buddy helps me out. "Elvis, aren't you going to ask me why I became a midwife?"

"I am now."

My uncle always craved the bully pulpit. He sits up and pontificates to the gallery and occasionally the jury. "This state made midwifery illegal for decades for reasons of pure racism. Congress abolished the importation of slaves into the United States in 1808. A joyous occasion? Not for those already enslaved. The evil planters needed more slaves to earn profits. No more Black people could be . . . 'imported' into this country, so the slave population depended on a high birth rate. The oppressors turned to the established medical establishment—meaning White males—to make sure it happened. White doctors supplanted the traditional midwives, who'd treated expectant mothers bound in slavery with compassion, with respect for their spiritual beliefs and their physical needs. I'm sure it won't surprise you that most Southern doctors didn't treat slaves with compassion. That stayed true for a hundred years after the Civil War. Modern medicine was forced on poor and Black women by a controlling establishment. Midwives provided care that White male doctors wouldn't. So states like Alabama tried to force midwives out of existence by making the profession illegal. When the practice became legal again in 2017, there weren't enough licensed midwives to go around. I'm an old White male, but there's a shortage of midwives in Alabama, so I'm filling a need until I'm no longer needed."

"Are you familiar with a structure off Pioneer Lane that might be called a log cabin?"

He sits back. "It was your home for the first four years of your life. It's been vacant since your parents skipped town and left you with me. I tried to take you back there a few times after they left, but I could tell when we approached that you thought they'd be there. It was too painful. So I just ignored the place, and you forgot about it. Didn't see a point in mentioning it when you got older. Traumatic and, besides, it's a worthless shack in the woods. I guess now it's all yours if you want it."

A recollection from pre-abandonment—I lived in a pioneer *log cabin*. Buddy Henderson had to know something about the place. So I subpoenaed him—and discovered the truth.

"And yes, I let Destiny Grace Harper hide there," adds my ever-impatient uncle. "I read online about the district attorney's attempt to force Destiny Grace to undergo a procedure on her unborn twins and how Destiny Grace ran off to avoid the hearing. Then I got a call from Lillian Wagers. Lillian was the midwife for the Church of Our Lord's Rapture. Kind and generous woman despite her kooky religious beliefs. She was a mentor to me. Until she was murdered."

Over the gallery noise, Barraclough admonishes the jury to ignore the part about murder, but I doubt that's possible.

"Lillian asked me whether I could help Destiny Grace with a problem multiple pregnancy," says Buddy. A matter-of-fact shrug. "The law requires that a doctor handle those, and Lillian wouldn't do anything illegal. But I would. So I helped. I hid Destiny Grace in the log cabin, I helped with the pregnancy, and I begged her daily to have the fetoscopy—until it was too damn late for the procedure to succeed."

"Did you see Destiny Grace after you gave her permission to use the log cabin?"

"Many times. I attended to her. I brought her food and drink; I made sure she had the recommended bed rest. When she went into early labor, she called me, and I came running. We didn't want Brandi to be there. What I was doing was illegal, and Brandi couldn't handle an arrest and conviction. I could."

"Why illegal? You're a licensed midwife."

"Like I said, in Alabama, midwives can't attend to multiple births or problem pregnancies. This was both."

Barraclough Mirandizes yet another witness. "You've been read your rights, Mr. Henderson. Do you want to continue?"

"He does not," says Destiny Grace.

When Buddy sends her an avuncular smile the likes of which I've never seen, it occurs to me it was a shame he didn't get to raise a niece.

"Destiny Grace shouldn't be sitting in this courtroom," says Buddy. "She should never have served a day in jail."

Barraclough sustains Kerr's objection and instructs the jury to disregard the commentary.

"Mr. Henderson, what was Destiny Grace's attitude toward her twins?" I ask.

He closes his eyes for a moment and lets out a weary sigh. *Oh, Buddy, how old you look.*

"Destiny Grace was obsessed with meeting Brooklyn and Lydia. Talked about it so much she was getting on my nerves. I'm not always a patient man. She'd speak to those babies for minutes on end, would leave her hand on her belly like pregnant mamas do when they comfort the little ones. I witnessed her praying for their health. She loved them."

"How do you feel about relying on prayer to cure illness without going to a doctor?"

"It's hoodoo. I believe in natural methods of healing, sure, but I also believe in doctors when necessary. But Destiny Grace was a true believer. I've been around long enough to know I wasn't going to talk her out of her beliefs."

"Tell us about the twins' birth."

Buddy's eyes flood with tears. I've never seen him cry. "Oh, man, this isn't easy. A dark, dark day. The babies suffered from the afflictions the medical professionals predicted they would. Still, we humans are always surprised when miracles don't happen. I told Destiny Grace I was going to call 911 whether she liked it or not. She said she didn't want to get me in trouble, so she made the call. While she was on the phone, I delivered the big baby, Brooklyn. Stillborn. My attempts to rouse her failed. Then little Lydia came, real fast, within five or six minutes, and she moved. But she wouldn't cry, and I tried all the techniques I'd been taught—mouth-to-mouth, patting her back, everything, but she wouldn't breathe, and she eventually died."

Destiny Grace weeps softly. I press forward so I don't become emotional myself. "How long did Lydia live?"

"Five minutes. At the most. We gave up trying to save her after ten minutes or so."

"You're certain both babies were dead when you left?"

"One thousand percent. I had to get Destiny Grace to stop trying to revive the tiny one. And that's when I made another mistake."

"Which was?"

Sweat droplets form on his brow. He wipes his forehead with his shirtsleeve. "Destiny Grace said she'd already affronted the Lord in so many other ways, and she begged me to take her away so the EMTs wouldn't force her to go to the hospital. She truly believed a hospital visit would be sinful. More than that, I think she wanted to die because of what happened. I took pity on her and brought her to my house. But she needed medical care. She finally agreed to go to the hospital, but only if I dropped her off and left so I wouldn't get into trouble. I did what she asked. I'm not proud of it, but I was afraid. I didn't want to get arrested."

"If you believed Destiny Grace was wrongfully accused, why didn't you come forward before this? Why did I have to subpoena you?"

"First of all, Destiny Grace made me swear I wouldn't jeopardize my freedom."

"Not a very good explanation," I say, and now I'm speaking for myself and not as Destiny Grace's attorney.

He doesn't take his eyes off me, but a haze forming over his pupils signals embarrassment—and remorse. "I feared going to prison. I still do. I believed when you took over as Destiny Grace's lawyer, you'd win an acquittal without my involvement. I've followed your career. You do good work. All that's a piss-poor excuse for me not doing the right thing."

I've had my hands resting on the lectern for a while, and now I drop them in a mixture of surprise and frustration. If he'd come forward earlier, this trial might never have happened.

"Why do you think you're here, Elvis?" volunteers Buddy. "Coincidence? *I* recommended that Destiny Grace hire Hazel Curnow, which meant hiring you. I thought if things went in the wrong direction, I could come forward afterwards, and Destiny Grace would get a new trial." He looks down at his hands, which are folded in his lap, as if he's just discovered their existence. "Then you subpoenaed me, so . . . thanks for giving me the opportunity to finally do the right thing." He looks at Barraclough and then at the district attorneys. They very well might arrest him, but not today.

I pass the witness.

Kerr ambles to the lectern, her mouth pressed together in a tight, contemplative frown. "Mr. Henderson, you believe the defendant, Destiny Grace Harper, should've had the laser procedure to save her babies, don't you?"

"I do. Because she wanted those babies so much, it was crazy for her not to have the procedure. Which was what I told her every time I saw her for as long as the procedure could still be effective."

"You also knew there was a warrant out for her arrest for her failure to appear at a court hearing?"

"I did."

"Yet you helped the defendant evade arrest."

"Yes. You and your office were wrong to try to force her to have the procedure."

"You were an advocate of abortion way back in the early seventies before the Supreme Court decided *Roe v. Wade* in 1973, weren't you?"

Kerr's on a fishing expedition, but the problematic fish in Uncle Buddy's historical pond are plentiful.

Barraclough overrules my valid objection.

"I was an early advocate of a woman's right to choose. I was a civil rights activist and an opponent of the Vietnam War after I left the army."

"As a so-called chiropractor, did you perform or help procure illegal abortions for women prior to 1973?" asks Kerr.

This time Barraclough sustains my objection on relevancy grounds. I do wonder how Buddy would answer. If I ask him later, I doubt he'll tell me—we don't have such conversations.

CHAPTER FORTY-TWO

After a ninety-minute break, a desperate Kelsey Kerr calls one rebuttal witness—the Reverend Jeremiah Tipple. Trying to turn the witness stand into a makeshift pulpit, he preaches. He tells us how the scripture provides that the body heals only through prayer *and* faith, not prayer alone. He insists that Destiny Grace flouted the church's teachings, which made her a nonbeliever. He maintains that her immoral behavior was antithetical to faith in God and that her decision to flee rather than to defend her beliefs in a court of law proves her lack of sincerity. All his testimony serves a single purpose—saving his church's sullied reputation.

"Do you believe your son sexually assaulted Destiny Grace Harper?" asks Kerr.

Up on the bench, Barraclough sets down his pen. I could successfully object, but I want the jury to hear this.

"I do not. Hunter is a devout man. He'll succeed me as pastor someday."

"But your daughter, Brandi, testified that Hunter tried to assault *her*. She testified that your other son, Clayton, stopped it."

"I don't know what happened, but it must've been a misunderstanding. Sometimes my daughter gets things wrong, and Clayton can be a hothead. Brandi has a lot of misguided loyalty to Destiny Grace, so there's that too."

Kerr quits, apparently satisfied with this testimony, but Graham has her chin cradled in her hands and her eyes closed—not a good look for the jury.

I approach the witness. "Did you just call your daughter and your younger son liars so you could protect your eldest son, Reverend?"

"That's not what I said, Elvis. I said my daughter sometimes misunderstands things."

"She misunderstood a sibling's attempt to sexually assault her? And your younger son, Clayton, is a hothead who also misunderstood?"

Tipple doesn't react, and I end the cross-examination. I don't dare ask whether he agrees that Destiny Grace did the right thing in refusing the medical procedure on the twins. He'll just use the opportunity to call her a whore and a liar whose babies got sick and died because she doesn't believe in God.

He stands down and approaches his family. Before he can reach them, Tamara motions for Brandi and Clayton to stand up, and the three of them hurry out of the courtroom, leaving Jeremiah behind.

CHAPTER FORTY-THREE

Barraclough excuses the jury for the remainder of the day, and Destiny Grace returns to jail. As soon as the jurors clear out, I make a motion for judgment of acquittal on the grounds that there's not enough evidence to convict—the technical term for asking the judge to boot the case out of court. Even judges who believe such a motion has merit rarely grant them. They generally send the case to the jury anyway, hoping for a not-guilty verdict. That way, if the freed defendant later commits a crime, the judge won't get the blame. Only the rare courageous judge will spare an innocent defendant the trauma of jury deliberation. Merle Barraclough isn't one of those rare courageous judges.

"The motion is denied," he says.

"Can you at least give us the reasons for your ruling? You heard Buddy Henderson's testimony. Complete exoneration." The words are not mine but Aruna Higgins's.

"I won't give a reason because I'm not required to," says Barraclough.

The judge's reply blasts Higgins right out of her seat. "The ruling is unfair, Judge. But that's not a surprise. You've been ruling unfairly since before this trial even started, when you tried to bar Mr. Henderson from acting as defense counsel. No, you've been ruling unfairly since the day you denied bail and made Destiny Grace Harper—who's a victim, not a criminal— languish in jail for months while you went hunting and drank your bourbon and barbecued."

"Stop talking and sit down, counsel!" growls Barraclough.

"Take a deep breath, Aruna," I say. "Take three deep breaths."

I might as well have asked a brakeless bulldozer to stop rolling downhill.

"The defense objects to a narrow-minded, boomer White male—"

"Judge, may I have a moment to confer with my colleague?" I ask, stepping forward and doing the best I can to interpose my body between Higgins and the judge's bench. "It's been a long day." Attorneys can become unhinged at the end of a trial, but I didn't expect Higgins to tear away from the jamb. She said nothing I wouldn't like to say myself, but we need this judge to make rational rulings, and she's going to antagonize him beyond repair—and get herself thrown in jail to boot.

"You'd better do more than confer, Elvis," says Barraclough. "You'd better convince her to shut her mouth." I can think of few judges who would let an attorney get away with the insults Higgins has hurled at him. He clearly doesn't want to harm her career.

"Do not continue on this potholed road, Aruna," I say. "He *will* hold you in contempt; he should've done it already. He jailed me for less. We need you in court tomorrow."

She pulls her shoulders back and says in a lowered voice, "Actually, Elvis, I'm just tomorrow's window dressing. A young, local female lawyer of color who sits quietly and looks pretty and diverse while you do all the work."

"Window dressing is the last thing you've been and the last thing you'll be. Trust me. We need you in court tomorrow. More accurately, Destiny Grace needs you. Please."

Higgins responds with a brusque "Yeah, okay" and takes her seat again. She doesn't apologize to Barraclough.

The lawyers on both sides endure a grueling afternoon arguing points of law about the critical instructions that the judge will deliver to the jury tomorrow morning. Then we leave the courthouse. I drive right past the Quartz Inn and merge onto the interstate.

"Where are you going?" asks Margaret.

"There's a Mexican restaurant just outside of Greenfield—Rosita's, about a twenty-minute drive. My favorite when I was a kid. My uncle would always order a Cadillac margarita or three."

"We don't have time. And you shouldn't drink. You've got to get ready for closing arguments."

"Oh, we have all the time in the world tonight, Margaret."

She thinks this over. "Smart move, E. Will you send the text, or shall I?"

CHAPTER FORTY-FOUR

A somber group files into the jury box. In a matter of hours, they'll begin deliberating over Destiny Grace Harper's fate. The four men wear jackets, and two of them, the construction worker and the rental car mechanic, wear ties for the first time. The veterinary technician, who wept during Brandi Tipple's second session on the witness stand, has applied makeup. The romance writer, a compulsive notetaker, flips through her notepad.

Late yesterday, Barraclough granted our request that he make an exception to the local rule that a jail inmate may only have a single set of clothing for court. Destiny Grace wears a blue dress LeAnn Harper found in the closet and altered to fit her daughter's diminished physical stature. Despite the alterations, the dress consumes Destiny Grace. I wear a charcoal-gray Fresco wool suit with no lining—it's still hot outside—and a traditional burgundy-striped necktie. I tie my hair back in a bun, so when I face someone, it appears I have a short haircut. I wear my tortoiseshell glasses rather than contact lenses because I couldn't sleep last night, and my eyes burn. No bolo ties or unusual accessories. This isn't the day to distract the jurors.

After all these years in practice, I still can't understand why the law uses legalese to instruct juries. Ten-year lawyers often can't navigate the nooks and crannies of the obscure instructions. At least Barraclough converses with the jurors. Too many judges read *at* them. He tells them capital murder includes the intentional murder of a person less than fourteen years of age or of more than one victim. He instructs the jury on what the law calls *lesser included offenses*—a smorgasbord of crimes of decreasing severity: second-degree murder if Destiny Grace showed "extreme indifference" to the lives of her twins, manslaughter if she recklessly caused their deaths.

Because the prosecution has the burden of proof, Kerr and Graham get the first and last words. Kerr will give Alabama's closing statement and then a rebuttal to our closing. Ordinarily she's well kempt, but today her blouse is untucked, and a strand of hair has escaped her tight bun, even though we've just started the day. Graham whispers to Kerr, who tucks in the blouse and fixes the hair before starting her summation.

"Members of the jury, we all agree that, if Destiny Grace Harper had the fetoscopic procedure, there was a 90 percent chance one or both of her babies would've lived. Without the surgery, the odds were 90 percent they would die. They did die. Exactly what the defendant wanted. She wanted her babies to die."

Kerr goes over the science behind TTTS and the miracle that is fetoscopy yet again. She levels a finger at Destiny Grace. "This callous, soulless woman was given a divine gift, yet here she sits, childless after refusing a gift from God. Why? Because she *intentionally* killed her babies." The chief prosecutor shakes her head in feigned astonishment. "If the dreadful medical odds of survival without surgery weren't low enough, the defendant did her best to lower them more. She didn't have a doctor at the babies' birth. No, she broke the law again and had a retired chiropractor at her side during a complicated birth of at-risk multiples."

Kerr's forehead glistens—literal sweat of the brow that makes her performance even more effective. "Lydia and Brooklyn—immaculate human beings. We can't say the same for their mother. She comes into this courtroom and invokes the Bible and Jesus as her excuses for committing the capital murder of two innocent babies; she claims to follow Jesus as her Lord and Savior; she claims her gospel counsels against medical care. Yet she carries a scar from a medical operation that a medical doctor performed at a Huntsville hospital. She took her mother to medical doctors for cancer treatment. Where's her faith in healing prayer? She doesn't have it and didn't have it. She's trying to excuse double murder.

"You heard the testimony—Destiny Grace Harper sold her body for money. She admits it. *She worked as a prostitute.* Ladies and gentlemen, actions speak louder than words, and the defendant didn't act like someone who's accepted Jesus Christ as her Lord and Savior. Her appeal to religion as a reason to avoid conviction is a bald-faced lie. She believes only in herself, in her own convenience, in her own pleasure." Slowing her pace, Kerr cites the testimony of Thomas Styles, Destiny Grace herself, and even LeAnn Harper. "Actions speak louder than words, members of the jury. Destiny Grace Harper's actions prove beyond a reasonable doubt she wanted her babies to die. She accomplished her evil goal.

"Now, what will Elvis Henderson say when he stands up when I'm finished talking to y'all? His arguments will boil down to this: it was fine and dandy to let baby Lydia and baby Brooklyn die so that defendant Harper wouldn't be inconvenienced. Because that's what the fetoscopy was for Harper: an inconvenience." Kerr engages the jurors one by one. "Now, I also expect

Mr. Henderson will argue that, because the defendant's twins were conceived as the result of a rape, she had the right to murder them. He won't use those words, but that's what he'll mean. That, of course, is not God's law, nor is it the law of the state of Alabama. You know what? The rape, if it really happened, gave the defendant a strong motive for murdering her babies.

"You'll also, I'm sure, hear about how easy it is to drive to another state to have an abortion, and that the defendant would've done that if she truly didn't want the twins. That dog just won't hunt, members of the jury. Let's say the reason she didn't abort the babies was fear, or delay, or denial because of the rape, or a concern for her reputation. Then she learns she's carrying twins suffering from TTTS. She learns the babies will die if she does nothing. In Destiny Grace Harper's mind, the TTTS wasn't a tragedy. The TTTS was the murder weapon. And it doesn't matter whether, in the days before the birth and death of Brooklyn and Lydia, the defendant prayed and lay on her back and sipped protein drinks. The defendant's no fool. You don't stop a bullet by trying to block it with a thick winter coat, and you don't stop TTTS by drinking milkshakes, and she knew it. That, members of the jury, is murder, beyond a reasonable doubt. The one thing every human being has in common is that we're going to die someday. But Brooklyn Harper and Lydia Harper never got a chance to live, and they didn't have to die the horrible way they did; they shouldn't have died at all. This case will soon be in your hands. The legacies of Brooklyn Harper and Lydia Harper are in your hands."

CHAPTER FORTY-FIVE

Barraclough says, "Mr. Henderson."

Aruna Higgins claims the lectern, which causes an electric hum in the gallery.

Barraclough's wiry eyebrows stretch toward the ceiling. "Oh. Ms. Higgins?"

"Thank you, Judge Barraclough." Higgins lengthens her spine, the posture of a lawyer making sure not to slouch at the beginning of the most important argument of her legal career. Self-conscious, yet at the same time authentic, and this jury needs authenticity.

Which was why I realized yesterday that Higgins should handle the closing. Though I was born and raised only a few miles from this building, I'm an out-of-towner. I'm a male. The jury now knows my uncle is a crucial witness. Until yesterday, I still wasn't sure that Aruna Higgins had the passion, commitment, or guts to take the lead. My view changed when she stood up to Barraclough.

Margaret approved. So did Ms. Curnow, according to Margaret, especially because Curnow is still upset at me for calling

Destiny Grace to the stand. "A severe lapse in judgment," she says. She believes that Uncle Buddy's testimony would've been enough to exonerate Destiny Grace. I disagree, because before the testimony about the sexual assault, the jury *did* hate Destiny Grace. The truth of her ordeal humanized her. I made the right decision calling our client to the stand for another reason— without the rape testimony, Brandi Tipple would never have recanted and told the truth.

Only Destiny Grace had reservations about Higgins handling closing argument. Why did she bother to hire our firm if Higgins was going to shoulder the final burden, she asked? She'd fired Higgins. I convinced her to take our advice anyway. I'm a good advocate.

Higgins smooths out her jacket. "Members of the jury, we aren't speaking about minor inconvenience to Destiny Grace Harper, as the district attorney would have you believe. We're talking about whether the government had the right to bind Destiny Grace's hands and feet and strap her to a gurney. We're talking about whether the State had the right to inject into her veins—against her will—a drug that would knock her unconscious. Imagine what kind of force it would take to inject a struggling pregnant woman with anesthesia and make a laser cut in her body and in the bodies of her unborn babies. That's what the State wanted to do when it tried to use the court system to force Destiny Grace to have the surgery." Much of a trial is a battle over semantics. The prosecution calls fetoscopy a *procedure*. Our side prefers the more ominous *surgery*.

"You know what, members of the jury? What the State wanted to do to Destiny Grace Harper sounds a lot like rape. You heard Dr. Panman give hard statistics showing how the courts aren't always right. You heard him say women should be able to trust their doctors and not have to fight them. Destiny

Grace said no to a violation of her body, and she had every right to say no. That's what the American College of Obstetricians and Gynecologists says, the top organization of experts in the field. A pregnant woman who says no to a government forcing surgery on herself and her baby has the right to be heeded. A woman who says no to the government's violation of her body isn't a murderer. That is not the law. And you should come back with a verdict of not guilty for that reason alone, without bothering with the issue of religion."

Higgins goes to the lectern to check her notes. I wouldn't have brought notes to the lectern, but better Higgins use a crutch than stumble. "Do you know, members of the jury, in 1985, the US Supreme Court held that a robbery suspect couldn't be forced to have surgery to remove a bullet lodged under his skin, even though the bullet could've proved the wounded man had committed a crime? And yet, Ms. Kerr—"

"Whoa, that's legal argument, not proper summation," says Kerr.

She's right. Long before Margaret and I became involved in the defense, Higgins argued these exact judicial opinions to the judge in an effort to get the case thrown out. The judge refused. Once that happened, these opinions became irrelevant until an appellate court addresses the issue. The jury decides the facts, not the law.

Higgins didn't run this part of her closing by me. And yet, maybe Higgins is onto something worth salvaging. I doubt Barraclough will go for it, but worth a try.

"May we approach the bench, Your Honor?" I ask. Requesting a bench conference mid-argument is a horrible look to the jury, especially so because I'm stepping in on behalf of a junior attorney. But it has to happen.

Barraclough beckons us forward with a liver-spotted hand.

"These cases go to the defendant's mens rea," I say. *Mens rea* is Latin for that illusive concept of "intent." "Every person is presumed to have knowledge of the law, including the defendant, so the existence of these cases goes to the issue of Ms. Harper's intent to commit murder. She's presumed to know that the law would not hold her actions murderous and therefore could not have had intent to kill." My argument is drivel, and the judge knows it, but when Kerr starts to point that out, Barraclough waves her off. "Run with it, Aruna. But not too far."

Kerr and Graham stomp away, both shaking their heads. Not much they can do about Barraclough's highly questionable decision—the prosecution can't appeal an acquittal under our system of justice, even if the judge made an error of law. The constitutional right against double jeopardy—the right not to be tried twice—prevents that.

I leave the bench heartened, but by the time I reach my chair, I'm worried. Judges often decide disputed legal issues in the expected loser's favor to diminish the likelihood that a higher court will throw out the jury's verdict based on judicial error. Maybe Barraclough made such a warped ruling in our favor because he expects us to lose.

Higgins returns to the lectern. "Here's what one court said in refusing to force a murder suspect to have surgery: 'A substantial intrusion into a defendant's body, without his consent, involving pain, trauma, and risk of serious complications, is offensive.' Members of the jury, if a suspected murderer has the constitutional right to avoid coerced surgery, a twenty-one-year-old pregnant rape victim should be accorded the same rights to protect her body."

Of course, the suspected murderer in that earlier case wasn't pregnant.

Higgins rests an arm on the lectern to let the point sink in and then addresses the gritty evidentiary details regarding what she calls Destiny Grace's catastrophic and heartbreaking journey from rape victim to political prisoner.

"The State has had months and months to provide evidence of intent to murder; they've come up with zilch, much less proved their case beyond a reasonable doubt. There's only evidence Destiny Grace Harper didn't believe in medicine but did everything in her power, short of surgery, to keep her babies alive. That's true from the start of the pregnancy to its finish. Recall Brandi Tipple's testimony—her *truthful* testimony, which she gave despite the risk of criminal prosecution. Recall LeAnn Harper's testimony. Recall Buddy Henderson's testimony. He, too, risked going to prison to come forward and tell the truth. Let's take a step back and think like reasonable people, which the district attorney hopes you won't do. Destiny Grace was raped and got pregnant. If she didn't want those babies, she would've gotten in her car, driven to another state, and had an abortion, and no one would've been the wiser.

"How low does the prosecution stoop? As a woman, I'm sickened and shocked by this, especially because the prosecution team consists of two women. They couldn't stop talking about Destiny Grace's sex life, using it to attack her credibility about her faith. Y'all know what that's called, members of the jury? *Slut shaming.* The shame isn't on Destiny Grace Harper. The shame is on the prosecution for treating a sexual assault victim that way." She wags an index finger at the prosecution table and spins back toward the jury. "Famous male religious figures and supposedly squeaky-clean politicians have had sordid sexual affairs exposed, cavort with prostitutes, father children out of wedlock—or father children with married women who aren't their wives. Yet those men are soon forgiven, their boo-hoo crocodile tears of contrition viewed as a sign of moral courage and heavenly redemption. Oh, how we like to forgive those not-always-holy men. Not so with women, in power or out of it. Destiny Grace was a mother who, upon instinct and faith, tried to protect her unborn twins the best way she knew how, consistent with her upbringing—with prayer and without intervention from the medical establishment. Sure, most of us might've made a different choice about the treatment, but that doesn't mean Destiny Grace is a murderer. No, ma'am; no, sir; she's the victim here, many times over. The victim of sexual assault; the victim of gross slander of her character; the victim of an overzealous prosecutor throwing her into jail and prosecuting a grieving mama who lost her darling babies to a rare and terrible disease. Destiny Grace named the twins—*Lydia and Brooklyn*. She spoke to them as she carried them in her womb; she wanted to meet them."

Several jurors nod.

"For all her human flaws, Destiny Grace Harper is a woman of God who prayed for the lives of her babies. The prayer went unanswered. So, so sad. I will leave you, jury members, with this from the book of Amos. 'But let justice roll down as waters, and righteousness as a mighty stream.' I implore y'all to let justice roll down like waters and come back with a verdict of not guilty. That's the righteous decision."

Kerr goes to the lectern for rebuttal, and I worry she'll steal victory. She doesn't, just largely repeats the same arguments. You get to a stage in a trial where there's nothing left to say.

Barraclough delivers some final technical instructions about picking a foreperson and asking questions of the judge, and then he sends the jury off to the deliberation room with the words, "Ladies and gentlemen, you may finally discuss this case. The decision is in your hands."

CHAPTER FORTY-SIX

Margaret Booth, LeAnn Harper, and I haunt the nearly empty courthouse, waiting in our windowless war room. The media members have left. I miss Callie Rocha. The courtroom clerk will call the reporters when the jury reaches a verdict and give them time to get to court. Higgins works on other matters but stays close.

I don't believe the lawyers' myth that a protracted jury deliberation favors the defendant. I've both won and lost trials after several hours and after several grueling weeks. So far, this jury has deliberated for three and a half days.

I avoid LeAnn. She doesn't seem to mind. Not once has she thanked us.

There's nothing heavier than the oppressive weight of not knowing. Why, oh why, don't law schools teach a course on how to cope with endless waiting? Margaret is as anxious as I am—worse. She continually paces, sits down and hops up, walks to the conference room door and back, taps fingernails on her table, and clicks the mouse of her dormant computer. I sit in one spot in a kind of torpor, as the doubt about my trial performance, coupled with a previous night of pulled pork and hush puppies, ravages my esophagus. I'm too anxious to get much work done on our other cases.

"Please sit, Margaret, or go out in the hall."

"Yeah, sorry, E." She sits for ninety seconds, gets up, and begins pacing again.

LeAnn spends most of her time in a far corner, reading a book by the juror who writes romance novels.

"I like romances—Kristan Higgins, Nora Roberts," says Margaret. "Any good?"

"Only if you enjoy reading about naive girls in their early twenties who fall for bad boys in their late twenties," replies LeAnn. "You can tell when the good boys show up, because they have all taken chastity vows. This trash is making me sick." Yet she keeps turning the pages.

Hours pass.

Margaret fiddles with her smartphone. She gasps.

My guts shrink like over-grilled pork chops.

"Have they reached a verdict?" I shout after a few seconds.

LeAnn exclaims, "Oh my lord."

Margaret points her right index finger skyward in the universal signal for *give me a fucking second*. She looks away from the phone, hurries over, grabs my arm, and pulls me toward the door.

"It's about a matter having nothing to do with this case, LeAnn," says Margaret. "Sorry to alarm you."

We move out of earshot.

"The standard DNA test," says Margaret. "It came back—"

"It's not Hunter?"

"No, I mean, yeah, Hunter is the father of Destiny Grace's babies. Totally. The other test. Arlette Coyle's fetus. There's a match."

Before I can make sense out of the words on the screen, Eddie Travis walks in. "The jury has reached a verdict."

CHAPTER FORTY-SEVEN

We take our places. The gallery is packed. Except for the sounds of human respiration, the courtroom has fallen silent. Callie Rocha sits beside her media colleagues, her pen and notepad at the ready and her smartphone balanced on her lap. Kerr and Graham wear matching gazes fixed on a point on the wall. Graham keeps pushing her glasses up her nose. Kerr knocks, knocks, knocks her knuckles on the table.

The jury files into their box. Several of the jurors look our way. One of the NASA widows cracks a slight smile. Jurors who return a guilty verdict don't often make eye contact with the defense team, much less smile. I give Destiny Grace a reassuring nod.

Mildred Chilton's phone buzzes. I flinch.

Barraclough takes the bench. "You have a verdict, is that correct, ladies and gentlemen of the jury?"

"We do, Your Honor," says the romance writer—now Madame Foreperson. Higgins gives a side-eyed glance.

Barraclough again: "Is your verdict unanimous?"

"Yes, Your Honor."

Destiny Grace grasps my hand, and although her small hand is lost in mine, her grip is so tight I feel a twinge of pain.

"Has it been signed by your foreperson?" asks the judge, following the rules and prolonging the torture.

When the foreperson says yes, Barraclough directs her to give the verdict form to Bailiff Travis. Judge Lethal Injection has gone through this process scores of times, but today, at least, he looks solemn. Eddie gives the piece of paper to the judge, who unfolds the form, clears his throat, sighs, flips to the second and last pages, purses his lips, and nods.

"This is the jury's verdict," says Barraclough. "In case number 210-749368, *State of Alabama v. Destiny Grace Harper*, Verdict, Count One, murder, 'We, the jury, find the Defendant not guilty of capital murder in the death of Brooklyn Harper.'" On this count, the jury also reaches a not-guilty verdict on all of the lesser included offenses—second-degree murder, manslaughter, child endangerment.

Destiny Grace breathes a sigh of relief. I do not.

"Count Two, murder, 'We, the jury, find the Defendant guilty of capital murder in the death of Lydia Harper, a child under fourteen years of age.' Signed and dated by the Foreperson."

A gleeful Kerr hugs Graham, who looks stunned and doesn't hug her back. Some of the media members—not Rocha—hurry into the hallway in pursuit of their scoops. Destiny Grace squeezes my hand hard again but otherwise shows no emotion. How the media will pounce on her lack of emotion. They'll write that she's plainly guilty; they'll write that she doesn't care; they'll call her a psychopath. Quite the opposite. She's trying to stop herself from shattering into a billion pieces.

I must play the confident voice of reason—the optimist certain of a reversal on appeal—but this is the first time I've ever fought back tears before I left the courtroom. Our side has

suffered a total loss. The acquittal on count one means nothing—less than nothing. The murder of a child under fourteen
remains a capital crime. I'd like to show my displeasure to judge,
jury, and media alike, but I can't continue to antagonize a hostile
jury—they'll return for the penalty phase to consider whether
Destiny Grace Harper lives or dies.

The tendency of well-meaning people (I do believe this misguided jury meant well) to act irrationally in the name of justice
amazes me. Neither side—not Kerr, not Dr. Woodruff, not the
medical examiner—disputed that Lydia Harper, although born
alive, would've died even with the best medical care available.
So no reasonable jury could've found that Destiny Grace committed murder by leaving the shack and causing the death of
the twin who survived the birth. This jury wasn't reasonable.
This jury wasn't true to its principles. The jury consists solely of
individuals who oppose abortion—individuals who all vowed
during jury selection that they believe the unborn are human
beings. Yet, they drew a stark distinction between the born and
the unborn, apparently finding that Destiny Grace didn't kill
the stillborn twin but murdered the baby who lived for only
minutes. Destiny Grace has been convicted solely because she
left the scene. An incomprehensible compromise verdict that is
no compromise at all. To those who have the power to decide,
the truth is malleable.

Destiny Grace lets go of my hand.

Barraclough directs the bailiff to show the verdict to counsel and the defendant so we can review it for form. Higgins,
more composed than I, takes the document, reads it carefully,
and hands it back to Deputy Travis. Barraclough asks whether
either side takes exception to the jury form, and Kerr and Higgins say no. Barraclough next inquires of each side whether it
wants to poll the jury. Kerr declines the offer. I accept it. I want

to force the people sitting in that box to state their position in open court—to acknowledge they believe Destiny Grace committed a crime that warrants the death penalty.

One by one, each juror reaffirms their irrational, unjust belief that Destiny Grace murdered one of her children with malice aforethought.

"It'll be okay," I whisper to Destiny Grace. "We have a ton of appealable issues."

"I want to talk to Hazel Curnow about all this."

Barraclough announces he has some business to attend to out of the jury's presence. After the jury departs, the judge leans back in his chair and directs us to sit down. I expect he'll discuss housekeeping issues relating to the penalty phase—scheduling, timing of witness, length of trial. I can barely think, much less focus on such procedural nonsense.

Higgins starts weeping. I can read her thoughts—she blames herself because she delivered the closing argument. I don't regret for a moment the decision to have her close. Nothing could've changed this bizarre result.

"You did a great job, Aruna; it's not your fault," I say, and she nods. But I haven't convinced her. If the roles were reversed, she wouldn't have convinced me.

"Listen up!" shouts Barraclough. "Y'all will want to hear what I have to say about all this."

The room quiets.

"I wish I'd gotten the chance to decide this thing when Ms. Harper was still pregnant. We could've sorted this mess out then, but she ran and pulled the carpet right out from under me." He folds his hands and raises his eyes to the ceiling. "I'm officially an old judge. So denominated by our state legislature, and soon to leave the bench. I got nothing to lose by doing what I'm about to do. When my grandson Christopher was just about a year old, he couldn't keep food down. I'll never forget it. He wasn't just spitting up like babies do, but the projectile kind of vomiting, like you saw in the old horror movies about demons and satanic possession and such. Vicki, my daughter, took the small fry up to Nashville, to Vanderbilt University Medical Center, one of the finest hospitals anywhere. The university doctor wanted to do what they call an upper GI. That meant little Christopher would have to drink barium, after which the doctors would X-ray him. Well, we all know now that with X-rays come radiation, and radiation is harmful. Vicki, like she always does, did her own research and balked at having the test. She told the doctor her decision, and he replied that performing an upper GI was important to rule out a blockage in the abdomen or even a tumor. Scary stuff. My wife and I, Vicki's in-laws, and even my son-in-law, the boy's daddy, we all of us wanted Christopher to have that test, but Vicki wouldn't go for it. Threatened to divorce my son-in-law if he pushed the issue any further. She pointed out that, other than the throwing up, Christopher was a happy baby with an appetite, and her mother's instinct told her everything would be all right. And you know what? Everything *was* all right a week later. But what if Christopher had not recovered? What if he'd passed because there was an undetected blockage? Would my daughter have been a murderer, or guilty of manslaughter, or any kind of homicide?" He shakes his head from side to side. "Uh-uh, no." He elongates the last word. "The evidence in this case is insufficient to find this Destiny Grace Harper guilty of anything other than relying on a unique interpretation of the Lord's word. The *only* evidence in the record—the testimony of the defendant herself, and of Brandi Tipple and the only other eyewitness to the birth, Buddy Henderson—shows there was no intent to harm the babies. Quite the opposite. And, in ruling not guilty on one count but guilty on the second, the jury's verdict is inconsistent with the evidence. Do I think the defendant made a bad choice? Absolutely. The consequences of her choice will haunt her for the rest of her life. But that's not for me to judge. My job is to judge the law, and that's what I'm doing when I say, pursuant to Alabama Rule of Criminal Procedure 20.3, I hereby grant, on my own motion, a judgment of acquittal of defendant Destiny Grace Harper on count two."

I turn and hug Destiny Grace, who doesn't respond. She hasn't recovered from the jury's guilty verdict.

Loud murmurs ripple through the gallery. Mildred Chilton regards her boss with the desolate, angry eyes of the betrayed.

Higgins smiles and pumps her fist.

"Holy shit," whispers Margaret. "We've won ugly, but we've won."

"As this trial proves, the law is about anything but beauty," I whisper back.

Kerr storms up to the lectern. "We ask you to reconsider your ruling, Judge. You've substituted your judgment for that of the jury, and that's manifest error."

"The State's motion is denied," says Barraclough. "Anything else?"

She pounds a fist in outrage. "The State of Alabama will appeal your ruling and seek reinstatement of the guilty verdict on count two. This is a blatant miscarriage of justice. Considering the guilty verdict and imminent appeal, the State requests the defendant be remanded to the custody of the sheriff's department without bail. She remains a flight risk."

"Denied."

Kerr's decision to appeal means the case isn't truly over. If the judge had showed the guts to grant our motion for acquittal *before* the jury reached a guilty verdict, an appellate court couldn't have reversed and ordered a new jury to reach a verdict because that would place Destiny Grace in double jeopardy. But the jury handed down a guilty verdict. The appeals court can simply reinstate that verdict without the need for a second trial—no double jeopardy. So, this case is not over. That being said, I'd rather be us than Kelsey Kerr. For once, the fix wasn't in. Destiny Grace is walking out of court a free woman—for the time being.

CHAPTER FORTY-EIGHT

On an afternoon three days after the trial ended, I sit at a back booth in an almost empty Gypsy's Factory Lounge, nursing a Southern-style iced tea—cloyingly sweet yet delicious, especially on a sweltering day like this. No live music—only a sound system. Just as Lynyrd Skynyrd sings the lyrics "All the friends I've got just got to come interrogate me" from the song "Don't Ask Me No Questions," Sheriff Dave Coyle walks in and slides in across from me. He's twenty minutes late. Despite the day's heat, he wears a coat and tie. Sweat glistens from his forehead, prominent because of his receding hairline.

"Get caught up in that Cole's Crossing traffic?" I say, foolishly unable to rein in the sarcasm.

"Police business." There's not an ounce of amicability in his deep voice. "I told you we should've met at the station."

"Like I said, I do not have fond memories of that place. For reasons you know well."

He lets out an impatient exhale and knits his brow. His glare conveys a hatred that hasn't dissipated over the many years since Arlette's death.

A server comes over and asks if Coyle wants something. He gives a dismissive wave and says, "I won't be here but a minute."

The server gives a thin smile. "Holler if you change your mind, sheriff."

"You said you have something to tell me about my sister," says Coyle. "This better not be some lawyer bullshit that wastes my time."

"I don't believe Arlette committed suicide," I say.

He sits back in his seat. "Neither do I. Never have, as you know. Oh, she tried it a few times, the poor girl, but they were cries for attention. She didn't take her own life. Are you about to confess to her murder, Henderson?"

"I'm not the father of Arlette's baby, either," I say, sliding a document over to him.

As he reads, his eyebrows raise.

That sample of my own DNA I gave as an afterthought after Clayton Tipple bloodied me during our parking lot altercation? Luckily, by the time Arlette died, the state had already started preserving DNA as a matter of policy. Clayton Tipple's DNA sample did much more than help identify Destiny Grace's rapist. According to the database, Clayton Tipple and Arlette Coyle's baby were half-siblings. Which means that the Reverend Jeremiah Tipple impregnated Arlette.

Coyle finishes reading and offers the report back to me.

"Keep it," I say. "For your murder investigation of Jerry and Tammy Tipple."

He chortles. "This proves nothing, Mr. Defense Attorney. Not in a court of law and not to me."

"I'm not done. After Arlette died, did you talk to Tammy about what she knew about the pregnancy? The trip to Florida?"

"Of course I did. The girls were best friends."

Now I'm asking questions I don't know the answer to, but

you can do that in a deposition to discover information—and this is my informal deposition of Dave Coyle. How long he'll tolerate me I have no clue. "What did Tammy say to you?"

His stare could refreeze the melting cubes in my iced tea. "She told me she only learned about Arlette's pregnancy after you got back from Florida, where you tried to force my sister to have an abortion. She said you were furious that Arlette didn't go through with it and that you probably killed her. Said she didn't tell the cops this because she was afraid of you."

Now it's my turn to lurch backward. Tammy set me up. In light of recent events, it all makes perfect sense.

"Dave, Tammy not only knew about the pregnancy and the planned abortion, she helped Arlette set up the appointment with the Florida clinic. Arlette told me that she'd confided in Tammy. Tammy was ready to tell your parents that Arlette was with her on that college trip that weekend. I've got—"

"I'm supposed to accept your word that Arlette said these things? Your word means nothing."

"Given the recent revelations about the Tipple family, you're absolutely supposed to take my word for it. But I wasn't finished. Take a look at this."

I hand him another piece of paper, old and crinkled, but still legible: Panhandle Women's Free Clinic of Tallahassee, Florida, followed by an appointment date, address, and phone number, all written by the same hand.

He slides the paper back. "So what?"

"That's Tammy Evans's handwriting."

"And you kept this note all these years? How convenient."

"Call in a forensic examiner if you don't believe me. Analyze the handwriting and the age of the paper. Get a sample of Tammy's handwriting. It'll confirm what I'm telling you."

"Why would you keep this?"

I shrug and take a sip of my tea. "I don't really have a good answer to that question." That's the truth. After Arlette died, I found the piece of paper when I was cleaning out my old Buick. Why did I keep it? To hold onto a small piece of Tammy? Or maybe Arlette? Or maybe I just have a strong instinct for self-preservation.

He stares at the paper for a long time. "Mind if I hold onto this?"

"Be my guest—so long as you log it in as evidence."

He studies the document some more, then puts it aside. "So you're telling me that the Tipples murdered my sister?"

"I'm saying that Tammy wanted to marry Jeremiah, and that wouldn't have happened if anyone found out that he'd gotten Arlette pregnant. That's right, isn't it?"

He nods. Both his parents and Jeremiah's parents would've insisted that Jeremiah do the right thing. Coyle pinches the bridge of his nose with two fingers, and when his eyes glisten, I perceive for the first time an emotion other than his loathing of me.

"All it would've taken was a paternity test to prove Jerry was the father and I wasn't. My uncle would've insisted on the test if I'd stayed around. He never believed I was the father. I used protection. And I'm sure Jerry was much more careless and much more active with your sister than I was. He once bragged to the guys that—"

He scowls and holds up a hand.

"Look, I'm just saying . . . I'd wager that when Tammy found out the truth, she went ballistic. Her best friend was betraying her, and her comfortable future as Preacher Jerry's wife was about to dissolve before her eyes." As for my romance with Tamara, I wasn't ever in the picture—I see that now. First, I was a diversion, then a patsy. "Tammy probably convinced Arlette to get an abortion because pregnancy would've meant scandal.

Your sister was so emotionally fragile, so impressionable that she'd listen to Tammy. So Arlette came to me and claimed I was the father to get me to take her to Florida. Probably Tammy's idea, too. Besides, I supported a woman's right to choose. Who else would've taken her?"

"You support murder."

I hold up a hand. "Like I told you way back when, I didn't force Arlette to do anything. She asked me. *I* turned the car around because I saw she didn't want it." I've spent my entire adult life beset with guilt, believing that I should've encouraged Arlette to walk inside the abortion clinic and terminate the pregnancy. I've wondered whether the baby was truly mine. I believed that Arlette committed suicide because she was too afraid to tell her parents about the pregnancy, and that an abortion would've saved her life. As it turns out, an abortion likely *would* have saved her life, because the Tipples would've had no reason to kill her. No, I'm not responsible for Arlette's death. Still, the truth doesn't lessen my regrets. The truth doesn't always set you free; sometimes it just tightens the bonds that imprison you.

"There you have it," I continue. "Tammy lied about her knowledge of the pregnancy, she wrote a note confirming the appointment with the clinic, and she had a motive to murder the friend who'd betrayed her and threatened to ruin her future. And given recent events, it's clear that at least some of the Tipples don't hesitate to use violence."

He shakes his head. "Not near enough evidence to indict anyone."

"No, but it's a first step in a reopened investigation. Who knows what more digging will bring?"

"That it?"

"That's it. Thank you for your time." I throw some money on the table and get up to leave.

"Henderson, wait. You're not denying that you had sex with Arlette, are you? That you worried that you maybe were the father?"

"No, Dave, I'm not denying either of those things."

"Then the fact remains that you also had a motive to hurt my sister because you believed you could've been the father. A baby would've fucked up *your* future, too."

"You have no evidence that I've lied to you. Can't say the same thing about Tammy. As for fucking up my future, you know who I was. I wouldn't have married your sister even if I had been the baby's daddy. I was going to get out of this town no matter what. Hey, I have a family history of parents leaving their kid behind."

He takes a moment to absorb this. "Get in that van of yours, Elvis. And don't come back here again."

CHAPTER FORTY-NINE

Two weeks have passed since Judge Merle Barraclough released Destiny Grace Harper from custody. The case against Hunter Tipple has gotten stronger. He attended law school in Little Rock, Arkansas. It turns out there's an unsolved rape of a prostitute in Delton, a suburb of Little Rock, in which the rapist hummed during the assault, made the victim swear on the Bible she'd never tell, and swore on the Bible that he'd kill her if he did. Oh, and the assailant wore a spicy cologne. The assault occurred when Hunter was in his second year of law school. A couple of years ago, Hunter went to Savannah on some church business—exactly the time when an unsolved rape occurred with a similar modus operandi. Except, this last victim preserved some DNA by managing to scratch the assailant during the act without his knowing—a preliminary match to Hunter. Two of the women who received hush money via LeAnn Harper have also come forward about his assaults. My one regret is that so far, there's no evidence that Hunter murdered Lillian Wagers. But all in due time. At least he's incarcerated without bail—a flight risk and a danger to society, Merle Barraclough ruled.

Leaning against my van in the Quartz Inn parking lot, I take a satisfying drag of my La Finca Nicaraguan cheroot. Margaret scrunches up her nose and fans the air though the smoke is nowhere near her. "Disgusting. Not to mention bad for your health."

"No disagreement from me." I take another puff and watch the smoke tendrils disappear into the Alabama morning sky.

When I was in law school, my remedies professor loved to tell jokes. Most were unfunny, many indecent by today's standards. One joke sticks with me, though. A fellow in a restaurant begins choking on a piece of meat. A man sitting at the next table says, "I'm a doctor; I'll perform the Heimlich maneuver." The doctor does so and saves the choking man's life. The victim sighs and says grudgingly, "Since you're a doctor, I suppose you're going to send me a huge bill. How much?" The doctor replies, "How about half of what you would've paid me while you were choking to death?" Yesterday, Destiny Grace, through her mother, fired us and hired a big-name law firm out of Atlanta, which has agreed to handle the appeal pro bono. The decision in this case has become big news, stoking the controversy surrounding women's rights and the rights of the unborn. And once Barraclough ruled in our favor, the case became much easier to win on appeal. Not a slam dunk, but not the uphill battle we faced at trial. Great publicity for a large firm. And the Harpers are upset we didn't win a full jury acquittal. Clients expect perfection, especially after the fact.

"Visit your uncle more often," says Margaret. "You can't make up for all these years, but . . ."

"Thank you, den mother."

"The truth is the truth. Buddy did a good thing."

"Eventually."

"He did a brave thing."

I take three more puffs on my cigar, then drop it on the

asphalt and snuff it out with the sole of a Jack Purcell. "See, you next time, Margaret."

"Successful travels, E."

I climb into the Ford Transit, start the ignition, and roll out of the parking lot and onto Interstate 65, heading north toward Nashville. Calinda Rocha lives in Nashville. About ten miles into Tennessee, a billboard pops up on the side of the road—*Daniella's D-Cup Divas, Live Nude Girls, Exit 6.* I move into the right lane and look for exit 6.

ACKNOWLEDGMENTS

Thank you: Dr. Jacob M. Appel, Daco Auffenorde, Terri Cheney, Derek McFadden, Matthew Sharpe, Les Standiford, Robert Wolfe, and James W. Ziskin; Jill Marr and Andrea Cavallaro of the Sandra Dijkstra Literary Agency; and William Boggess, Brendan Dineen, Candice Edwards, Daniel Ehrenhaft, Lydia Rogue, Katrina Tan, and Josie Woodbridge of Blackstone Publishing.